A BILLION Last Goodbyes

WICKED HOT BILLIONAIRES

JANE McBAY

cat whisker press
Boston

Copyright © 2025 Jane McBay
All rights reserved under International and Pan-American Copyright Conventions.

First Paperback Edition
ISBN: 978-1-957421-68-1

Published by Cat Whisker Press
Cover: Philip Ré, Rex Video Productions
Book Design: Cat Whisker Studio
Editor: Chloe Bearuski

Note to Readers: There are references to domestic bullying, and the main female character physically fights with her former lover. If this might be a trigger for you, please **reconsider** reading this book.

To those who love chocolate
as much as I do

This one's for you!

WICKED HOT BILLIONAIRES

A Billion Little Lies

A Billion Hot Kisses

A Billion Starry Nights

A Billion Last Goodbyes

A Billion Risky Games

A Billion Second Chances

1

Morgan

A blinking red light snags my attention away from a late-night coding session, instantly causing my heart to race. It's not that I've never seen a security alert before, but I usually deal with cybercrime. This alert indicates a physical intruder at the company I'm consulting for. No doubt about it. Not what I signed up for, yet I somehow doubt there's anyone else online this very moment seeing what I'm seeing.

Setting down my glass of Lemon, Lime, and Bitters, which has quickly become my favorite drink while working Down Under, I stare at the screen on the company laptop. Luckily, I had it turned on and running beside me on the dining room table of the short-term apartment rental, while working on my own computer.

The light stops blinking. That's curious. Someone's breached the side entrance of Henley Confectionery's Sydney division and then turned off the main alarm. A moment later, the schematic security map shows me smart lights turning on as whoever it is navigates the ground floor.

Well, shit!

With a click, I bring up the video feed, which shows a tall figure in a hoodie, hood up and head down, moving quickly across the ground floor. My fingers fly across the keyboard, pulling up access logs. No authorized entries scheduled this late. Grabbing my phone, I dial the police while continuing to watch both the lights and the video.

I hear a recording. "The number you dialed is not in service." Of course it isn't, because 911 means nothing in Sydney, Australia. Quickly looking up the proper one, I dial again, 000.

"Hallo, do you have an emergency?"

"There's a break-in at 42 Market Street," I tell the dispatcher.

"Break and enter, mate? Have you got eyes on the bludger from where you're at?"

The bludger? Making sense of the question, despite the late hour, I answer. "No, I'm watching on a security monitor from my apartment."

There's a pause. "42 Market?" Another pause. "That's the Henley Candy Company."

"Yes, it is."

"Your security screen shows some drongo busting down a door, or what's the go?"

Frowning, I make another stab at interpreting what this Aussie is asking. I've only been in the country for four days, barely settled into my new temporary home, ten thousand miles from Boston—and from Ethan. And I've barely started investigating the cybertheft I've been hired to solve.

"No, nothing like that. Just an alert that someone has entered the building. Are you going to send the police?"

"What's to say it's not just some worker having a late one?" he asks.

"Who works at midnight?" I demand.

The dispatcher chuckles. "Me, for a start, mate. And sounds like you, too."

I make a huffing sound, feeling frustrated with the pace of this exchange. The dispatcher adds, "Look, it seems like Henley's got their own mob of security blokes. Until their lot rings us up, I won't be sending the coppers 'round."

"Are you serious?" The intruder has made his way from the side door, down a short hallway, past a janitor's closet and the restrooms, toward the upscale lobby. Automatic sensor lights continue to flick on, lighting the person's path while showing me his progress through the building. It's like playing a video game except, in this case, I can't do anything to neutralize the enemy.

"Listen mate," my disinterested Aussie desk cop continues, "unless you're keen to give us your details and swear on your mum's grave that some duffer's gone and knocked in a window or plowed their ute or sedan through the joint, my hands are tied. Reckon it's just a poor bugger ducking in for some late-night lollies."

To my amazement, he hangs up. On one hand, the dispatcher could be right. After all, the alert only blinked for a few seconds before whoever it was disarmed the alarm system. But watching the trespasser traverse the polished hardwood floor of the Henley's lobby, lighting up my security dashboard like a Christmas tree, I think he's wrong.

I don't think anyone is there for candy. *Lollies*, indeed! Besides, the only candy in the Sydney headquarters are the sample boxes in the break room, which I discovered on day one. Everything else is at a factory off-site.

Since I was called in to discover how someone is siphoning off a small but growing stream of the profits via the Internet, I can't help wondering if this midnight disturbance is related.

The dispatcher mentioned Henley's own security company. Unfortunately, I think at this moment, that's me. The friendly looking guy at the front entrance who checks people in and out with his clipboard is hardly Mission

Impossible level security. As far as I know, he goes home after letting in the cleaning crew. Apart from that, the confectionery company relies on secure codes, keycards, and strong locks.

When an elevator is engaged, I keep my eyes glued to the intruder's progress, tracking his digital breadcrumbs. Up, up, up, all the way to the executive floor.

"Damn!" I know for a fact the CEO is away, and there's just no way any of the rest of the C-suite would be going to work at this hour. No way in hell.

The apartment Henley's HR put me up in for the three-month contract is only two blocks from Market Street. Stuffing my feet into running shoes, I sprint along the empty street with my cell phone clutched in my hand.

Turning the corner, I head for the side entrance, all the while telling myself that this is a good idea. I might be a five-foot-six-inch woman, and the prowler is definitely a man by the build I saw on the monitor, but I can take care of myself. The door clicks open with my override code, and I slip inside.

The steel-and-glass building feels different at night. Instead of Sydney's sunny view through the massive windows, there's simply blackness reflecting the lights and my own face back at me. Pink pajama pants that are practically indistinguishable from sweatpants, an oversized long-sleeve cotton T, and my hair in a damp braid after my shower. Not exactly a sleek spy, but I do have a black belt in kung fu, so I'm almost a ninja.

Almost. My footsteps echo off the gleaming dark wood floors, and I take the stairs in case the trespasser sees the elevator's indicator lights. Sure would be nice if the police were on their way.

The building only has four floors, so I'm not even winded when I reach the top. Before I open the stairwell door, I check my phone screen, checking which smart lights have powered on. After the elevator reached the top floor, hoodie-man went directly to the CEO's office suite. I creep down the wide, carpeted hallway, keeping my breathing level as years of martial arts training taught me. I say a silent thanks to my parents for making me go to training at the dojo, even when I wanted to skip out for a date or stay home and veg.

With all my senses on alert, I hear him before I see him. He's tapping on a keyboard. Then, through the open door of the corner office, I finally catch my first glimpse. Black hoodie and jeans, broad shoulders, bent over the front of Luke Henley's desk. Luckily, because otherwise he'd be facing me. The moment before I act, my pulse thunders in my ears.

Launching forward, I sweep my leg in a perfect arc, making steady, jarring contact. His feet fly out from under him, and he crashes sideways with a surprised grunt, bringing a few papers down with him. Before he can move, I'm on top of him, straddling his chest, my forearm pressed against his throat.

"Don't even think about it." I dig my elbow harder into his larynx, not sure what I think he's thinking, but it's my first real-life takedown, and I want to sound menacing and in control.

"Spread your arms wide." Staring down at a handsome face, right into his golden-brown eyes, which are still wide with shock, I have a feeling I should know him. And not only because his mouth looks particularly kissable.

As he takes in my appearance, he relaxes, despite being on his back and helpless. I guess, because I'm female, he's not taking me particularly seriously.

"You're in big trouble," I say, belatedly realizing the problem I'm in. I can't move and lift my arm from his throat, or he'll be able to start fighting back. We are basically stuck like this until morning and someone shows up for work. His gaze narrows and, unbelievably, he lets out a choked laugh.

"Not the welcome I was expecting." His voice is barely above a whisper, while his tawny eyes crinkle with amusement, despite being in *and under* my control.

That voice . . . an American accent like my own. Something is filtering through my late-night thoughts, and I ease up on his windpipe just a little. In that moment of indecision, he rolls me. I never did get him to spread his arms out.

Now, he's using those very strong muscles to pin my hands to the floor on either side of my head while he sits on me. I'm grateful he's keeping his weight on his knees and not my stomach.

He rubs his neck sideways against his shoulder without releasing his hold on me, and I'm sure it hurts. I wasn't trying to crush his trachea, but I hadn't been gentle, either.

"I'm Luke Henley," he says at last, his voice still gravelly. "And you are?"

Oh, God! I just attacked my boss.

2

Luke

The stranger scrambles backward, her pretty face flushing an embarrassed shade of red as she bumps into my desk. My smile widens despite the twinge in my throat where her fierce, pointy elbow had been.

"Shit! I'm so sorry!" She's adorably flustered. "I'm Morgan Anders. The new cybersecurity consultant. Well, temporary consultant. I saw the breach alert on my monitor, and then the dispatcher wouldn't send anyone, and I thought—"

"That you'd take matters into your own hands?" I adjust my sweatshirt, pushing the hood down my back, watching her with growing fascination. That this slip of a woman, with wide blue eyes, a long brown braid, and . . . *pajamas?* That she took me down is impressive as hell. I'm compelled to tell her that.

"I have to say, I'm impressed. Though next time, maybe verify the identity of your target before going for the windpipe?"

Her chin lifts defiantly, displaying her pulse racing at her throat. *Interesting.* My imagination conjures me wrapping that thick braid around my hand, using it to tug her head back so I can put my lips on that fluttering heartbeat. On the other hand, she'd probably do some fancy warrior move again, putting me on my back.

"I was just doing my job," she insists.

"By physically assaulting the CEO?" I can't help teasing her. It's been a long time since anyone surprised me like this. "That's dedication." *Or lunacy.*

Heavy footsteps in the hall interrupt whatever she was about to say. Two officers burst in with weapons drawn, and I don't fight the urge to step in front of Morgan.

"Hands where we can see 'em!" one barks.

After raising mine, before I can speak, Morgan comes out from behind me, her hands raised, and I admire her composure even as I move to defuse the situation.

"Stand down," I say firmly. "There's been a misunderstanding. I'm Luke Henley. I own the company. This is my security consultant, Ms. Anders."

"*Cyber* security," she chimes in, which is laughable since she could replace our lobby guard without any problem as building security.

The officers lower their weapons but look skeptical. "Just got word about a break-in," the first one says.

"That would be my fault," Morgan admits, shooting an apologetic glance my way. "I saw an unauthorized entry and called it in. I didn't realize it was Mr. Henley."

"Because I forgot my keycard in my luggage," I explain, watching how she shifts uncomfortably. "Rather than go back and hunt for it, I used the override code. I guess I set off the alarm first. Ms. Anders was simply being thorough in her duties."

The second officer, graying and stocky, holsters his weapon. "Right then. You're saying everything's bonza here?"

"Perfectly fine," I assure them, rubbing my throat. Not because it hurts much anymore, but because I enjoy the slight guilt that flashes across Morgan's face. "Just a zealous security consultant doing her job."

The first officer eyes Morgan with obvious skepticism. "Bit unusual, isn't it? A sheila taking down potential burglars?"

Morgan bristles and I step in before she can respond. Her fire is entertaining, but I don't need this situation escalating. "Ms. Anders is highly qualified. In fact, I'd say her response tonight proves we made the right choice in hiring her."

The officers take in my notes from the flight now on the carpet and my laptop that I must have knocked askew before I went down. It probably looks suspicious, but I'm too jet-lagged to care.

"If you need any verification," I reach for my wallet.

"No worries, Mr. Henley," the first officer says quickly. "Now I've had a proper look at you, I recognize your face. Just doin' our duty, checkin' things out."

After they finally leave, Morgan lets out a long breath, which draws my attention to her lips. She has a full lower lip that makes a man want to sink his teeth into it and a cupid's bow upper lip that I want to see smiling. What's more, despite how she obviously came out without any makeup on, her mouth is a deep rosy color.

"I really am sorry," she says, tugging at her over-sized T-shirt self-consciously. "I should have—"

"Verified my identity before executing that amazing take-down?" I can't stop myself from asking.

"If you were a malicious intruder, extra seconds chit-chatting and asking questions could have gotten me killed," she points out.

I nod. She's right. I hate to think of her sneaking up on someone, then asking for their ID. I could have turned around with a knife or a gun.

"Where did you learn moves like that?" *And what other moves do you know?*

"Ten years of martial arts training," she says, before offering a small smile with a shrug. A bit self-deprecating for such a bad-ass. "My parents insisted," she continues. "They said if I was going to be independent, I needed to know how to handle myself."

Thinking of her handling something else, I move to the sparse bar cart, an excuse to put some distance between us and hide my body's strong reaction to her. Must be my tiredness sending inappropriate thoughts winging through my brain. Like how I already want to see what's under her shapeless layers. The late-night Sydney skyline creates an intimate backdrop that isn't helping my jet-lagged judgment.

"Drink?" I offer, knowing I should send her home but not wanting to. Not yet. When she hesitates, I add, "I think we both could use one after that excitement."

I find myself holding my breath until she nods.

"Whisky or … whisky?" I hold up the amber bottle with a bright blue cap, watching her track my every movement with eyes of similar blue. I don't explain that the liquor is more for show, kept in my office as a treat when my granddad drops by. Gramps likes Melbourne-distilled Starward, whereas I'm more inclined to a cold beer, an expensive glass of cab, or French brandy.

"I guess I'll take whisky," she says finally, going along with my little joke. While I pour, she moves around the massive expanse of my office, like a cat on the prowl, and I'm profoundly aware of her at every moment.

As I take a replenishing sip, I observe her scanning the bookshelf, my laptop, and finally, she's standing in front of the one piece of art in the room, a painting of my grandparent's ranch in the Hunter Valley.

When I approach her, she turns her gaze to me. It's analytical, professional, but there's something else there, too. Handing her the glass, I let my fingers brush hers deliberately. A slight flush blooms up her neck. I'm toying with her, which isn't nice. But wrung-out as I am, I don't feel "nice."

"Tell me more about how you ended up tackling me tonight." I give her some space and brace my ass on the edge of my desk, trying to look casual rather than drop-dead exhausted.

Morgan leans her shoulder against the wall, her legs crossed at her ankles, before taking a sip. I track the movement of her throat. She doesn't do any exaggerated choking like some women do, as if they've never had hard liquor before.

"I was monitoring the security feeds from my apartment when I saw the breach alert. Actually, I wasn't really monitoring this place at all," she confesses.

I raise my eyebrows at her abrupt countering of her own sentence.

"I mean, I'm technically off the clock. I was actually coding a private project, something that might . . ." She lets her words drift off, obviously making a conscious effort to stop rambling. Her clarifications and backtracking shouldn't be as charming as they are, but I'm thoroughly entranced.

"Anyway, I happened to have my work laptop beside me, and noticed the moment you let yourself in. After the police dispatcher refused to help, I decided to investigate."

"Because your apartment is close by?" I guess, knowing we have a few furnished rentals we keep for company guests.

"Two blocks away." She gestures toward the windows with her glass. "When I saw movement on the executive floor, I knew something was wrong."

"Why?"

"Because I was told you were away, and it didn't make any sense that someone from the C-suite would be working.

I mean, maybe someone from accounting, perhaps being driven mad by numbers not quite adding up. Or maybe a chocolate designer who's desperate to try out a new truffle flavor."

Clamping a hand over her mouth, she effectively shuts off the stream of words, and I have to hide my smile in case she thinks I'm laughing at her. Because I would owe her a serious debt if it hadn't been me traipsing around in here, deciding I had to read a quarterly report that my VP texted was alarming for the very reason Morgan is here. Cyber theft. It could've waited till morning, but I was driving by.

Morgan takes another sip of whisky before adding, "And I knew the cleaning crew would have already finished."

"So you rushed over here alone?" I can't keep the edge from my voice. The thought of her confronting an actual bad guy makes my chest tight. "That was risky."

"Says the man who had his black hoodie over his head and triggered his own security system," she fires back, and I'm charmed by her boldness.

"Fair point. Though in my defense, I just got off a fourteen-hour flight from Singapore. My brain isn't firing on all cylinders."

She shifts into qualified-expert mode. "The override codes should be changed more frequently. I can set up a program with high randomness that sends out a new code weekly to—"

I cut her off. "Morgan." Her name feels unusual but pleasant on my tongue. I don't believe I've ever met a *Morgan* before. "We can discuss security upgrades tomorrow, sometime after coffee. When I got off the plane, I was still kind of jacked and had seen a text from our VP about the continuing theft. I should've gone straight to bed. But I honestly can't take in any idea more complicated than the message on your T-shirt."

She looks down. "Eat. Sleep. Debug. Repeat." is written in white cursive on her dark-blue shirt. Seems like someone has forgotten one of the best aspects of a full life—satisfying sex.

Setting my empty glass on the edge of my desk, I push to my feet. I'm more than ready to go home. But drawn by something I'm too tired to resist or to filter, I can't help adding, "I'm intrigued to have discovered my cybersecurity consultant is skilled enough to take down someone twice her size."

"I wouldn't say *twice* my size," she deflects, though she has to tilt her head back to meet my eyes. "And size isn't everything in martial arts."

"Clearly not." My gaze drops to her mouth before I can stop it. The tension between us is palpable, dangerous because of its intensity and how swiftly it flared. That is, it might be a problem if we weren't both responsible, professional adults. Even if one of us is in pink pajama bottoms, and the other is almost loopy with lack of sleep.

"You know," I say, my voice lower than intended, "most people who meet me for the first time don't immediately try to incapacitate me."

"Most people who meet you probably know who you are beforehand." She drains the last drops of whisky and steps toward me. My stupid male libido thinks she's going to make a move, maybe even go up on tiptoe to kiss me. But she simply places her glass next to mine. *Cool as a cuke.*

On the other hand, I notice her hand trembles slightly as it pulls away. "If you'd been facing me, I would've recognized you from your company photo on the website."

"Hard to recognize someone in a hoodie," I agree, leaning a little closer, unable to help myself. "But those photos are all suits and fake smiles. This," I gesture to myself in casual clothes, "is much more . . . authentic."

"Show me," she challenges.

Just like that, this woman has caught me off-guard again. "Show you *what?*" The possibilities seem endless to my foggy brain.

"The real smile," she explains. "The one that isn't for a corporate headshot."

Without thinking, I give her a smile usually reserved for family and close friends. Her response—a soft "Yeah, like that"—makes my heart race, shooting heat straight to my groin.

The moment stretches, charged with tension, and her glance is now trained on my mouth, until her phone buzzes. For a second, with our gazes locked, we both ignore the sound. Then she draws it from her pocket. A quick glance and the change is instant. Morgan stiffens, steps back, and makes her excuses about leaving.

"It's really late. I'm so sorry," she apologizes needlessly, as if she'd been holding me against my will. "Nothing like a long flight and then being tackled by your newest hire. Anyway, bed time." Her eyes widen at her own words. "I mean for *me*. Obviously, you can go to bed whenever you like. Of course. Again, sorry."

It's hard not to like her, with her awkward, long-winded chatter. But it's also hard not to be a little disappointed in what I think nearly happened. Then I shake my head. What an ass I am for supposing anything. She's temporary. I'm her boss. And for all I know, she has a significant other waiting at home.

"Of course," I say, professional mask firmly in place for the first time since she attacked me. "We can discuss security protocols tomorrow."

At the door, she pauses and turns, catching me staring at her shapely ass. "Mr. Henley?"

"Yep?" I reply, sounding strangled.

"Next time you forget your keycard, maybe just call building security instead of testing my combat skills?"

I laugh, but as I watch her walk away, I know I'm in trouble. Because temporary or not, Morgan Anders just became the most interesting thing in my life.

And I haven't even begun to process the fact that the first time I've ever been physically bested, it was by a woman. And it turned me on.

Kiss. Fuck. Sleep. Repeat.

3

Morgan

I arrive at the office early, hoping to avoid any awkward encounters. My dove-grey pantsuit and vibrant fuchsia blouse feel like armor after last night's pajama-clad tackle. My temporary spot at a desk in the IT suite gives me a clear view of the state-of-the-art, large security monitor hanging on the wall opposite. It includes a continuous, cycling display of the hallways on all four floors including, unfortunately, the corridor outside Mr. Henley's office.

Not that I'm looking every minute or so, but naturally, I can't resist an occasional glance. Eventually, about ten minutes after I arrive, I'm rewarded with a glimpse of his imposing figure striding down the corridor toward the executive suite. Squinting, I take in every detail in the three seconds he's onscreen. His bespoke light-gray suit makes him look more of a powerful CEO than his jeans and hoodie, but no more attractive. How could he be *more* than drop-dead perfect?

With a click of the keyboard, I could change the display to a steady view of the lobby, or even a schematic showing green lines like I was looking at last night. It would be preferable, but it's not my call.

"G'day, Morgan." Jack Thompson, head of IT, stops by my desk a half hour later. It's *his* call. And in the few days I've worked with him, I've discovered he has a bit of a Napoleon complex. Taller than me but not by much, he struts rather than walks. He likes to have the wall monitor show live feeds all day, as if he's king of the castle, surveying his domain and all its people.

In truth, Jack and his staff of two mostly handle hardware issues and software crashes, just like I did in grad school.

"Morning," I reply, keeping my eyes fixed on my screen while I click my keyboard to hide my work. Jack picks up the tiny succulent I brought in to liven up my sterile bit of company real estate. He looks closely at the little red pot and miniature green plant before setting it back down, next to my Boston Red Sox mouse pad. Then he starts to wander.

I don't need to track him visually to know he's positioning himself to loom over my shoulder – his signature move. By the time he does, it appears as though I'm reviewing the building's security protocols, which is what everyone thinks I'm here to do.

After a silent moment, he circles around to the front, so I have to look up at him. Putting me here instead of being sequestered in, say, a janitor's closet was a mistake, by my way of thinking.

"Heard you had a right proper blue last night." His forced smile doesn't reach his eyes.

Of course he heard. I don't ask how, or what a "proper blue" is, but I can guess that's why he was running thirty minutes behind today. Must've already had an earful.

"Just doing my job," I say, dropping my gaze to focus on my screen.

"Just making me look bad," he gripes under his breath.

Jack doesn't know why I was hired when, by rights, he should be the one to do a company-wide cyber security audit. And *that* annoys the shit out of him, meaning I annoy the shit out of him by my mere presence.

Just then his staff shows up, Brad and Zoe, IT techs carrying their obligatory massive cups of coffee that will get them through, maybe, the first hour of the workday. They nod in our direction before settling behind their monitors.

"Righto," Jack says. "Got a meeting in ten to sort out security protocols." He taps my desk twice with a thick pointer finger. "Upstairs conference room. The CEO wants to have a look at the new security measures himself and specifically asked for you to rock up."

My fingers freeze over the keyboard. *Great. Just great.* Luke Henley knows why I'm really here, so why haul me upstairs? Jack's slight sneer as if there's a bad smell under his nose tells me that neither one of us is happy about the request for me to "rock up."

Once he's seated in his glass-partitioned office, I snatch up my purse and head to the ladies' room, only encountering Noah Matthews from sales as he gets on the elevator. He's one of the few people whose first name I know. Friendly guy with a white-toothed smile, he holds the doors open.

"Sorry," I say, "not going up, not yet. Can't chitchat." And I dash past and down the short side hallway, by which I first saw Luke Henley enter last night.

I really should use the ten minutes to brainstorm some sort of coherent suggestions because I'm not currently doing the cyber security audit, nor do I have any firm recommendations for new cyber protocols. Not yet. The former will happen naturally as I hunt the cyber thief, auditing every last Internet account and email, every byte that flows through the Henley Confectionery servers. When I'm done, I won't be simply making recommendations. I'll put new procedures in place before I leave to make sure nothing like the current payment hacking can happen again.

Meanwhile, a girl's gotta look her best. After reapplying a pale-pink lipstick for confidence, I take out my comb. Last night's post-shower braid left my long hair slightly wavy when I undid it this morning. A little like an 80s' perm. I wish today of all days it was smooth and sleek, not beachy. After a decent attempt, my hair still looks unkempt and, to my eyes, unprofessional.

Scrabbling in the bottom of my gray leather bag, I find a thick, silver barrette. Soon, I'm sporting a low ponytail at the nape of my neck. Then I give myself the once over. No coffee stains. I spin around. No loose hairs hanging off my butt. I glance at my feet. No toilet paper stuck to my blush-colored, high-heeled pumps. Good!

Returning to my desk and stowing my purse in the drawer, I gather the company laptop I'm borrowing. Seeing Jack still in his office, I take off, hoping to get to the conference room before anyone else and prepare myself for seeing Luke Henley.

I'm not the first one here. There's a woman preparing the room, making sure all the chairs are pushed in, the water pitcher is filled, plenty of glasses in the center of the table, and . . . two open boxes of assorted chocolates! One at either end of the table.

"Seems a bit early in the day for candy," I say, thinking this svelte, well-dressed employee will agree, but she frowns.

"This is Henley Confectionery," she points out like I'm a simpleton. "It's never the wrong time for our chocolates."

"Right," I agree, wishing I'd kept my mouth shut. Taking a seat in front of one of the boxes, I breathe in the delectable aroma. My mouth waters, even though I don't normally think about candy, at least not until after lunch.

When I look up, the woman is still staring at me. Waiting.

Reaching out, I take a random chocolate square and pop it in my mouth. An intense burst of sweet flavor melts across my tongue—a rich, creamy chocolate center with a hint of orange and vanilla. Immediately, my mood relaxes and lifts. More than that, I crave a second one almost as soon as I swallow the first.

"Delicious," I say softly. She nods at me as though satisfied that I've joined the Henley cult. After taking another look around, she leaves.

The glass walls with their open vertical blinds offer no privacy, and I'm acutely aware of every person who walks past and see those before they enter. Two men come in, introducing themselves to me as Jeff, head of accounting and Theodore, the CFO, each taking a chocolate after they sit. It's like I've stumbled into a cult.

Regardless of how weird it seems, I snag another one, thoroughly enjoying what I realize is a flow of serotonin and dopamine, among my brain's other responses. When Luke enters, I'm not as nervous as I was a few minutes ago. Having had the prior warning of how devastatingly handsome he looks in his perfectly fitting suit, I don't ogle him. *Much.* Up close, there's no sign of the previous night's jet lag in his appearance.

We lock gazes immediately, and the same jolt of awareness hits me as it did last night.

"Good morning, Ms. Anders," he says, completely professional. Only the slight quirk of his lips betrays any memory of our midnight encounter.

"Mr. Henley." I nod, proud of how steady my voice sounds. Right behind him is his assistant, an enthusiastic guy, a little younger than I am, whose name I've momentarily forgotten. *Dave or maybe Dan?* It's no wonder I'm drawing a blank when he's in his boss's shadow.

For that matter, I can barely recall my own name while Luke's undivided attention is on me. I'm about to try for small talk when he puts a finger to the side of his mouth and nods at me.

I startle. Is it a secret code telling me something? *About the cyber thief?*

I shrug, letting him know I have no clue. He simply smiles.

"You have chocolate on your face," Dave or Dan announces. Loudly.

What?! So much for professional. There's a stack of cocktail napkins next to the water pitcher, so I snatch one of those and wipe like my mom used to wipe peanut butter and jelly off my mouth and cheek. Scrubbing fiercely. I know I've destroyed my perfect lipstick and lost my cool, painfully aware of how everyone is now focused on me.

Luckily, Jack Thompson enters next with both his IT team, which feels like overkill, but makes him seem important while taking attention off of me. I hope no one in the building has a computer meltdown because they'll be shit out of luck. Charlotte Bauer, the company's VP arrives, as well as a woman I've never met wearing a visitor's tag, followed by the lobby security officer.

Luke takes the lead, seated at the conference table head. "As you all know, I hired Ms. Anders to evaluate the effectiveness of our company's cybersecurity infrastructure and protocols."

I glance around to see heads nodding, and Jack shoots me a too-wide smile. I want to send him an equally fake, over-the-top two-thumbs up. If he only knew I was there not so much to evaluate and make suggestions as to solve a very real and costly cybercrime that is happening even as we sit here.

"I'm sorry I was away when she arrived, but I trust you've all made her welcome." He looks at Jack.

Before Luke can continue, the security officer speaks up. "'Scuse me, Mr. Henley, but I'm a bit lost with all this cyber gadgetry and whatnot. Not really my cuppa tea, mate."

A couple people laugh, but not in a mean-spirited way. Luke nods. "I'm aware of that, Henry. But I asked you here and invited your boss because of something that happened last night. For those of you who don't know, this is Ms. Carson from Chelle Security."

That explains the visitor's pass. The middle-aged woman wearing her dark hair in a short bob sends a nod as greeting around the room. It seems no one knows her.

"We had a break-in of sorts around midnight," Luke announces.

There are a few gasps from those who didn't know about last night's incident. Henry looks perturbed, and Ms. Carson immediately offers, "I'll put a night watchman on at once. This evening!" She frowns. "When we were hired, we were told this was a low-risk company without the need for a 24/7 physical presence."

"I still think that's the case," Luke tells her. "The intruder was me, as it turned out."

Murmurs go around the table. "And the *break-in*"—he uses air quotes—"was only detected by Ms. Anders as a blip on her screen. Which is why I want to focus mainly on cyber security. I know she hasn't had time to complete her evaluation of our security protocols, but I'm hoping she has formulated the barest of plans after what she's observed so far."

His eyes lock on mine, and a frisson of electricity passes between us. So hot, it would fry my laptop's motherboard. "Do you have some ideas to avert another incident like last night's?" Luke asks.

Boy, do I have ideas! Visions of being on top of him after I knocked him to the floor fill my head. I could have leaned down and kissed him, although that might not have been very welcome with my elbow in his neck. All I know is when he rolled me, it was erotic AF. If he'd put his big hand under my T-shirt and palmed my breast, I probably would've been OK with that.

"Yes," I say, then clear my throat since the single word came out in a whisper. "Because of last night's unintentional security breach, I can tell you where the system's vulnerabilities lie." I launch into a short presentation—*really* short because Luke did, in fact, put me on the spot. I go over the current vulnerabilities, particularly in how quickly the alert can be defused rather than having the police notified. I recommend some initial upgrades. At least the technical details help me focus on something other than the CEO's distracting presence at the head of the table.

"These changes seem excessive," Jack says. "Our current system—"

"Failed to properly identify an unauthorized entry last night," Luke cuts in smoothly.

"How could it be unauthorized when it was you?" Jack asks.

Collective silence indicates the impertinence of the IT head's ballsy question. But Luke remains calm, obviously not threatened. "My late-night screw-up proves the need for a system rework, and although it wasn't her initial focus when hired, Ms. Anders has the capability to implement it. I agree with her that it's prudent to change the security codes at least once a week. All department heads will get the random code through a secure server."

He pins his IT head with a stare. "As long as you use your keycard, Jack, you won't need to remember the ever-changing override code, if that's a problem."

Jack's jaw tightens, but he stays quiet.

Next, Luke looks at Ms. Carson again. "I want Chelle Security to react should the building ever be breached again, no matter the brevity of the initial alert. Just because it only took me a second to punch in the correct code, that doesn't mean next time it won't be a real intruder. I want the police notified to come over every single time there's an alert. Is that understood?"

"Yes, Mr. Henley." She's clearly not pleased to be dragged into this.

"I find it inexcusable," Luke continues, "that our consultant had to be the one to not only alert the police but to come investigate."

"Yes, Mr. Henley," Ms. Carson repeats, and I feel sorry for her. This wasn't her fault. I hope she doesn't think I was complaining or trying to get her into trouble.

As the meeting comes to a close, I'm about to escape along with everyone else, when Luke says, "Stay back, Ms. Anders. I have a few questions."

"Should I stay, too?" Jack asks.

"Nope," Luke says, effectively cutting him off at the knees, as surely as my leg sweep.

Once we're alone in the conference room, Luke closes the door. The glass walls leave us exposed, but somehow the room feels more intimate.

"You did well," he says. "Despite the short notice."

"About that," I start, "it seems I'm stepping on toes."

"My fault, but I needed to establish your authority quickly. Jack Thompson isn't going to make this easy for you."

I raise an eyebrow. "You noticed?"

"I notice everything." His voice drops lower. "Including how different you look today compared to last night."

Heat creeps up my neck. "Well, I wasn't exactly dressed for work then."

"No," he agrees, his eyes traveling over my suit. "Though I have to say, the T-shirt and pajama pants had a certain charm."

My phone buzzes in my pocket, and I ignore it. But Luke's gaze flicks to where the sound came from, and something in his expression shifts.

"So," he says, all business now. "About those security upgrades. I know they're not your main task, but how soon can you implement them?"

The abrupt change in tone reminds me to keep my focus where it belongs. "I can program the system to start spitting out random override codes to all your department heads by this afternoon. And every seven days after that."

Luke nods. He seems to have already finished with this topic despite being the one to ask me to stay and talk. In any case, I forge ahead. "Mr. Thompson's staff can make sure the codes sync up to the outer doors simultaneously."

"Good," he says. But when his expression turns serious, I know last night's security breach is no longer on his mind. "It's early days yet," he says, lowering his voice. "I don't suppose you've made any progress on the matter we hired you for."

By *we*, he means him and his sister, Lark, who runs the New York City Henley Confectionery headquarters. When my Boston boss put me on a conference call with Lark Henley and with her brother, who was on the other side of the world in Sydney, I was thrilled to take this job, solving cybercrime. Exactly what I wanted, especially when Luke Henley said I would need to be onsite. Away from Boston. Away from Ethan, my boyfriend of three years.

"I haven't solved the theft yet," I tell Luke, "but I've only been working on the problem for a few days."

"Fair enough. Let me know when you make progress." He gestures toward the door, and I start moving.

"And Morgan?" he adds when I'm nearly out. The way he says my name, as if I'm something sweet and forbidden, causes my skin to tingle. No one's ever made my hard, manly name sound so sensual before.

"Yes?" I manage, back to a breathy whisper.

"Try not to tackle any more Henley employees in the meantime."

I can't help but smile. "Even if they deserve it?"

His answering grin makes my heart skip. "Even then."

As I leave, my phone buzzes again. This time I check it, and my stomach drops. Two texts from Ethan:

Missing you. Thought I could stand 3 months apart. Now not so sure.

Let me know when free to talk. Discuss moving up your return date??

Guilt floods through me. *What am I doing?* Flirting with my boss when I have a would-be fiancé waiting for me back home? Ethan gave me three months to decide if I wanted to marry him. We've been apart less than a full week, and I'm already . . . *What? Attracted to someone else?*

I need to get my priorities straight, and Luke Henley is definitely not one of them.

4

Morgan

Friday afternoon social gatherings are part of the culture at Henley Confectionery, a cheerful tradition that transforms the workplace into something more communal and welcoming. Several coworkers assured me this isn't an elaborate ruse to start the weekend early, but I suspect it is. And I'm here for it. Totally.

After a long week of scanning every employee's digital fingerprint, I could use a drink or two to unwind. It might also be the way I'm fighting my wildly inappropriate attraction to Luke Henley while avoiding any chance of running into him and, at the same time, fielding Ethan's ever-more demanding texts.

Most companies would use a break room for a little after-hours gathering. But Henley Confectionery has a rooftop lounge and a deck, offering a view of Sydney's skyline and the chance to catch some sun. I get off the elevator to a cheerful room with clusters of high-top tables on one side and a spacious sitting area with oversized chairs and a big sofa on the other.

Through the floor-to-ceiling windows, the city is ablaze with late-afternoon fiery orange hues, literally painting the harbor in liquid fire. And this weekly event looks to be well-attended, not like office birthday parties back home, where a few show up so as not to seem like assholes, eat a quick piece of overly sweet cake, and leave as soon as politely possible.

Luke Henley's employees seem like they're here to enjoy themselves with people they consider friends. Some, already holding acrylic wine glasses or plastic beer cups, have moved outside where fairy lights ramp up the lively social atmosphere. I'm duly impressed.

I'm also glad I chose to wear my favorite jeans, an emerald-green T-shirt, and strappy sandals with a little heel. The casual Friday dress code here is a lot more relaxed than back in Boston, and if I hadn't listened to Zoe in IT, I would have shown up in my usual work attire *sans* jacket and in flats instead of pumps, as if that was dressed down enough. But there are women here in flowery little skirts and even one or two sporting tank tops.

Unfortunately, as I scan the room, half dreading half anticipating seeing Luke, the knot in my stomach tightens. I probably should've gone back to my apartment or ventured out on my own for my first full weekend in the city. I'm still hesitating at the entrance, suddenly imagining sharing this view with Ethan. I think he would love it, and he'd have dragged me into the middle of the crowd already, grabbed us a couple drinks, and started chatting to strangers in his effortlessly friendly way.

Why aren't I head-over-heels and ready to marry him?

"Morgan! You made it." Noah Matthews from sales approaches. His warm Australian accent is a pleasant interruption to my brooding. He's carrying two glasses of wine, and his charming smile seems genuine. "Reckon you'd fancy a drink."

"Thanks." I accept the glass gratefully and follow him to a high-top table. Noah's been friendly all week, his easygoing demeanor blooming into flirtation that I have zero interest in returning.

He stopped by my desk with coffee the day after I arrived. I hadn't even met Luke yet. The next time Noah came into the IT suite, he gave me the low-down on the best, nearby lunch places and placed on my desk a rubber duck stamped with "I ♥ Sydney" on its back and wearing sunglasses. It makes me smile each time I look at it.

He's boyishly handsome in an easygoing way, with curly, sun-bleached hair and laugh lines around his eyes. But his attention makes nothing inside me sit up and take notice.

It's actually rather nice and a relief to be utterly relaxed around a man. Polar opposite to both Ethan and Luke, and even Jack, all for different reasons.

"How ya findin' things 'round here?" Noah leans against the table, close enough that I catch a whiff of his cologne—something crisp and oceanic.

"Still adjusting to the time difference," I admit. "And trying not to say 'elevator' when I should say 'lift.'"

His laugh warms the space between us. "Must be quite a big wallop to your system compared to Boston."

Taking a sip of wine, I wonder how he knows where I'm from, recalling I've only told him I'm from Massachusetts. But office gossip travels faster than the speedy kangaroos that I'm dying to see. He probably knows a lot more, and it's going to be difficult to keep my real purpose a secret.

"Big change," I agree.

"So, what's it like on the other side of this big rock?" Noah prompts, leaning closer. I take it he means half a world away.

"Different," I say, but thinking of Boston brings Ethan to mind.

"Different good or a real shocker?" Noah asks.

Before I can answer, my phone buzzes, right on cue, as if thinking of my boyfriend has conjured yet another text. I ignore it. I've been getting texts from Ethan all week—*at all hours!*—and I've been answering them when I'm alone.

No, I'm not changing my plans.

No, I haven't made any final decisions.

No, I'm not coming home early.

"Different good, because Sydney is new, which makes it exciting," I reply. "But I haven't been out much to see anything yet. I've heard your beaches aren't rocky like a lot of ours are. New England is generally rocky," I add, trailing off because it's been a long week in a strange land, and I'm fried. But Noah is nodding as though my conversation is scintillating so I continue.

"Like you, we have distinct accents across the US, although I don't have what you might have heard is a classic Boston accent." Not growing up in the heart of the city, my speech is decidedly non-descript.

"*Pahk* the *cah* in *Hahvahd yahd*," Noah says, and I laugh at his attempt to mimic the hard-core Bostonians, realizing that Aussies are "r" droppers, too. "Nothing like those New York accents," he notes. "Though I never heard one from Mr. Henley. Maybe he lost it when he came Down Under to live with his nan and pop as a teen."

At hearing Luke's name, heat floods my cheeks. I glance around without meaning to and find him watching us from across the room, arms crossed, expression unreadable. His assistant is jabbering in his ear, but he's clearly not listening. When our eyes meet, his lips curve into that devastating half-smile that makes my heart stutter.

"What else?" Noah asks, and it takes me a few moments to catch up to our conversation.

"About Boston?" I ask, willing myself to keep my gaze on his friendly face. "Our coffee culture is something people go to war over, with Dunkin' Donuts usually winning. And we have the best clam chowder. Your turn," I say.

Noah shrugs. "Can't beat the Sydney lifestyle," he insists, as if that is the beginning and end of it. The look in his eyes tells me an invitation is coming. "If you ever want a friendly guide, I can take you to some hidden gems, away from tourist spots. There's a great place on Manly Beach."

Before I can laugh at the name that invokes a sandy stretch covered in buff dudes, flexing their muscles, the air shifts and I hear footsteps. A glance sideways reveals Luke at my elbow, and my insides do that stupid flutter thing it's been doing all week.

He's ditched his suit jacket and rolled up his sleeves, revealing strong, tanned forearms and a watch that makes me do a double-take. If I had to guess, I'd say the dark-blue strap is alligator hide, but what catches my attention is beneath the crystal-clear face, the internal workings are showing—a bunch of little dials laid bare under the two hands keeping time.

Regardless of his super-cool watch, his casual appearance only makes him more appealing. *He'd be perfect on Manly Beach!*

"Ms. Anders," he says formally, while his eyes hold something warmer. "Enjoying our Friday tradition?"

"I am. It's like nowhere I've ever worked." I take a large sip of wine and decide to stay quiet. No babbling.

"Morgan here's still finding her feet in Sydney," Noah tells Luke. "Reckon I could show her 'round the place, give her the proper local experience, ya know?"

Something flashes in Luke's eyes. "That's thoughtful of you. Though I'm sure Ms. Anders is capable of finding her way."

"Still," Noah persists, "it's always better with a local." He's looking at me again, waiting for an answer.

"Maybe," I tell him noncommittally. "I've got a lot going on right now."

"Trust me, mate, we all do." He leans in conspiratorially, like we're sharing a secret. "But crikey, sometimes you've got to make time for a bit of fun, yeah? Can't be all work and no play. That'll make you a dull sheila, no mistake."

On cue, my phone buzzes again, and I'm wondering if Ethan is psychic with his extremely bad timing. Since both men are staring at me, probably unable to fathom how anyone can ignore a text, I pull my phone from my back pocket and glance at it.

The bakery reopened. Bought your favorite cookies and put them in the freezer for when you come home.

The guilt is immediate and sharp. What am I doing here, letting Noah flirt while thinking about Luke, when my boyfriend is *impatiently* waiting for an answer back home?

"I should probably head out," I say, draining my glass and avoiding eye contact with either man. "Early morning tomorrow."

"It's Saturday," Noah points out, but he's smiling, apparently not good at taking a hint. "At least let me walk ya home?"

I'm about to respond when Luke cuts in. "Actually, Ms. Anders, I need to discuss something with you before you leave." His tone brooks no argument, and Noah straightens up and steps back.

"Of course, Mr. Henley." I hope my voice doesn't betray how my pulse just doubled.

"Another time then," Noah says, and his eyes promise he means it.

$♥$♥$♥$

Luke

I've been watching Morgan from the moment she arrived in that shimmery green shirt that clings to her breasts like molten chocolate poured over a couple scoops of ice cream. I can't bullshit myself about maintaining purely professional interest. She's hot. And besides her unbelievable hotness, something about this woman is stoking every visceral craving I have.

I notice the way she keeps subtly shifting away from Noah Matthews' advances. How she touches her phone whenever it buzzes almost without realizing, her expression clouding. And I'm acutely aware of the soft curves of her body in those well-worn jeans that make my hands itch to trace the seams.

Purely professional? *Not even close.*

When Noah suggested walking her home, something snapped. I spoke without thinking, inserting myself into their conversation with a flimsy excuse about work. Now, as we step into the elevator together, I realize I haven't actually planned what to say.

"So, what did you need to discuss?" Morgan asks, her voice carefully neutral.

The doors close, and suddenly the space feels too small, too intimate. She smells like vanilla and wine, and I want to press her against the wall and taste both on her lips.

"I thought you might need rescuing," I confess, watching her reflection in the polished doors instead of looking directly at her. She's not Medusa, for God's sake, although she definitely has an unearthly power over me. Braving this woman's enticing charms, I face her.

She raises an eyebrow. "From Noah? He seems harmless enough."

"Harmless isn't exactly a glowing recommendation." The words come out more derogatory than intended.

In low-heeled sandals, Morgan has to tilt her head back to meet my eyes. "I wasn't aware I needed your approval for potential da . . . friends."

She nearly said "dates." The thought of her dating Noah—or anyone—brings a sour taste to my mouth. I'm not usually territorial, but Lark and I brought her halfway around the world, so I suppose I do feel protective.

"You don't," I assure her. "But Matthews is the type who won't take no for an answer. I know because that's how he got the job." Then, as if it's any of my business, and sounding like a maiden aunt, I add, "For some reason, I had the idea there was someone back in Boston. Someone who texts you. A lot."

I'm hoping to hear the messages are from family and friends who miss her, not a significant other. *Wrong.*

Her face falls slightly. "It's complicated."

Damn. The worst kind of significant other is a complicated one. The elevator doors open to the lobby, and I gesture for her to exit first.

"I'll walk you home." I make it a statement rather than a question, because I'm not looking for permission.

"We can talk about *complicated.* Or whatever you like."

Outside, Sydney's night air wraps around us like silk, warm and slightly humid. Morgan walks beside me, her heels making the barest of sound against the pavement. Two blocks, one down and one over, like a chess move. That's all we have before we reach her apartment, and I'm already regretting the moment I'll have to let her go.

"So?" I prompt, as if we're best buds at a bar.

She sighs, and in the sinking sunlight, I catch the vulnerability in her expression. "His name is Ethan. We've been together three years, and before I left, he asked me to marry him."

My chest tightens. I wasn't expecting that level of involvement. Nor did I mean the next question to jump from my mouth. "And you said?"

She sighs. "That I needed time, which is why I jumped at this job." She laughs, but it's hollow. "I don't know why I'm telling you this, but Henley Confectionery provided three months breathing space and also the perfect excuse to get some distance and figure out what I really want."

I can't believe I'm going to be this nosy, but I want to know the answer just about as much as I want my next breath. "And what do you want, Morgan?"

She stops walking. The city lights paint her skin in soft gold, and all I can think about is how perfectly she fit against me that first night, even while trying to keep me pinned down.

"I don't know," she whispers. "That's the problem."

We're outside her building now, and I know I should say goodnight and turn around. Fast. Instead, I step closer, close enough to see the flutter of her pulse at her throat. "Maybe I can help you figure it out."

Her breath catches, and for a moment, I think she might close the distance between us and let me kiss her. Then her phone buzzes again, and the spell breaks.

"Goodnight, Mr. Henley," she says softly, stepping away.

Watching her disappear into the building, I know I'm in dangerous territory. As she said, she's only here for three months, and the first week is already over. What's more, she's my employee and practically engaged. But standing here in the Sydney sunset, I realize I don't care about any of that.

I want her. And unless I know nothing about women, I'm sure she wants me too.

5

Morgan

I smell the flowers as soon as I enter the ground floor IT suite. A riot of vibrant colors spills from a vase perched on my desk, the sweet scent encircling me like a warm hug. Carnations, happy yellows, bright pinks, and sunny oranges, burst forth in stark contrast to the muted tones of the office, reminding me of last night's sunset.

My first thought is that they're from Luke Henley, followed really quickly by the notion that Ethan must have sent them to remind me he's waiting and that he loves me. My breath catches, however, as I notice the small handwritten card tucked among the blooms.

"Hope you have a great day! - Noah."

Groaning inwardly, I roll my eyes at the audacity of my persistent coworker, despite having given him no encouragement. As much as I appreciate his thoughtful gesture, my focus should be entirely on unraveling the mystery of the cybercrime plaguing Henley Confectionery, not fending off unwelcome advances.

So why did I hope they were from Luke for a split second? *Because his advances aren't unwelcome*, I confess to myself.

Taking my seat, I push the vase to the far corner of the desk and open the company laptop that Jack provided on day one, giving me unfettered access to everything being handled on and through the company servers. Regardless, the heady aroma of the roses serves as a reminder that I'm not just a happy-go-lucky employee, doing her job before going back home to my loving fiancé.

The juxtaposition of welcoming fragrance and inexplicable tension in my life isn't lost on me. And I can't forget Luke Henley's undeniable presence a few floors above. A few minutes later, I head to the break room one floor up. My passion for Lemon, Lime, and Bitters, which everyone calls LLB, caused me to drink the last of an embarrassingly large supply yesterday evening. I treat it the way I used to drink Mountain Dew in grad school to keep me peppy while programming.

Today, I'll have to switch to coffee, not without a little trepidation. Not because I don't enjoy it, but I'm not lying when I say the intricate coffee machine here at Henley Confectionery has bested me each time I've tried to use it. Which is a total of twice.

The break room is empty apart from the fragrant aroma of chocolate and nuts. Henley's is the only company I've ever worked at with a supply of complimentary high-quality candy at all times. Some places offer bowls of foil-wrapped Kisses or lemon balls or—*the worst*—red licorice!

On the counter next to the stainless-steel refrigerator, there's a stack of boxed chocolates, with the top one unsealed. If I don't find anything I like, I can open the next one in the stack. Luke's assistant told me that on my first day. So far, I've always found one I like in the first box.

Grinning like a kid, I lift the lid and choose what I now know is a dark chocolate-covered caramel. It disappears into my pie hole before I face the machine that looks like it belongs in a spaceship. I read the little labels on the various buttons, but some are worn off, which doesn't make it any easier. After a few moments, I lean over and eat another caramel. They are my weakness. This one has nuts, too.

Chewing, I pick up a cup, placing it under the spout. Got that part down pat.

"Need help?"

I jump at Luke Henley's voice behind me and try to swallow the candy at the same time. To my horror, I choke, and some brown goo oozes out of the corner of my mouth, which I quickly cover with my hand.

Stepping closer, the CEO slaps my back until I hold up my free hand to stop his enthusiastic ministrations. He grabs a bottle of water out of the fridge and hands it to me. I wish I could speak and thank him, but my teeth are stuck with caramel and coated with nuts and chocolate.

Turning away from him, I take a swig and reach for a napkin, and work on getting all the candy down my throat. When I finally look at Luke, I'm hoping I'm clean and tidy, although my lipstick is once again long gone.

"Thanks," I say, saluting him awkwardly with the water bottle, which causes a few drops to spill onto the floor. "I think I can manage." I turn back to the machine, with my heart racing and my cheeks burning at being so ridiculously uncool.

"Really?" From close behind, he reaches around me, his chest brushing my back. I gasp, but all he does is press a couple buttons. "Because you'd been staring at the coffee maker for a long time before I walked in."

The machine whirs to life. As if I've never seen coffee made, I keep my eyes firmly on the filling cup, watching as frothy milk is added. He didn't ask how I take my coffee, and I don't care. At this point, I'll take it however it comes. I remain motionless. It seems an eternity before the coffee reaches the brim, with Luke standing still behind me. Finally, when I reach for the cup, he moves back, and my entire body instantly misses his warmth.

I don't face him right away, taking a moment to collect myself and my freshly brewed coffee. Something about this man rattles me, which makes no sense logically. He's just another handsome face atop a mouth-wateringly perfect body. I'm not bad looking myself, so I've had no shortage of guys coming on to me in my adult life. Ethan is good-looking, too, proving it's not about looks. Rather, I swear I could close my eyes and "feel" where Luke Henley is. What's more, I want to move closer to that spot.

There's nothing rational about how my body is locking in on his energy and digging it. *Big time.*

When I turn, his golden-brown eyes are fixed on me as I knew they would be. "Thank you, Mr. Henley."

"Luke," he corrects quietly, the tone of his voice making parts of me clench in response.

My cheeks feel even hotter, as do other places. I am in utter lust with this man. To cover my embarrassment, I lift the cup to my lips.

"Careful," he warns, and I freeze again. "The machine makes great coffee," Luke says, "but it's often a bit too hot. I've got to get someone to turn down the temperature."

Amen to that. It always feels like an inferno when he's around. He looks amazing in a tan suit and a plain white shirt. No tie. Kind of Aussie outback meets Wall Street.

"Everything okay?" Luke asks into the silence.

"Fine." I force a smile. Indicating the coffee with a nod of my head, I explain, "I'm out of LLB." His eyebrows shoot up, and he appears to be fighting off a laugh.

"It is tasty stuff," he agrees finally. Then he opens the fridge again to show me an entire shelf of it. "Next time you have a hankering for anything, just ask me. I bet I can satisfy whatever you're craving."

My eyes are probably as round as tennis balls. There's no mistaking what he's saying. Although I could be totally imagining the double-entendre. Nodding, I smile, pivot, nearly spill coffee on my blouse, and head for the door.

"Morgan," he calls after me, and I halt. Coming up beside me, he's holding a lid. "I think you need this."

Now I'm sure Luke is laughing at me. Taking the lid, knowing he touches my fingers on purpose because he's enjoying my discomfort, I square my shoulders and walk out. I deserve to humiliate myself. After all, what kind of woman leaves her fiancé behind so she can seriously think about their future and accepts flowers from another man while flirting with yet another man at the same time?

Fortunately, I don't see the sexy CEO again all day. I've been following cyber trails, hunched over my laptop for hours. I met with the VP for about half an hour, even though Luke insisted during our first phone call that he trusts everyone in the C-suite.

I also had a friendly chat with the head of accounting and one of the shipping managers. They're all curious as to why I need to speak with them, but nice enough to give me their valuable time. I do my best to put each at ease, letting them know their input as to operations helps me craft the new cybersecurity program. It's all BS, but most people like to talk about their jobs.

At quitting time, with no breakthroughs, while I'm packing up to walk home, Noah appears. With a little dread, I've been expecting him, but I lie.

"Glad you stopped by," I say. "Thank you so much for the flowers. What a treat on a Monday morning."

"Spotted the lot of 'em and straight up thought of you," he says. "Pretty and bright." He leans forward, entering my personal space. "And sweet smelling."

My smile is forced. "I need to tell you something," I say, and his expression falters. "I have a boyfriend back home. A live-in one."

"*Oh.*" For a moment, Noah looks downtrodden, but he rallies quickly. "I can respect that." He sticks out his hand, and I have to take it. "Mates only, fair enough. And why not? If I was Nicole from sales instead of Noah, you'd let me walk you home or show you the touristy bits or hit the beach with me, right? Nothing flash, just a couple of cobbers having a ripper time."

"I suppose so," I begin, thinking it might be nice to have a friend in Sydney. "But you're *not* Nicole. You're—"

"As safe as a koala takin' a nap," he promises, then he frowns. "Been through a rough patch lately, had me heart broken proper. Reckon I saw you and thought maybe I could bounce back quick smart, yeah? But truth is, mate, I'm just a bit lonely these days. Since you're new to our neck of the woods, thought maybe we could hang out, no worries. No drama. Let me be your Aussie tour guide. Now that I know the lay of the land where your heart is concerned, I promise there'll be no pressure, no flirting, no innuendo."

He smiles, and it's genuine. I appreciate how Noah showed me his vulnerable side.

"You're only here for a few months," he reminds me. "Might as well see the sights with a local. Most of us are fair dinkum, but there's always a few dodgy blokes who'll try to have you on or take the mickey. Be a shame if you copped a raw deal from some galah when you could have a proper mate showin' ya 'round instead."

I consider, do my best to translate, and decide to trust him. As long as we're being honest with one another, why not? Besides, if I'm with Noah at the beach or at a bar, other men will leave me alone. Like having my own personal bodyguard.

"All right," I agree.

"Then I'll walk you back to your place," he says.

"I don't see why not, but I'm not inviting you inside. Agreed?"

"Fair go, then. But maybe some other night, you'll have me 'round. We can get some tucker delivered. What's your fancy?" Noah asks as we head out of IT and cross the lobby. "Got the lot here. Pizza, Indian, kebabs, chook shop, Thai," he rattles on.

"What's a chook shop?"

He laughs. "Chook's what we call chicken." Noah rubs his hands together, his eyes practically dancing. "Crikey, I know this ripper joint that serves up the most bonza bird you've ever laid eyes on. Done proper crispy or spinning on the spit, with a mountain of hot chips that'd make your noggin look tiny!"

With my mouth watering, I'm starting to change my mind about tonight since nothing in my nearly empty kitchen rivals any of that. "Actually," I hear myself saying, despite my better judgment, "maybe we could—"

"Ms. Anders." Luke's voice cuts through the evening air, making both Noah and me turn. He's standing a few feet away, his suit jacket draped over one arm, looking like he just stepped out of a magazine cover shoot. Actually, he's just climbed out of the back seat of a car, which drives off, merging into Sydney traffic. I stare at him. The way his white shirt stretches across his shoulders should be illegal.

"I need to speak with you," he says, his golden topaz eyes giving nothing away. "Now."

Noah shrugs good-naturedly. "No worries, mate. Another time then, yeah?" He gives me a friendly wave and heads off, leaving me alone with Luke and my rising irritation.

"It's after hours," I point out, but the CEO ignores me, holding the door open and clearly expecting me to go back inside. "And Noah was just walking me home."

I bite my tongue. *Why did I explain that?*

"This has nothing to do with Noah," Luke says, following me into the lobby. His hand settles on my lower back, guiding me toward the elevator, and my skin tingles through my blouse. "My family's been calling, wanting updates on the investigation. We haven't spoken about it since last week, and I meant to catch you before you left."

The elevator arrives with a soft ding, and we step inside. As the doors close, I turn to face him. "I would have updated you if I had anything concrete to report. I'm still gathering data, following trails. These things take time."

"Time," he repeats, moving closer. "Like the time you're spending letting Noah show you around Sydney?"

I narrow my eyes. "You said this had nothing to do with him," I snap, my temper flaring. Ethan can be a little controlling at times, and that's the last thing I want or expect from my temporary employer. Lifting my chin, I take a step closer, too. "Besides, what I do in my off hours—"

His mouth crashes down on mine, cutting off my words. For a split second, I'm too shocked to respond. However, when his hands cup my face, I tilt my head to give Luke better access, and rational thought flies out the window. His lips are firm but gentle, coaxing rather than demanding, and I melt into him with a small whimper. At the same time, with the heat sizzling between us, I breathe in whatever cologne he's wearing.

It. Is. Heavenly. Woodsy, silk sheets, spice, and manliness. I think no matter what happens, I have to ask him what it is and keep a bottle beside my bed.

The elevator dings again for each floor, but we don't break apart. Instead, Luke backs me against the wall, one hand sliding into my hair while the other grips my hip. I clutch his shoulders, feeling the solid muscle beneath his shirt, and part my lips on a gasp. Taking full advantage, he deepens the kiss until the elevator stops. As the doors start to open, we spring apart, staring at . . . an empty corridor. Luckily!

My heart pounds so hard I can barely hear anything else. I touch my lips, still feeling the imprint of his kiss, the taste of coffee, and something distinctly *Luke* lingering on my tongue. *What have I done? What have I let him do?*

Luke steps out, and I follow on shaky legs. "Morgan," he says softly, reaching for me.

I hold up my hand. "No. We can't." My voice trembles. "I have someone back home who trusts me. And you're my boss. This is—"

"Complicated," Luke suggests. "You warned me before." He runs a hand through his disheveled hair. I must have done that, I realize with a jolt, messed it up like a woman feeling serious desire. "Because you're temporary? Because of Ethan?"

The sound of his name on Luke's lips is like a bucket of ice water pouring over my head. I actually shiver. "All of the above," I manage, but it comes out on a whisper. "Plus, I'm here to find out who's stealing from your company."

"And you already know Noah's innocent?" Luke's expression hardens.

The abrupt change in topic throws me. "What does Noah have to do with this?"

"Maybe nothing, but who knows?" Luke moves closer again, until I can see the gold flecks in his topaz-colored eyes. And it takes all my willpower not to back up like a chicken. "You're investigating cyber theft in my company," he says. "I told you I trust my executives, but I could be wrong. They should still be on your list. As for Noah and everyone else, they're all suspects until proven otherwise."

"Including you?" The words slip out before I can stop them.

His eyes darken. "Definitely not. I'm the only one in the entire company you can talk to about this. So why don't we go to my office and talk about what you've found so far? Unless you'd rather discuss this in the hallway?"

But I don't make a move. "You can't do what you just did."

"What *we* just did," he clarifies.

"What *you* initiated, getting into my personal space. Whether in Australia or the US, as you know, there are laws."

Luke Henley doesn't look the least bit worried. "Are you going to press charges?"

I don't hesitate. I'm not playing games. "No."

He nods. "I don't mean to be arrogant—"

I make a sound of disbelief that interrupts him. He grins.

"Really, I don't. I thought I read you right. If I was wrong, then it'll never happen again. Do you want me to promise nothing will ever happen again between us, Morgan?"

He's not playing fair, saying my name like it's a lover's song. Besides, I'd be lying if I said I wanted him to promise that. I should say I do, but I don't. Regardless, it cannot happen again, now or soon . . . or maybe ever. If I'm strong.

"Your office," I say firmly. "And *just* talking."

"Just talking," he agrees, but his slight smile tells me he's thinking about the kiss too.

Then I point out, "And I never said Noah was innocent of the cybercrime, only harmless in other ways." All the ways that the CEO most definitely is not.

Luke rolls his eyes at the distinction. Following him down the hallway, watching his firm ass in his fitted slacks, I try to focus on the case, on my job, on anything but the lingering warmth of his lips on mine or where his fingers gripped my hip through my skirt. But deep down, I know I'm in serious trouble. Because that kiss wasn't mere physical attraction or momentary weakness.

It felt like coming home.

6

Luke

For two days, I've managed to avoid Morgan Anders. Mostly. I still catch glimpses of her through the security feed, which I can view on my laptop. A couple times, I've rewound footage just to watch her walk across the lobby, her long brown hair swaying whether she wears it down or in a ponytail.

Like a lovesick teenager, I notice every detail—how she always takes the stairs up but the elevator down, how she brings her own lunch and eats at her desk while working, how she fidgets with her phone whenever it buzzes. Which is often.

The kiss haunts me. I can still taste her, still feel her pressed against me in the elevator. But I managed to do the right thing afterward, keeping our discussion strictly on business. I even let her leave alone, though everything in me wanted to walk her home.

Now, staring at the same document I've been trying to read for the past half hour, an email from Lark, I know I can't stay away any longer. Not when there's a legitimate reason to see her. Grabbing my jacket, I head down to the IT department.

Morgan's at her desk, absorbed in whatever's on her screen. I already know she's wearing slim navy slacks and a cream blouse from my morning's virtual voyeurism. Up close, I notice her hair is twisted in some intricate knot that makes me want to remove the pins or bands or clips, or whatever the hell holds it in place, and watch it tumble down.

I clear my throat, and she jumps slightly.

"Mr. Henley," she says formally, though her cheeks flush pink.

"Ms. Anders." I lean against her desk, careful not to disturb the vase of now-wilting flowers from Noah. "I'd like you to accompany me to our factory in Wetherill Park today."

Her eyebrows rise. "The factory?"

Glancing around, seeing there's an IT tech at her desk, with her eyes on us, I say only, "I've been thinking about potential security breaches."

Actually, I want to discuss a thought that occurred to me, that the cyber theft could be originating from somewhere other than this building, including from our production facility. But until we're alone, all I can add is, "Besides, you should see how we make the candy you've been so enthusiastically sampling."

A small smile plays at her lips. "Are you suggesting I've been eating too many chocolates, Mr. Henley?"

"Not at all." I grin, remembering her stuffing two into her mouth at once. Then a wickedly erotic thought enters my over-charged brain about what else her sweet mouth could hold. Trying to keep the mood light, I say, "I noticed in the break room, you favor the dark chocolate turtles."

Her blush deepens. "When do we leave?"

I have a meeting and a few things I have to do. "After lunch," I suggest. "About 1:15. I'll come back here to collect you."

She glances at her screen, probably considering her workload. Then she nods as I know she will because I'm the boss. In a couple of hours, I'm back at IT, watching her close down her laptop, shove it into a satchel, and grab her purse.

Jack comes out of his office just as we're leaving, his eyes full of envy. He's a good tech head, but he could never do what Morgan's Boston boss said she can do—catch a thief who's leaving no trace, no fingerprints, nothing except, I hope, a careless digital breadcrumb.

In the parking garage, I lead her to my car—a black Audi R8. It's fun to drive, and I'm looking forward to the short jaunt westward to the factory. Morgan glances from the sleek car to me, and her eyes widen slightly.

"Nice," she says, sliding into the passenger seat. The man-child inside of me pumps my fist into the air, hoping I've duly impressed the girl. But I keep a cool exterior, despite this being the single most awesome vehicle I've ever owned.

"It gets me where I need to go," I say, and close her door. I sound like a prick. No one buys this car to simply go from A to B. I bought it for the style, the V10 engine, and the absolute joy of driving this well-engineered machine. Cranking it on, I let it purr for a moment, and then say something she may not believe. "Sometimes I miss my red ute from my teenage years on my grandparents' ranch." I was sixteen and loved driving that truck all over the dirt roads and hills and through their vineyards.

"Your what?" she asks.

"Sorry, *ute* is short for utility vehicle," I explain, pulling out onto the street. "But it's not a UTV, or utility terrain vehicle. Here, a ute is what we call a pickup truck in the States. Got it?"

Morgan laughs, which is a wonderful sound. Rare, too, since usually, we're locked in some epic battle of control—losing it or keeping it—or breathing hard as we try to maintain our distance.

"I can't picture you in a pickup," she says.

Interesting. "No? What do you picture me in?" Out of the corner of my eye, I see her turn, so I glance over. Our eyes meet briefly and the tension between us instantly returns, filling the small, luxurious interior. I have to look away first or risk killing us both.

"Something *exactly* like this," she says quietly.

The drive to Wetherill Park takes about forty minutes, during which we maintain a careful conversation about work for the first half, then relax and wander into more personal territory. I tell her how I was born in the States, but spent a lot of time here with my grandparents on their ranch and, later, helped in the candy factory during school holidays. Eventually, I moved to Australia full-time.

Morgan returns the personal info data dump, telling me she has two sisters back in Boston, both parents alive and well, and that she got her start in everything computer-related from her dad.

We don't mention the kiss.

At the factory, Jim Peters, our longtime manager, meets us at the entrance. He's a barrel-chested man with silver hair and weathered skin from years of surfing.

"G'day, Luke," he says warmly, then eyes Morgan. "You must be the security sheila from the States?"

"Morgan Anders," she introduces herself, shaking his hand firmly.

Jim leads us through the facility, past gleaming machines and conveyor belts carrying rivers of confectionery. The air is thick with sweet aromas—chocolate, vanilla, caramel, and roasting nuts, and Morgan is instantly mesmerized by the sights and the scents.

Workers in white coats and hair nets nod as we pass, and I answer her questions, since Jim is always a yard ahead, checking gauges with the scrutiny of a submarine commander.

"I feel like I'm walking with Willy Wonka," she quips quietly, so only I can hear. I love that soft whisper of hers.

"I do occasionally wear a top-hat and tails," I tease. "Where is my extra-large candy cane when I need it?" Then I think of Jim's tanned face and nearly white eyebrows and can't hold back a short laugh. "If I were you, I wouldn't tell Jim you think he's an Oompa-Loompa." She shoots me an exaggerated grin, as recognition dawns on her face.

In one of the quality control areas, Jim insists we try the latest batch of sea salt caramels, plucking them directly off the moving conveyor belt. Morgan's eyes close in bliss when she bites into one, and I have to look away from her expression of pure pleasure. I want to see that again in a decidedly less-wholesome circumstance, preferably both of us bare-assed, and me having just elicited from her the biggest orgasm of her life.

"These are amazing," she says, licking a spot of chocolate from her thumb. The innocent gesture furthers my fantasy, sending heat straight to my groin.

"Wait'll you try our new product," Jim says proudly. "Dark chocolate with macadamia nuts and . . ." He trails off as his phone rings. Checking the number, he adds, "Sorry, need to take this. Show her the nerve center, yeah?" Everyone at the factory talks to me like I work for them, because at one time, I did.

Once we're alone in the climate-controlled IT hub above the factory floor, Morgan's professional demeanor returns. In the first room, she examines the setup with curious eyes, asking technical questions I barely understand of those who keep all the robotic mixers, coating and dipping machines, one-shot mold filling machines, small bag fillers, and even the roasting ovens chugging along via computer programming.

Of course, there are real people at every stage with the ability to override, speed up, and slow down any part of the production, and I have worked each job, even loaded the pallets, while learning the business. My sister, Lark, did, too.

Currently, Morgan is peering over an employee's shoulder at a screen showing our high-speed robotic palletizer, which does the loading task better than I did. Meanwhile, I look at her incredible curves in those tailored, figure-hugging slacks. *Down boy!*

Next, we go into the sales and security room. It's less busy and noisy in here where there are simply three desks. I introduce Morgan to Jenny and Alinta, occupying two of them. They handle any issues with orders or shipments, although it's mostly automated.

Opposite them is where Mark sits, but he's not around. His screen shows a security feed to the perimeter and another one that revolves among all the factory rooms and hallways. Seeing Morgan in this environment, taking it all in with confidence and capability, only makes her more attractive.

When we head downstairs, she says, "I saw security personnel outside when we came through the gate. Do they patrol at night?"

"They do. In our Sydney offices, there's nothing much to lose apart from laptops and that coffee machine you're so fond of."

She makes a face, and I laugh before adding, "But here, we've got expensive inventory and highly specialized machinery. Can't let any of that get stolen or tampered with."

Morgan nods. "Can I get remote access to everything on those computers once we're back at the office?"

She's gone beyond my pay grade. "I don't know. Can you?" I ask.

This engenders a wry smile from her. "We'll make sure I can before we leave," she says, before I hold open the door to the tasting room.

When she enters, her glance flits over the sterile steel drawers with glass fronts, holding candy samples, and the sparkling-clean counters in which we can see our reflections.

"Wow," she mutters. I remember how I felt my first time in here. I think I ate myself sick in about twenty minutes, but then, I was a kid.

"Jim left us a sample of the chocolate-coated macadamia clusters," I point out, and we both head to a shiny steel tray with half a dozen identical candies. "Ready?"

"Ready," she says. Staring into one another's eyes, we both put an entire chocolate in our mouths. It only takes a second for the burst of sweet flavor, which deepens to a satisfying richness, followed by the creamy nuttiness. I don't know if she can taste it, but there's vanilla in this recipe as well as honey.

"That's almost obscenely delicious," she says. Without hesitation, she takes another one and wolfs it down. I know we make an awesome product, but earning Morgan's high praise gives me an extra boost of happiness, mixed with pride.

"To think it all started in my nan's kitchen," I say and point behind her. She turns to see the framed photograph of their homey kitchen, before the ranch endured upgrades and expansions. Morgan goes closer.

"Looks quaint and pretty," she muses.

If she could see the place now, it's anything but quaint. "Maybe I'll show it to you sometime," I say, not really thinking about whether my invitation is advisable or appropriate.

She turns to give me a long look before nodding, and I wonder if I've crossed a line even more than when I kissed her in the elevator. Because in the blink of an eye, Morgan is back to business.

"The security here is actually better than at headquarters," she says. "And not just because of the presence of 24/7 guards outside. From what I saw, the software for the orders and sales is a different system entirely."

"Is that significant?" I ask. She bites her lip while thinking. I'm fascinated, watching her teeth sink into that plump lower lip of hers. *Have mercy!*

"It could be," she says. "I'll have to mull it over."

"Another chocolate?" I offer.

She gives me the most adorable lopsided grin. "Maybe just one." It takes her so long to look through all the possibilities and choose, I want to grab a few of every kind and insist she try them all. We'll definitely take a few boxes for the road.

Finally, she tries what we call, for purely marketing purposes, a *Parisian.* A smooth, dense, chocolate-custard center, infused with coffee, vanilla, elderflower, and caramel, is coated in tempered dark chocolate. The last production step is rolling the truffle in milk chocolate flecks before the outer chocolate shell is entirely cool.

"I've found another favorite," Morgan says, leaving a little on her lip. Her tongue comes out but misses the chocolate piece entirely. At last, given this stellar opportunity, I cannot keep from touching her.

Brushing her lower lip with my thumb at the same moment as she closes her eyes and gives a hum of satisfaction, our fairly innocent encounter jumps into the erotic zone in seconds. As I stroke her plump lip, her eyes remain closed for a long moment before they languidly open.

Falling into her blue gaze, all the air leaves my lungs. And whatever remains in the room is electrically charged like we're in the middle of a lightning storm.

A second kiss is not optional. It's mandatory. I lower my mouth to hers, and she tilts her chin, offering herself. Not much tastes better than a woman who has just eaten a Henley chocolate. Well, maybe a few things, but we might get to that later. In the meantime, I have her trapped between the counter and my growing need, hoping I've read her right.

When her arms go around me and her hands actually rest on my ass, I feel empowered. Pressing my hips against hers, I'm grateful she's wearing high heels, putting her mound at the exact right level.

Morgan moans when my tongue slides between her lips. Then wonder of wonders, she sucks it. *Well, hell!* Our kiss continues because there's nothing to stop it except her and me, and neither one of us seems willing. Until somewhere nearby, a door slams, breaking the moment. We don't jump apart, but we do return to our senses, and slowly, I back away.

Even before we see him, Jim is talking as he rounds the corner and enters the tasting room. Maybe he didn't want to surprise us doing exactly what we'd been doing a few moments earlier.

"There you are. Sorry I took so long," he says. I only wish he'd taken about an hour longer.

The three of us return to the main floor and finish the tour. Jim does send Morgan home with an assorted box, as if she can't have Henley candy every day of the week. The drive back to Sydney is quiet, filled with unspoken words and growing tension.

"Dinner?" I offer because candy does one thing spectacularly, make your blood sugar rise and crash, leaving you hungry for real food. At least, it does for me. Surprisingly, Morgan says yes, when I was expecting to be brushed off.

This isn't a date, I remind myself, just a work dinner at the end of a long day. I'm careful not to take her anywhere dark or romantic. No tablecloths or candles. I know those would freak her out. We end up at the Squire's Landing, a brewhouse at the Overseas Passenger Terminal. In our work clothes, we fit in perfectly with the rest of the tired Sydney workforce, grabbing beers and burgers.

Without Morgan noticing, I pay a little extra so we have a window table and can see the illuminated Opera House, which juts out into the harbor on the other side of the busy quay. Being a billionaire has its privileges, which I rarely exploit.

We eat in companionable silence, and I learn she likes fried spring rolls as much as I do, and bacon with mango chutney on her burger. She mentions her excitement at digging into those other computers remotely via the factory's server tomorrow.

"You really are a techno geek, aren't you?"

Morgan takes that as a compliment, just as I intended. After dinner, the ride to her building is only thirteen minutes. I park, knowing I should drop her off and leave. *Fast.*

Instead, I turn into the parking garage under the corporate apartment rental and take a visitor's spot.

"I'll walk you up," I say, and it's not really a question.

In the elevator—*why is it always elevators with us?*—Morgan stands as far from me as possible. But when we reach her floor, she turns to me with a look in her eyes that says she has come to some decision.

"Would you like to come in?"

I should say no. I have every reason to say no.

"Yes," I say. "Very much."

7

Morgan

As I unlock the apartment door, my heart pounds so hard I'm sure Luke can hear it. My fingers tremble slightly holding the key, and when his hand brushes my lower back, a shiver runs through me. His touch is light, probably meant to be reassuring, but it only heightens my awareness of what I'm about to do. *With him.*

Stepping inside my temporary home, I flip the switch, showering us in an artificially harsh daylight glow. Luckily, it's dimmable, and I push the bar down to a level so we don't need our sunglasses. Everything in here is gray and white and chrome, reminding me of the tasting room I was in earlier today.

There's no hallway. Basically, in two steps, we're in the main room housing a kitchen to my right that consists of one long counter with a sink and appliances. In front of it is a glass table and four gray chairs. The rest of the room consists of a gray area rug over the faux wood floor and a single gray sofa with a glass table, both situated before a floor-to-ceiling sliding door. Beyond it is a balcony, invisible at this time of night.

"What it lacks in hominess," I quip as I drop my purse and laptop satchel on the dining table beside my personal laptop, "it makes up for in minimalist modernity."

Luke grimaces, and I recall his company is paying for it. "Not that I think there's anything wrong with it," I add in case he's offended. Hurrying over to the gaping blackness of the huge slider, I work the metal drawstring that brings down the pale-gray shades.

"Nothing wrong with it if you enjoy living in a glorified doctor's office," he says. We both laugh, and I relax a little, even though he seems like a massive, 3-D, full-color figure arbitrarily dropped into a black-and-white photo.

"It's not that bad," I tell him. "Sure, it's a lot of gray. A lot! But at least I'm high enough that I see treetops instead of cars out the windows." Also, it's my own fault for not adding any personal touches, apart from my breakfast dishes in the sink. I wish I'd shoved them in the dishwasher this morning, but I'd lingered too long in bed and didn't want to be late for work. "Besides, the bed is comfy."

I freeze as soon as I've uttered those words. We both swing our attention to the open door revealing the bedroom with its decidedly unmade bed.

"For sleeping, I mean. Probably for other things as well, but I only know it for sleeping. I've surfed the internet while lying there, too, of course, and eaten a bowl of ice cream. Don't we all, but usually . . ."

When Luke closes the distance between us, I swallow my rambling words—*thank God!*—and brace myself to accept his kiss. As soon as his mouth covers mine, my tension and most of my muscles melt like warm chocolate, and my brain grinds to a halt. His hands roam down my back until he gives my ass a gentle squeeze before tilting me against him. He's already hard as a rock.

Wow! He can't tell yet, but my own body has reacted by drenching my panties. It's a startling feeling, not typical at all, a little frightening in the intensity of my reaction. And it's the little slither of fear that makes me push my hands against his chest and break the kiss. I don't mean to be a tease, but I've entered unfamiliar territory.

Breathing hard, I blurt out, "Would you like a drink?"

Luke's eyes widen for a moment. I think he's getting his raging libido under control because he nods, maybe sensing my conflicted emotions.

"Sure. That would be great." His deep voice carries a hint of strain that matches the tension I feel. Unfortunately, right about then, the voice inside my head, which desperately needs silencing most of the time, reminds me I don't have anything to offer him besides water, a half-drunk can of LLB, or whole milk for making coffee on the weekend.

Moving toward the fridge, all of four steps, I'm still wondering what the hell I'm doing. His presence behind me is almost tangible, like our waves of attraction are creating an actual force field. Moreover, now that he's kissed me again, I'm acutely aware of the intoxicating scent that's been driving me crazy since our first kiss. His cologne is probably labeled *Eau de Desire*.

"So, water, milk, or LLB?"

Without laughing at me, he says, "Water's fine." Class act. So why am I hiding with my head in the refrigerator?

Shutting it, I grab two glasses and fill them from the tap. When I turn, he's moved silently away, giving me space. Poking two fingers between the blinds, so the streetlamp glistens off his wristwatch, he's faking interest in the dark night, and I stare a moment at the sexy attractiveness that is Luke Henley. Muscled shoulders and arms, rock hard thighs, from what I've felt. Six-foot-three, if I'm guessing correctly. And his soft hair and unusual golden-brown eyes. *Damn!*

But it's not any of that. At least not *only* his looks. I'm not that shallow, although any woman would be forgiven if she were turned on around him. Because of my current situation, I could fight the lust. After all, Ethan is no dog. In fact, he's a hottie who I'm lucky to have in my corner. Yet I can honestly say I've never had such a strong, knock-me-off-my-feet reaction to him, or to any man, as I feel for Luke. And that's the nut of it.

It's this overpowering zippity-zap connection that makes me hyper-aware of everything he's doing and saying. It's the way he makes me tingle. It's how I want to know his thoughts. *Weird.* Hopefully not obsessive weird.

Taking a deep breath, I join Luke and touch his shoulder. After all, he can only politely pretend interest in the nothing-view for so long, while thoughtfully giving me a chance to regroup myself. When I hand him his drink, our fingers brush, and electricity zings through me. Taking a long sip of water, I try to calm my racing pulse, but the tepid liquid does nothing to ease the heat building inside me.

"Ice cubes?" I blurt out. Something I actually have. Setting my glass down on the coffee table, I start to dash away again. Before I can take a step, he snakes out a hand and holds my arm.

"Morgan," Luke says softly, setting his glass down beside mine without letting me go. The way he says my name makes my knees weak. "We don't have to—"

I cut him off by pressing my lips to his. *Oh yes*, I think. *Yes, we do.* My lady-bits would form a mutiny against my brain if we didn't. My body has never been so revved and ready.

Responding immediately, he pulls me close as the kiss deepens. His hands slide into my hair, finally releasing it as he finds and undoes the two clips, which he tosses somewhere. I don't care. All I care about is the way his mouth moves against mine, how his body feels pressed against me.

After a long and thorough face-suck, Luke rests his forehead against mine. "Are you sure about this?"

Am I? *No. Yes. Maybe.* My mind is a whirlwind of conflicting thoughts, but . . . "I'm sure about right now," I say.

That seems to be enough for him. His mouth captures mine again. I moan as his hands roam my body, learning my curves through my clothes. My own hands are clasped behind his neck. Like a superhero, he lifts me off my feet, and I lock my legs around his waist, drawing him closer crushing my breasts to his chest.

"Bedroom?" Luke murmurs against my neck. I know he's asking permission rather than directions.

I nod, unable to form words as his lips trace a path down my throat. He carries me through the open doorway and sets me down gently beside the bed. In the glow of the streetlight coming through the window, our clothing starts to drop. Swiftly, desperately, we undress ourselves and each other, not exactly savoring each new patch of bare skin. But I manage to look my fill and appreciate what I see, including a bird tattoo on his upper arm. His body is everything I imagined—strong, tanned, perfect.

When he's fully naked, I can't help but stare, and he speaks first.

"You're magnificent," he says, his voice rough with desire. I don't contradict him because his expression is making me feel that way. His hands skim down my sides, and I shiver. "So beautiful."

Then we're on the bed, and everything else falls away. There's only Luke's mouth teasing my nipples until they stiffen, Luke's hands with his fingers trailing down my stomach and across my pussy, making my hips buck off the mattress. And then Luke's skilled tongue, retracing every part of me that his fingers already touched. He takes his time, learning what makes me gasp and moan, what makes me arch against him begging for more.

As it turns out, I beg a lot in this first half hour, especially when his tongue sucks my clit while his fingers slide inside me and find my G-spot. When I'm shaking from the way he keeps bringing me to the edge of a climax before backing off, when I'm saying his name, pleading for him to finish me off, at last, he dons a condom.

Luke nudges my legs apart with his knee, settles between my thighs, and enters me with a reverent gentleness that belies the hunger in his eyes and his raw strength. He's using restraint that I'm not sure I want right now. My trembling body welcomes him completely, hot and slick with need. So. Much. Need.

Each deliberate inch of his thick cock stretches me deliciously until he's buried deep, filling me so perfectly I can barely breathe. *How have I never had sex like this before?* And we're just getting started.

"Morgan," he whispers against my throat, his voice strained with self-discipline and control. "You feel incredible."

I can't speak. I have to bite my lip to keep from coming because of how ready he has made me.

"Mm," I murmur in mindless response, taking in a ragged breath along with his intoxicating fragrance, fir tree and fire and vanilla, intensified from the heat of his skin and his racing pulse.

Luke begins to rock, and I try to move underneath him, but there's little I can do except receive. The weight of his body is both grounding and exhilarating. Each powerful thrust sends waves of pleasure coursing through me, while pinning me to the bed.

When I think I can't take any more without shattering, his strong hands grip my hips, guiding me to arch beneath him. Our bodies find a natural rhythm, moving together as if we've done this countless times before.

"I have to," I manage to say, not sure what I mean except I'm going to come soon. I can tell by the tension in his back, under my clawing fingertips, that he will, too.

Wrapping my legs around his waist, changing the angle, I draw him even deeper. He responds with a groan that vibrates through both our bodies, his pace quickening as sweat breaks out at his temples.

"Luke," I gasp, my nails scraping down his back, "don't stop."

"I couldn't if I tried," he confesses before dipping his head to capture my nipple with his mouth. The unexpected intensity of these dual sensations sends me over the edge. My release crashes through me, my pussy tightening around his thrusting length as I tilt my head back and take everything he can give. I'm expanding out of myself, floating away with pleasure, while also impossibly focused on where our bodies are joined.

He releases my breast with a gentle bite and rises up to look into my eyes, never breaking his rhythm. Luke watches me climax, his expression fierce with desire before his own control shatters. With a final thrust, all his muscles become taut. He stills deep inside me and comes, my name a prayer on his lips. "Morgan, yes!"

Afterward, we lie tangled in the sheets, my head on his chest, listening to his strong heartbeat. His fingers, which I now know can do extraordinary things to me, trace lazy patterns on my back, and I feel more content than I have in . . . forever.

"What are we doing?" I whisper into the darkness.

Luke's hand stills. "Probably something stupid," he admits. Then he tilts my chin up to look at him. "But I don't regret it. Do you?"

I should. My main emotions should be guilt and shame. I have about a billion reasons why this was a bad idea. But looking into Luke's eyes, seeing warmth and appreciation, I can't bring myself to regret it either.

"No," I say softly. "I don't regret it." At least not this second. Time enough for that later.

He kisses me again, gentle this time, full of promise. We do it again later, and I won't be able to claim it was a frenzied accident brought on by unstoppable lust. It will be deliberate and fulfilling and absolutely exquisite. But when he nuzzles my neck, giving the sensitive skin a thrilling nip, my phone buzzes somewhere in the living room. We both freeze. Neither of us wonders who it might be. We know.

"Ignore it," Luke suggests against my skin, and for once, I do exactly that.

Tomorrow, I'll deal with the consequences. Tonight, I just want to be here, in this moment, with this man.

8

Luke

Sunlight filters through the blinds, painting thin golden bars across Morgan's naked back as she sleeps beside me. Her brown hair tumbles across the pillow, and her breathing is deep and even. There's something unnervingly intimate about watching someone sleep, more intimate in its own way than the sex we shared during the night.

My phone tells me it's just past six, but I have no desire to leave her bed. Not with her luscious curves pressed against my side. It's an unusual contentment, just to be here. It's not like I've never stayed the night or had a woman stay at my place, but I'm typically up and out before daybreak.

Last night, there was no question of my leaving. Not when Morgan tucked herself against me after our second round, her body soft and pliant with exhaustion. This morning, I can't think of any reason to slip away. I want to eat breakfast with her, and see her with tangled hair and sleepy eyes, no makeup, and, hopefully, a big satisfied smile.

I must have disturbed her, because she turns to face me, although her eyes are still firmly closed and the cutest little whistling sound comes from her nose. She tucks her arm beneath her pillow, the other rests between us, squashing her perfect breasts.

Sometime in the night, one of us kicked the sheet down to the bottom of the bed. Now, I enjoy an unfettered view of a gorgeous shoulder—*when did I think shoulders were so sexy?*—her mouthwatering nipples that seem to send a signal right to her clit when I suck them, the deep curve of her waist, and the flare of her hip. I want to trace every inch with my tongue again, wake her with my mouth, and lose myself in her for another hour or three.

Last night was extraordinary. Not just the physical aspects, though the way my body reacted to hers was mind-blowing. There was something else I haven't experienced before. Not with Anong, my summer fling last year. One of the two hundred thousand temporary visa holders, she and I fulfilled one another's need for companionship and sex. Ultimately, she wanted to go back home to Thailand unless I married her, and that was never in the cards.

But this feeling of something else with Morgan, I also never felt with Isla, to whom I was briefly engaged in New York. That realization sends a jolt of alarm through me. This is strong and fast! I should worry about getting ahead of whatever *this* is, and decide whether to nurture it or crush it. But in this quiet morning moment, I allow myself to simply enjoy Morgan's warmth, curled against mine.

Not wanting to wake her, I resist as long as I can, but I'm like a child with a new toy. Finally, I move a strand of golden-brown hair from across her shoulder, laying it behind her head on the pillow. She stirs, those blue eyes blinking open slowly.

For a beautiful moment, she smiles up at me, unguarded and content. My heart catches, and I know I could be happy if I woke up next to her every morning for the rest of my life.

Then, for her, reality crashes in. I can see it in the way her expression shifts and how her eyes widen. She starts searching for the sheet. Finding it across her knees, she draws it higher as she sits up.

"Morning," I say softly, hoping to ease the situation, which is growing immediately tense.

"Hi," she responds, voice husky from sleep. The sound sends heat straight through me. "What time is it?"

"Just after six. We're earlier than we need to be. It's not like I'll fire either one of us for being late." My attempt at levity doesn't work.

"I should shower," she says, her expression neutral and her gaze not meeting mine. "And you probably need to go home to change before work."

I push myself up against the headboard. When she stares at my nudity, her face looking increasingly more unhappy, I grab for some sheet. For her sake, I cover myself.

"Morgan, if this is your uncomfortable 'let's pretend this never happened' conversation . . ."

"No," she interjects quickly, then more softly, "No, it's not." Her eyes finally meet mine, and the vulnerability there makes my chest tight. "Not exactly. I just . . . I don't know what *this* is." Funny how she mimics my own thoughts. "Or what it means," she finishes.

My hand reaches for hers, and she doesn't pull away. "It means we're attracted to each other. It means we acted on that attraction." I pause, choosing my words carefully. "It doesn't have to mean more than that unless we want it to."

Something flickers in her expression. Relief? Disappointment? Before I can decipher it, she nods. "Right. Attraction."

An uncomfortable silence stretches between us, filled with the unspoken difficulties that the morning-after inevitably brings. I don't want to pressure her, so I release her hand and stretch. The morning light reveals details of her space I missed last night while in a lust-induced craze— a worn paperback on the nightstand and a small, unframed photo of Morgan with two women who must be her sisters and her parents. Kind of jarring in this sterile apartment, as if she brought personal decorations to a hotel.

And the significance of both the book and the photo are heightened in that they're what she chose to bring ten thousand miles with her.

Following my glance, she says, "Mom and Dad and my sisters, Katie and Pru." I start to reach for the book, but she blocks me, making me curious. More so when she diverts my attention from it.

"I've got a spare toothbrush," Morgan offers, climbing out of bed, taking the sheet with her, clutched to her chest. The sight of her bare back and shoulders as she retrieves a robe from the closet makes me want to drag her back to bed.

"Thanks." I watch her disappear into the bathroom, leaving me alone with my thoughts and the lingering scent of her on the sheets.

This isn't what I expected when I walked her to her door last night. I expected sex—I'm not naive—but I didn't expect to feel so possessive. And protective. Neither word quite captures it. All I know is that watching Morgan retreat into the bathroom with her guard up again makes me want to break down every wall she's rapidly built since she opened her baby-blues.

Connected, that's it. With each kiss yesterday and during the night, we felt connected. And now, we're not.

I look over at the photo of a younger, happy Morgan with her family, and then, because I can't help myself, I pick up the book. Rainer Maria Rilke's *Letters to A Young Poet*. Opening it, two things fall out, a piece of paper with a handwritten note that says, "To keep you company while you're away from me. Love, Ethan." My stomach clenches because he has just become a real person, and I've spent the night thoroughly screwing his girlfriend and enjoying ever second.

To make it worse, the second thing that lands on the sheet is a photo of Ethan and Morgan. An actual printed four-by-six matte photo of them, standing in front of . . . I look closer. I think it's the castle at Disney World.

Not exactly a romantic European vacation together, I think unkindly. Obviously, I can give her the world twice over, but being snide and belittling the guy who has shared her life for three years doesn't make me the better man.

He's dark-haired and clean-shaven. Good looking, I guess, if you like his type. I catch myself actually sneering, either at myself for being a bit of a bastard or at him for letting Morgan go away for three months.

He should have come with her.

He should've known better.

He most definitely should've protected what was his.

As if I'm holding hot coals, I shove the two items back under the front cover and drop the book onto her nightstand. Curiosity killed the cat, as they say. I'd have been happier if I hadn't snooped, that's for sure. Now I have his face in my head.

Hearing the shower come on, the nearly overwhelming temptation to join her under the hot spray drives me from the room. I'm not a saint, but I'm also not certain I'd be welcome anyway, and it would suck to be rebuffed after last night.

Instead, I dress and close the bedroom door behind me to give her some privacy. By the time she comes out, I'm drinking coffee and reading emails on my phone, while leaning against her kitchen counter. She's one hundred percent office-Morgan again, wearing a caramel-colored blouse and slim cream-colored skirt that somehow look both professional and impossibly sexy. Her hair is pulled back in a sleek ponytail, so different from how it was splayed across my chest last night.

She stops short, and I know what that look means, which is confirmed by her next remark, "You're still here."

That irritates me. "Have you had a lot of guys rush off in the morning?" I shoot back, then wince. Wrong thing to say. It only popped out because of seeing Ethan's picture.

With her cheeks blushing, she lifts her chin. "How many guys I've had is none of your business."

"True enough," I say quietly, "and I'm sorry. That was out of line. Just so you know, I would never leave without saying goodbye. That would be a shitty thing to do." I shrug the tension from my shoulders and start again. "I made coffee."

Morgan backs down, too, nodding before sending me a small smile. "Thanks. It smells good." She pours herself a cup, and I take note that she drinks it with milk but no sugar. After all, having nibbled on every part of her body, I think I should learn how she likes her coffee.

"You didn't want to shower?" she asks.

"I'll head home to shower and change." Then, in case she's interested, I add, "I live about thirty minutes away, in Point Piper."

Morgan nods, sipping her coffee. I wish she'd start rambling in that charming way she does. Or at least ask me questions. I think about letting her know my apartment is in the most expensive neighborhood in Sydney, with truly awesome views of the harbor and with neighbors who run the gamut from Hollywood's elite to literary giants and politicians. But I know she won't give a damn.

Besides, I hardly need to impress her with my real estate when her permanent base is half a world away. Maybe if I had a home in Boston, I could light up her eyes. Anyway, I try to revive the woman I woke up with.

"I know a little of Boston. I have family with a house on Beacon Hill. What neighborhood do you live in?"

But Morgan has closed down as though I've already had way too much of an opening into her private life and she doesn't want to share anything more about herself, let alone learn about me. I think if I asked her what her favorite color was, she wouldn't answer.

All she does is shrug and say, "Not Beacon Hill, that's for sure." Then she sets her cup down. Touching moment is over. "I'll let you get going. If you live half an hour away, we'll be able to arrive at least an hour apart, by the time you've showered and changed."

I can't help my eyebrows rising toward my hairline. "You're worried that someone will figure out we slept together if we enter the building at the same time?"

"We did drive away in the same car midday yesterday," she points out, heading to the door. "So, yeah, probably wise if we don't give anyone a reason to suspect."

She's right for reasons I haven't worked out yet. My company doesn't have any hard-and-fast rules about no employees dating, but I wouldn't want people to talk about how quickly we jumped into bed. I'm still processing how much I wanted her, how hard I flirted and charmed and pressed to make it happen. Then there's the very real fact of how much more I want her now.

"Understood," I say finally, though I hate the necessity of it.

I see relief mixed with something else in her expression. And when she yanks the door open, I can't help but feel I'm being thrown out. There's an awkward moment as I pass by her in the small space. Morgan gazes out into the hallway, then at the floor. Neither of us seems to know how to say goodbye. *Do I kiss her? Shake her hand?* The absurdity of the latter makes me smile.

Dammit, I'll kiss her if I want to, assuming she lets me.

Leaning down slowly so she can turn away that's her choice, I brush my lips against hers, swiftly and keeping it light. She doesn't flinch or slap my face, so that's a win. Yet she also doesn't meet my eyes or return the kiss.

"I'll see you at the office," I say, and she nods before closing the door with a firm hand.

Outside her building, the Sydney morning is already warm and bustling. In my car, I take a moment before starting the engine, trying to sort through the jumble of emotions.

Desire? Certainly. *Regret?* A little, for her sake, because she seems shaken.

Beyond both, however, there's definitely something deeper, something that makes me want to turn around and go back to her. To make it right and get us back to where we were *before* we had sex. Or make it OK that we did.

Since I have no idea how to do that, I get the Audi's engine revving and drive home. And I'm a fool for already counting the minutes until I see her again.

$♥$♥$♥$

Morgan

As soon as Luke leaves, I close the door and sit down at the kitchen table to finish my coffee. Coffee that the CEO of Henley Confectionery just made after giving me the most incredible night of sex. Before my butt has settled onto the gray chair—*I may never like gray again*—I jump up and lock the front door with a satisfying click of the deadbolt.

When I slump back down in the seat, I realize how futile that was. The horse has left the barn, jumped the paddock fence, found a muscular topaz-eyed stallion, and had her lights fucked out.

"Crude, Morgan," I reprimand myself out loud. Not like me, but then it's not like me to have sex with a stranger. Certainly not while I'm in a long-term relationship. Should've never asked him upstairs. *Duh!* Should've locked that door last night.

Groaning, I put my forehead down on the cool glass table, giving myself a bird's eye view of my shoes. Today, I put on the least sexy work pumps I have, with medium-high, thick heels, best for a rainy day. I guess I wanted to appear unattractive to Luke.

Rolling my head until my cheek is flat against the surface, I take in my apartment from this sideways vantage point. My life feels as though it has shifted off its axis, and now the room matches. My boss's opinion of my shoes shouldn't matter one bit. But what Luke thinks of me does, in fact, matter. A lot. *Ugh!*

What is wrong with me? Maybe there's some kind of potion in the Henley candy I've been consuming daily in the break room, and even more at the factory yesterday. I'd like to shift the blame from my spineless, weak self to the chocolate . . . or to Luke. Yet I can't. I invited him upstairs.

Entirely out of character.

When I woke up, I was thoroughly shocked at how easily I'd fallen from my personal moral high ground. Not to mention how much I still wanted him to touch me. I almost invited him into the shower.

Ethan deserves better. And I usually am so much better than this slutty, wild behavior. How am I going to face him when I return to Boston? How am I going to face Luke when I go into work?

Double ugh!

9

Luke

The office seems different. Same walls, same people, same hum of activity, but everything is charged with new meaning, and I haven't even made it past the lobby. As soon as I walk through the main doors, I spot Morgan at the far end of the ground floor, in the doorway of the IT department, talking to my VP.

When I get closer, she notices me, and our eyes meet briefly. A flush rises on her cheeks, and my body responds immediately to the memory of those cheeks being heated for very different reasons.

I can't help but walk directly toward her as if she's reeling me in with a fishing line.

"Morning, Mr. Henley," she says formally after I close the space between us.

"Ms. Anders," I respond, matching her professional tone. But I can't help adding, "I hope you had a pleasant evening."

Her eyes widen slightly before she composes herself. "Very pleasant, thank you." The words are innocent enough, although the look we exchange is anything but.

I almost forget Charlotte is standing there, until she says, "I'll ride up with you, Luke. I've got a few figures to go over." Then she snaps her fingers. "Hey, I found out what you two did, and I'm not happy."

I think I lose a year of my life and probably sprout a few gray hairs. Glancing at Morgan, who's gone chalk-white, I ask, "What do you mean?" I wonder if Charlotte can hear my thumping heart.

"Your impromptu factory tour," she says. "I spoke with Jim this morning about adding a second line for the caramels only. We've been going back and forth about it, and he said you were there yesterday." Charlotte shakes her head. "I can't believe you didn't bring back some of the new chocolate-covered macadamias for the rest of us."

I force a thin laugh, lacking any genuine amusement, while my cyber security consultant looks as though she might pass out. "Next time, I promise," I say before giving Morgan a reassuring nod. "Ms. Anders really enjoyed everything she tasted."

That suddenly sounds filthy, like a really dirty joke, given what we were both doing with our mouths and tongues during the night. If Morgan could go any paler, she would, and I regret my words. But she manages to rally when Charlotte looks at her.

"I thought the factory was amazing," Morgan gushes. "Really clean. Sparkling clean, in fact, and the tasting room. I mean, wow! That's a lot of samples to taste. I think I ate too many. Did I?" she asks me, but I can tell she's on one of her rambles because she doesn't for wait an answer.

"You're right, Ms. Bauer. The macadamia chocolates were incredible. We really should have brought back a box. Maybe twenty. *Haha.* Well, I better get to work." Too rattled to even say goodbye, she turns and disappears into the IT office.

I'm not sure what Charlotte thinks of Morgan going all air-headed Barbie, but I stride to the elevator, knowing she'll follow. Taking her mind off our peculiar encounter, I start pressing the up button—*coolly, about a billion times*—and start talking about caramel production, which I continue until we reach the C-suite. Charlotte heads toward her office, convinced that we need more caramel.

Throughout the morning, I find myself watching the security feed that shows the IT department, just to see Morgan hunched over a laptop. It's unprofessional of me, borderline stalking, but I can't help myself. When my phone rings at lunchtime, I'm almost relieved for the distraction.

"Luke, it's me." My oldest sister's voice jerks me back to reality, but I'm silent until I close my laptop on the sight of Morgan eating a salad. *How can a salad be so seductive?* "Are you there?" Clover demands.

"Sorry, I was distracted." I clear my throat. "What's up?"

"Adam and I just landed in Sydney," she announces. "Surprise!"

I straighten in my chair. "What? Why didn't you tell me you were coming?"

"Because then it wouldn't be a surprise, genius." I can hear the eye-roll in her voice. "We're heading to the hotel to drop our bags and regroup, then thought we'd swing by. Unless you're too busy being 'distracted'?"

"No, no. That's great." My mind races, wondering how to navigate introducing Clover to Morgan. My sister has an uncanny ability to read me. "Wait, why aren't you staying with me, or with Gramps and Nan?"

"We're going to the ranch in a couple days, but we wanted to take it easy here first. It's harder traveling with a toddler than you might think. Which is also why we're not staying with you in your bachelor pad."

"*Ha!* You make it sound like I have bearskin rugs and a waterbed." Lark and I purchased the luxury apartment to be near the office when we were both still working together in

Sydney and neither of us was prepared to buy a house that needed a gardener and a pool company.

"Besides, you know I have the space," I add. "We can put a crib in Lark's old bedroom."

"No can do, brother dear." Her voice lowers. "We brought our nanny, and we're in a suite at the Langham."

I cannot fathom that my sister is now the kind of person who travels with help. The fact that she felt she needed to whisper the words makes me laugh. "Understood. You need room for the nanny. Just come on up to my office when you get here."

"Hold on," Clover says. "What's up?"

Already? "What do you mean?" *Did my voice just crack?*

"You didn't ask me if my nanny is hot."

For the second time today, I have to fake my laughter. "Is she?"

"No, I'll see you soon."

After hanging up, I head down to the first floor, telling myself it's to give Morgan a heads-up about my sister's visit and not just an excuse to see her. Jack Thompson eyes me as I approach Morgan's desk, and I wonder why I didn't use my executive power to call her up to my office. This woman has me behaving like a junior intern! In any case, Jack has never seen so much of me before we hired our new consultant.

"Ms. Anders, do you have a moment?" I ask, keeping my voice neutral.

For a second, I see last night in her eyes before she masks it. "Of course, Mr. Henley."

We move to the small conference room in the IT suite, and once the door closes, the mood between us changes instantly. Not caring how it looks, I draw the blinds across the entire interior wall. *Bye-bye, Jack!*

Morgan doesn't look too happy about being alone with me. "What are you doing?"

"My sister's coming," I blurt out, not quite the smooth transition I'd planned. "She and her husband just landed in Sydney. They'll be here later today."

"Oh." Morgan blinks. "That's . . . nice?"

"I wanted to warn you. Clover has a way of seeing things."

Morgan's eyebrows raise. "Things?"

I step closer, unable to help myself. "She'll take one look at me and know something's changed. She always does."

"Has something changed?" Morgan asks softly, her gaze steady on mine.

The question hangs between us, loaded with meaning. *Has it?* Last night shifted something fundamental. At least, for me. I guess I shouldn't assume anything for her.

"You tell me," I counter, reaching out to grasp a strand of her hair that has come over her shoulder, tempting me. Wrapping it around my finger, I start to tug her closer.

Morgan's breath catches, her lips parting slightly. The temptation to kiss her right here, despite being a few feet away from my employees, is almost overwhelming.

"Luke," she whispers my name like a warning and a plea all at once. "Not here."

I release her reluctantly, and she immediately reaches back to check her hair clip, making sure the ponytail is still tidy.

"Sorry." I shouldn't be rattling her at work or making her feel the least bit insecure. Taking a deep breath, I attempt to collect myself. "About my sister—"

"You don't need to worry," Morgan assures me, her neutral mask sliding back into place. "I'm quite good at keeping things . . . compartmentalized."

The word stings more than it should. *Is that how she feels?* For her, what we did is something that needs to be separated from her real life in the States. But then, what did I expect when she keeps Ethan's photo and his smarmy book beside her pillow? She probably texts him while looking at it every night before she goes to sleep.

Except for last night when I was there, making her beg for release, hearing her practically yell my name.

But, hey, let's shove that in a compartment, OK?

"Good to know." My tone is cooler than intended. Her expression falters momentarily, and I regret my knee-jerk reaction. I am simply blown away by how strong my attraction is to this woman, and I want it to be mutual. "Clover and her husband probably won't stay long this afternoon. They've brought my niece, Ivy."

An awkward silence ensues, and I add, "Anyway, come to think of it, I doubt you'll even need to interact with them."

Morgan nods, clasping her hands behind her back. "Well, if there's nothing else . . ."

"There's always something else with you," I murmur, making her blush deepen. "I'll catch you later." *Or maybe I won't.* She's not exactly giving me repeat-act vibes.

As we exit the conference room, Jack looks up from his desk, curiosity plain on his face. I nod politely and head for the elevator, feeling Morgan's eyes on my back the entire way.

$♥$♥$♥$

Morgan

Clover and Adam arrive at two, my sister's energy filling my office the moment she bursts through the door. Adam follows more sedately, offering me a handshake while his wife proceeds directly to a hug.

"You look different," my older sister says immediately, pulling back to study me with narrowed eyes. *Damn!* She's good. I wonder that she didn't become a detective instead of a graphic designer.

"It's been six months," I remind her, gesturing for them to sit. "People change."

"No, it's something else." She circles my desk, perching on the edge like she owns the place. "You're . . . I don't know. Glowing?"

Adam snorts, earning a questioning shrug from Clover. "Men don't glow, princess."

"This one does. Or maybe you could call it beaming bliss." Her scrutiny makes me uncomfortable. She always could read me like a book. "Did something happen?"

"Maybe he just got laid," Adam quips, because we have that kind of brotherly relationship.

Third fake-fucking laugh ensues, which only makes Clover stare at me harder.

"Nothing out of the ordinary," I lie smoothly. A whopper of a lie, too, because everything to do with how Morgan has affected me is extraordinary. "Business is good. The new Parisian collection is exceeding projections. How's Boston?"

"Cold when we left it," Adam says, accepting my change of subject. "Though with the little one, we barely notice the weather. We're too busy serving our new tyrant mistress, usually trying to stuff her octopus arms and legs into various sweaters and snowsuits."

"Seriously, how is my favorite niece?" I ask, grateful for the diversion. "When she's not being a tyrant?"

"Even then, exhausting," Clover sighs, but her smile is proud. Talk about beaming bliss.

"Even with a nanny?" I tease. "Who may or may not be hot."

"Not," Adam chimes in, earning a glare from Clover. "What?" he asks. "It's not like I noticed." Then he sends me a look, a man-to-man message of *he's damned if he does or doesn't.*

"Ivy's walking now," Clover continues. "Well, more like stumbling with purpose. Mom says she's exactly like me at that age—stubborn and fearless."

"Perfect Henley traits," I say, although Clover is now a beloved member of the Bonvier family.

"Speaking of Henleys," Clover continues, "Lark sends her love. She's been talking about you a lot lately. I think she misses her brother."

"Sounded like she missed Australia," Adam says. He's always brutally honest, but I ignore him.

"I miss her," I admit. "Before Dad retired, it was fun sharing this job with Lark." Then we had about a year of chaotic change. First, it was me heading up the New York office, leaving Lark here, and then the messy engagement with Isla, and then I landed back in Sydney. "Running Henley New York suits her, though, doesn't it?"

"You know Lark," Clover says. "She plays it close to the chest. Sometimes, I think she simply enjoys change, though, and she may be getting antsy."

Adam stands, stretching. "Are we doing the grand tour?" he asks, without much enthusiasm. He's seen it before, and it's just an office building, after all.

"I could, if you like," I say, rising to my feet, "but you might want to just go sit on a beach. I recommend Bondi. Because that plane trip will definitely catch up with you like a slap in the face from Attila the Hun."

Clover and Adam exchange a glance, then she nods. She's not the type to slow down, but I hope she'll listen to her *little brother*. Then I think of something I know she'll enjoy.

"You should go to the factory before you head to the ranch. I was there yesterday. It's as magical as ever. Ivy might be too young to enjoy it, but she'll love the aroma."

"Too young for candy?" Clover scoffs. "Not with my blood running through her veins." Then she yawns. "Maybe we'll go tomorrow. But I really wanted to spend time with you."

"Early dinner tonight, and you can keep me for as long as you like," I offer. "We can eat at your hotel, so you'll be close to Ivy and the *not*-hot nanny."

Adam laughs, and my big sister shakes her head. "How will you ever keep a straight face when you meet her?"

"I promise, I'll be on my best behavior." Then I add, "But I'm not trying to push you out the door. Not yet. Do you want to grab coffee in the break room and some candies or—"

"I want to meet Morgan Anders, of course," Clover says. *Well, hell!* "Why?" I bark.

"Calm down." My sister's tone makes me realize I've gone from congenial to tense in a split second. "Lark asked us to check in on her. That's all. Even Mom and Dad are concerned about the scope of the cybertheft. After all, what affects Henley Confectionery affects us all."

"Of course," I say neutrally, having regained my cool.

"I'm up for coffee," Adam agrees. "Let's combine the two."

"And then we'll get out of your hair until dinner," Clover promises.

We head out of my office, and I'm relieved to get moving. Standing still under Clover's scrutiny felt like being under a microscope.

As we walk through the executive floor, Clover leans against my arm, clasping my hand, and dropping her voice. As if Adam, striding along behind us, can't hear every word.

"So, who is she?"

I nearly stumble. "Who is who?"

"Don't play dumb, Basil." The use of my given name, which I've always hated, tells me she's serious. "The woman who's got you looking like that."

"Like what, exactly?"

"Like you've been shocked with a cattle prod, but in a good way." She grins. "I know that look. It's the same one Adam had when we first met." She glances behind at her husband.

"She's right," he says, sounding resigned to the fact.

I sigh, knowing denial is pointless. "It's complicated."

Clover's eyes light up. "*Complicated* is my favorite kind of story. Is she here? Do I know her?"

"No, you don't know her," I say truthfully. "And yes, she's in Sydney. Temporarily." The last word comes out sounding more bitter than I intended.

"*Ah,*"Clover nods sagely. "The temporary part being the complication?"

I guide them toward the elevator. "Among other things."

"Let me guess. The new itch you want to scratch already has someone in her life." At my stunned expression, she shrugs. "I'm a good guesser. Besides, it's always another person or distance that messes things up. Sometimes both."

The elevator arrives, saving me from responding. We ride down in silence, but Clover's knowing smirk tells me this conversation is far from over. And now, when she meets Morgan, my sister will have her antennae way up. I'm simply not a "clandestine affair" kind of guy. Lark and Clover used to say I was crap at hide-and-go-seek, too.

As we approach IT, part of me hopes Morgan is away from her desk so I can spare her the force of nature that is Clover Henley Bonvier. Of course, another part desperately wants to see her again. After all, it's been two hours.

10

Morgan

When Luke appears at my desk for the second time today, I'm already on edge. Every time I catch a glimpse of him—*which I try not to do but can't seem to stop myself*—my body responds with a tremor of awareness that's almost painful. Last night plays on an endless loop in my mind, making it nearly impossible to concentrate on anything else.

"Ms. Anders," he says formally, though his eyes hold a glimmer of pure fire that makes my stomach flip. "My sister would like to meet you."

My fingers freeze over my keyboard. "Why?" Not a very gracious answer. Looking past him, I take a peek through the glass at a tall, broad-shouldered, dark-haired man facing away from me. The swish of a coral-colored dress on the other side of him must be Luke's sister, but her husband's physique shields her almost completely.

"What happened to my *not* needing to interact with her?" I ask. "That's what you said."

Jack scents something interesting happening and comes out of his office. "Isn't that your *other* sister?"

I shoot Luke a questioning look. He shrugs. "That's pretty much how everyone refers to Clover, since she's not Lark, who used to run things with me here."

"The Bonviers are from Boston," Jack says, making sure I know that he knows them already.

I'd forgotten that Luke's older sister is married to Adam Bonvier of Bonvier, Inc., a marketing agency whose international headquarters is in—*oh, God*—Boston! *What are the odds?*

"Yes," Luke confirms, his expression carefully neutral. "They arrived this morning, Jack. And now my sister wants to meet Ms. Anders to learn where she stands with her security assessment of our family's company."

Jack deflates visibly, and I feel a twinge of sympathy despite his antagonism toward me. "I'll tell them how tight a ship you run," I offer.

Jack barely nods before disappearing back into his office. He slumps in his chair, and I'm starting to think a glass wall is as stupid as a screen door in a submarine. Sometimes, one needs privacy.

"That was nice of you," Luke says.

"Jack's not so bad," I shrug. "Just territorial."

"Like me," he murmurs, sending a shiver down my spine. "Anyway, if you're not too busy. . ."

I jump up. "Of course not. You're the boss," I remind him, earning a strange look. Maybe he's forgotten that uncomfortable fact, but I haven't. Not for a second.

"Before you go," he says quietly, for my ears only, "Clover already figured out I have the hots for someone, and she knows that someone is only in Sydney for a short while."

I literally gasp, prepared to pepper him with questions when he gestures for me to precede him into the lobby. "They can see us," he reminds me. "Let's go."

Clover Henley Bonvier is striking. About my height, she has cheekbones like a model, and shiny, smooth, honey-colored hair in chunky layers past her shoulders. When she looks at me straight on, I see the same intriguing, golden-brown eyes as her brother. But when I grasp the manicured hand she's holding out, it's her shoes I mention first.

"Those are the most gorgeous sandals I've ever seen." They are nude, with a comfy but sexy wedge under her pink-painted toes and a spiky, sexy heel at the other end. They're both casual *and* glamorous. *Impossible!*

Luke and Clover's husband start laughing, and I guess I've stumbled onto a major joke.

"Don't mind these hyenas," Clover says. "I love shoes, and I'm not ashamed of it. These are Christian Louboutin," she adds, which means nothing to me, except I can tell they're expensive AF. "Loubi Queen Alta," she adds, and both the men start laughing again.

I pretend to have heard of the brand before, while Clover takes their teasing in stride. Her smile reminds me of Luke's. But when she glances down at my ugliest, dowdy footwear, I cringe. I can see she disapproves, but all she says is, "This impossibly handsome hyena is my husband, Adam Bonvier."

"Nice to meet you," I say, shaking his hand. She isn't exaggerating about how attractive he is. Super dark-hair, a chiseled chin, he's Luke's height and build but with more of a . . . a devilish look to him. And his slate-gray eyes make me immediately like the color again.

"This is our cybersecurity consultant," Luke introduces me finally. "Morgan Anders. From Boston."

"I recall Lark mentioned that," Clover says. "Small world. Which part?"

"Back Bay," I answer. "Though I spend a lot of time in Cambridge for work."

"We're on Beacon Hill," Adam says. "Not too far. You should look us up when you're back home."

My glance darts to Luke before I can help myself, and he's watching me carefully. Something flickers in his eyes that I can't read.

"That would be lovely," I say, while inside, I'm thinking, *No way is that happening.* Imagine how creepy it would be if Luke thought I was getting close to his family in order to keep tabs on him.

"Let's go to the break room," he suggests, cutting through the awkward moment. "Ms. Anders is particularly fond of using the coffee machine, not to mention enjoying the free chocolates."

I cringe and defend myself. "Who doesn't like free candy?"

"Exactly," Clover agrees. "Best perk of working for Henley Confectionery. Certainly can't be dealing with my numb-nuts of a brother."

"I'm sure Mr. Henley is a perk, too," I say, instantly realizing how weird that sounds. Maybe even sort of revealing. I try to laugh it off and act casual, but my nerves are frayed from lack of sleep and the constant awareness of Luke's presence. I'm afraid the sizzling current flowing between us is visible.

Clover smiles at me, and I can see in her eyes that she's already wondering about me. Luke wasn't kidding about her "seeing things." Only my own sisters could pick up on my interest in the Henley CEO as fast.

Zoe from IT and Noah are in the break room, seated at one of the tables and drinking coffee. They jump up when we arrive.

"You don't have to leave on our account," Luke says.

"No worries," Zoe says. "We've got about ten minutes left on our arvo break, so we're duckin' down to the corner shop for an ice cream."

Noah offers his usual friendly smile. "Gotta make it worth comin' back to stare at our screens." As he passes me by, he winks like we have some secret pact. Then he stops in the doorway, looking only at me. "You want me to bring you back something, love?" he asks.

I have to will myself not to look at Luke. I sense he'll be wearing a disapproving expression. And I wish Noah had called me "mate."

"No, thanks. Another time."

When they've left, Luke makes a show of demonstrating the space-age coffee machine, which I've mastered. After making coffee for his family, he hands me a cup of mocha-coffee with froth. I catch his eye. Both of us are remembering the moment when his body was pressed against mine in this very room, and I look away quickly.

Adam leans his tall frame against the far counter and scoops up the first box of chocolate to see what's in it.

"So, Morgan," Clover says, perched on a stool, sliding her fingernail under the gold foil seal to open a new box of chocolates. "Lark tells me you're the best of the best for investigating our kind of cyber breach?"

I hesitate, glancing at Luke. "I—"

"Perhaps this isn't the best place to discuss it," he interrupts smoothly. "No one internally knows why she's really here."

"Whoops," Clover says. "My bad." She looks down and chooses carefully. It's a plain solid square of dark chocolate.

Adam selects a chocolate turtle and pops it in his mouth. "These are incredible," he says after swallowing. Smart man, unlike me, who tried to talk with a mouthful.

"That's twice now I feel badly for not bringing back some of the new macadamia clusters," I say without thinking.

"Bringing back?" Clover asks.

"I went to the factory yesterday," I explain.

"Did you?" she asks, her eyes at her brother. "I thought you said you went on your own."

"I didn't say that," Luke grinds out, while I mentally kick myself. "And Ms. Anders is correct. We should have brought back some for the staff to try. The chocolate-covered macadamia nuts are going to be a hit. They're exceptional."

His eyes lock with mine, and heat floods my face. I can't seem to stop reacting to Luke's every move or glance. Clover doesn't miss the exchange, her gaze flicking between us with growing interest. Most likely, the invisible dots are easy to connect.

"I really would like to hear more about your work, Ms. Anders," Adam says, oblivious to the tension.

I interrupt him. "Please, call me Morgan."

He nods. "Coincidentally, we've been looking to upgrade my company's cybersecurity protocols. There have been some concerning incidents lately."

"What kind of incidents?" I ask, professional interest piqued.

"Nothing confirmed yet."

Clover snorts. "No doubt in my mind."

Adam shoots his wife a fond smile. "We suspect some of our branding campaigns were leaked to a competitor. They won the client basically with our own designs." He frowns. "Files were sent from within my building, I believe, but I don't know from whom or how to figure that out." Then he shrugs. "Probably not as interesting as whatever you're dealing with here."

"Actually," I say, warming to the topic, "patterns of theft can be surprisingly similar across industries. I'd be happy to share some generalized insights."

"Perfect," Clover interjects with a smile that reminds me too much of Luke's. "And since I want to know how your work is going here, why don't you join us for dinner tonight? We're staying at the Langham. Luke has already suggested eating there."

Luke looks a little sheepish, as if he got me dragged into this. "Supposed to have excellent munchies," he says.

Clover nods. "We can discuss Henley's cyber security issue more privately there and maybe get a twofer, if you can give Adam an assist."

My stomach drops. *Dinner with Luke and his family?* I haven't even had twenty-four hours to process what occurred between us. I search for an excuse, *any* excuse.

"I wouldn't want to intrude on your family time," I begin when my sleep-deprived brain can't come up with anything better. A curse on four-in-the-morning sex session number three. Or was it three-in-the-morning and our fourth time?

"Nonsense," Clover waves away my concern.

"A foursome is always better," Adam adds, and all three of our heads whip round to stare at him. Innocently, he sips his coffee.

Clover rolls her eyes, then focuses on me again. "He means around a dining table, unless you had other plans."

Luke clears his throat. "I'm not sure Ms. Anders—"

"Is free tonight," Clover finishes for him, arching an eyebrow. "Are you, Morgan?"

Both siblings turn to me, and I feel caught in some invisible tug-of-war. Luke's expression is carefully neutral, but suddenly a little hint of a smile appears. It occurs to me he *wants* me there.

That makes me even more nervous, because sometime between his leaving my apartment and my arrival at work today, I decided what we did could never happen again. Not until I've had a facetime-to-facetime, heart-to-heart talk with Ethan. I owe him that. And when I'm around Luke, I'm too easily swayed. Too ready to lean against him, to let him kiss me, to kiss him back and then . . .

Still, I can't think of a valid reason to decline that wouldn't seem rude.

"I suppose I could make it," I concede.

"Excellent!" Adam says, selecting another chocolate. "Seven work for everyone? With jet lag, either Clover and I will be up all night or asleep before the salad course."

Luke laughs. "I want to see my niece first. Shall I bring her a slobbering puppy or her first bike?"

"He thinks he's funny," Clover says to me. "Do you know where the Langham is?"

Before I can explain that I'll ask the Uber driver, Luke says, "I can pick you up, Morgan, since you don't have a car."

My eyes widen slightly at the suggestion. Being alone with Luke in his Batmobile again, so soon after everything that happened, seems dangerous. But I can't figure out how to turn him down gracefully or believably.

"That's settled then," Clover says with a clap of her hands. "We should probably let you both get back to work. I think the jet lag is already hitting me. I need a nap on the beach and a swim in the hotel pool before dinner."

Adam tells me, "My wife is part fish, and she'll never turn down an opportunity to swim. Personally, I just want to stretch out and close my eyes."

"If you're ready to relax, it means Ivy is probably wide awake and bouncing off the walls," Clover says. "We've brought our nanny," she finishes, looking embarrassed.

"A good idea," I tell her. If she thinks I'm going to accuse her of being a snobby rich woman, she's wrong. She's a very smart rich woman. Anyone with sense would bring a nanny when they travel this far and have the funds to pay for help.

As we walk back toward the elevator, Clover links her arm through mine. "How are you liking Sydney so far? Luke's shown you around, I hope?"

Her innocent question carries undertones that make me nervous. As if her brother and I have been joined at the hip and dating.

"It's beautiful," I say carefully. "I haven't had much time for sightseeing, though. Going to the factory yesterday was my only outing so far, except for a few strolls I've taken through the city."

"Then my brother has been working you too hard," Clover says, her tone casual but her eyes sharp as she studies my face. "Nor is he being the best host. Those three months are going to fly by, and you'll wish you'd experienced everything you possibly could while here."

I've certainly experienced a few things I hadn't planned on.

Luke intervenes, "Morgan's been buried in our cyber mess. She doesn't have time to waste on beaches and scenic walks."

"Is that right?" Clover looks between us, and I swear she can see right through our carefully constructed disinterest in one another.

"It's true," I confirm, grateful for Luke's rescue. "I tend to get absorbed in my work. And I'm also working on a personal coding project in the evenings."

Except for last night when her brother was making me climax over and over.

"Remember how driven you were with your business?" Adam says to his wife. "Before Ivy mellowed you."

Clover shrugs. "Maybe we'll have time to go shoe shopping," she suggests. And I wince because she obviously thinks I'm sorely lacking in that department. I'll have to prove her wrong tonight.

"I'd like that," I say, again thinking, *Unlikely as snow in July*. On the other hand, I'm Down Under where it does snow in July, but I'll be long gone by then. I extricate my arm from hers as we reach the building's entrance.

This awkward interaction is almost over, although I've signed up for an entire evening of it. Adam checks his phone and then places his hand on Clover's lower back. "Let's enjoy some nap time," he says to her.

To my surprise, she blushes. *Well, well.* Then he grins at me, and I think again what a devastatingly attractive guy he is. "Morgan," he says, "it was a pleasure. Looking forward to dinner tonight and picking your brains."

"They're yours for the picking," I say, managing a genuine smile for him. Adam seems straightforward and guileless, unlike his perceptive wife whose eyes continue to assess me.

Luke walks them outside, and I take the opportunity to escape back to the IT suite, my heart pounding. Once at my desk, I collapse into my chair, trying to process what just happened.

I'm having dinner tonight with Luke and his family.

After sleeping with him.

After breaking my commitment to Ethan.

Out of the corner of my eye, I see Jack watching me curiously. When he catches me looking, he quickly returns his attention to his computer screen.

By the time Luke enters the IT department, I've composed myself enough to appear busy with work.

"I'm sorry about that," he says quietly, standing beside my desk. "My sister can be persistent."

"It's fine," I lie, not looking up from my screen. "They seem nice."

"Morgan." The way he says my name forces me to meet his gaze. "You don't have to come if you're uncomfortable. I can make an excuse."

For a moment, I'm tempted to accept his offer of a way out. But I'm not a coward. I want to make sure I can eat with this man and not try to tear off his clothes. I vowed this morning that I would behave better than I have been, and I intend to prove to myself I can do just that.

What's more, the professional part of me wants to help Adam Bonvier, too, since networking with one of the richest men in Massachusetts can only be beneficial. If my private project turns out to be a success, I'll need a good marketing agency.

That's my main reason for going to dinner—*not* because I want to spend more time with Luke. *Sure, it is.*

"I'll come," I tell him. "I'll be ready by six-thirty."

11

Luke

I've been distracted ever since my family left, unable to focus on much beyond tonight's dinner. The thought of Morgan with my sister and brother-in-law has me strangely pleased and not as anxious as I'd imagined. I want Clover to like Morgan, and vice versa, while simultaneously wanting my sister to stop analyzing every glance that passes between us.

By the time I pull up to Morgan's building at six-thirty, I'm in completely different clothes than what I put on after a quick shower. Black jeans and a short-sleeve black polo. *Done.* Why the hell was that so hard? Yet at home, I undid and retied my tie three times before realizing I never wear one with family, and Clover would know I was trying to impress Morgan.

Shedding the stupid sport coat and uptight slacks, I have no idea where my tie landed after I tore it off and threw it across my bedroom.

When I arrive, I text Morgan, thinking it's not a good idea to go upstairs to her door. She emerges from the building a few minutes later, and the sight of her steals my breath. I stand up straight from where I was leaning against my car. She's wearing a simple sleeveless, navy-blue dress that skims her curves and falls just above her knees, paired with strappy gold sandals that accentuate her delicate ankles.

Her hair is loose, flowing over her shoulders in soft waves. It's the first time I've seen her in anything besides office attire, pajamas, or her birthday suit.

For a moment, I forget this isn't a date. My body is paying tribute, if only she knew. I should start silently chanting: *We're colleagues headed to a friendly dinner.*

"You look beautiful," I say as she approaches.

"Thanks," she replies, tucking a strand of hair behind her ear. "I didn't pack many dinner options."

As we drive to the Langham, conversation isn't exactly strained, but it's not chatty, either. We've crossed too many lines to return to casual small talk, but neither of us seems ready to address what happened. It's hard to believe it was only last night—and the early hours of the morning—when our bodies were still wrapped around one another.

"About your sister," Morgan says finally. "She seems to think that we . . ."

"Are attracted to each other?" I finish when she trails off. "That's all she knows. But don't worry, she's discreet. She won't say anything inappropriate." At least, I hope she won't.

"I'm not worried about that." Morgan stares out the window. "I'm worried about how I'll feel when she asks about my life back in Boston."

The mention of her other life sends a pang through my chest. "Just tell the truth," I advise, though I'm not sure what version of truth I want her to share.

"Which part?" she asks, her voice barely audible. "The part where I have a boyfriend waiting for me, or the part where I slept with you anyway?"

The bluntness of her words makes my fingers tighten on the steering wheel. "I was thinking more about your job and your family."

"Right," she says, sounding embarrassed. "Of course."

We ride the rest of the way in silence, though I'm acutely aware of her presence beside me—the delicate floral scent of her perfume, the occasional rustle of her dress when she shifts in her seat, the way her fingers fidget with her small tan purse. More than anything, I want to touch her again.

When we arrive at the Langham, the doorman greets us with practiced elegance, and I guide Morgan through the opulent lobby with a light touch at the small of her back. The brief contact sends electricity through me, and I notice her subtle intake of breath. Her heels tap on the marble floor as we pass a glossy black baby grand. The hotel is stylish, without being either stuffy or minimalist.

"Low score for the gray chairs," I quip, feeling Morgan relax a little when I do.

"Higher score for the blue ones," she adds. "This place is more eclectic than I imagined a billionaire and his wife would stay in."

I chuckle, because to me Clover is just my sister. "I swear she and Adam have that same cream-colored sofa at her home. To be honest, the Langham's style reminds me of her, right down to those fresh flowers and the accent pillows."

The Observatory Bar is on the ground floor across from the reception alcove. As we enter between open art deco, gold-etched glass sliders, I scan the elegant but intimate bar and eatery. Long black-and-white marble bar on the left side, a variety of seating options in the middle, old-fashioned bar trays, reminiscent of the twenties scattered around, and a marble fireplace with a large mirror overhead dominating the right-hand wall.

If I'm not mistaken, that's a bottle of Louis XVIII cognac under glass on the mantle. Perhaps I can convince

Adam to buy it before the evening is over. *What's the point of $5000 brandy if you don't drink it?*

The place is filled at this hour, buzzing with conversation, clinking ice cubes, and forks scraping across plates. Despite the fact that we're a little early, Clover and Adam are deep in conversation, seated at a corner table to the left of the fireplace. They've commandeered the side with a small sofa, leaving the upholstered armchairs for us.

"There they are," I murmur to Morgan, nodding toward my sister's distinctive honey-colored hair. We start across the parquet floor that gives the room a welcoming atmosphere.

Clover spots us and waves, her face lighting up when we draw close. "You made it!"

"Traffic was lighter than expected," I explain, bending to kiss her cheek. "And Morgan's apartment is literally ten minutes away."

Adam stands to shake Morgan's hand. "Glad you could join us. I've got a lot of questions about cyber security."

"I'll do my best to help," she says, visibly relaxing at the prospect of discussing work rather than personal matters.

As we settle into our seats, a waiter comes over to take our drink orders. Morgan requests a glass of chardonnay, while I opt for Tasmanian apple brandy, neat. Clover and Adam are already nursing cocktails.

"So," Clover says once the waiter departs, "how was your afternoon? Did you make any progress?"

For a moment, I think she's asking about Morgan and me, but quickly realize she's referring to the cyber theft.

Morgan leans forward slightly. "The strangest part is that shipments are going out only from what appear to be legit orders, but the money coming in simply isn't adding up. There are also discrepancies in how the orders are processed. It's subtle, but definitely deliberate. I'm close, though. I don't think it will take the full three months."

That's the first I've heard of her possibly not needing the entire length of her contract. It's unsettling. She could solve the problem tomorrow, which would be a good thing for the company, but then be on the next flight home. *Which I would hate.*

Adam's expression is thoughtful. "A totally different problem than I'm having, which is more like espionage, to be honest. Our networked printers show no record of anyone printing out anything, so I'm convinced the design files are being accessed and sent in-house. Of course, no one's going to admit it, nor even allow for the possibility that they have a spy on their team."

"It's often someone who knows the system well enough to navigate around security protocols," Morgan explains. "In your case, it could be someone with legitimate access who's sharing information and has the knowledge to cover it up."

As they dive deeper into technical details, I find myself watching Morgan. Her confidence when discussing her field is captivating. The nervous woman from the car ride has vanished, replaced by a knowledgeable expert who commands attention. I sit back, sip brandy, and don't participate in the discussion.

"Luke's eyes glaze over whenever we talk tech," Clover teases, bringing me back to the conversation. "He was always more interested in the 3-D world than anything on a computer."

"I just prefer the hands-on aspects of production to staring at a screen," I say in my defense.

"What he means," Clover tells Morgan with a conspiratorial smile, "is that he loved playing with the machinery in the factory. Our grandfather's foreman used to watch Luke like a hawk watches a mouse, or my brother would experiment with running the huge mixers at full capacity on double-time or increase the speed of the conveyor belt until candy was flying off." She starts to laugh and Luke joins in.

"I did do that," I confess.

"Your father never ran the company in Sydney?" Morgan asks.

"No. He moved to New York and met our mother, and then opened up the US division," I explain. "He trained with Gramps, of course, but never was in charge here. It made sense that eventually one of us grandkids would take over the Australian headquarters."

"I never worked in the candy company in either country," Clover says, "but I loved coming here and playing in the factory."

Our drinks arrive, and after looking at the menu, we take a vote on whether to stay put and eat here or go five minutes down the road to Elements steakhouse at Walsh Bay.

"On the one hand," Clover says, "Walsh Bay is historic yet super cutting-edge, and I've heard Elements is fantastic."

"On the other hand," Adam says, without missing a beat, "we'd have to stand up. And since we started our day in Auckland, after our Major-General here"—he hooks his thumb at his wife—"generously allowed us an entire night's sleep in New Zealand before getting back on our jet this morning, that's the least appealing thing about any choice that isn't right here."

The vote is unanimous to remain at the Observatory.

"Besides, it's prime dinner hour," Morgan says, leaning back and crossing her legs, which garners all my attention. "We might not have gotten a table someplace else anyway."

I hope she's not offended when all three of us laugh. "What's so funny?"

"You're not only with Henleys, who have contributed a ton to Sydney's economy and its art scene," Clover says frankly, "but you're also with Adam. If the steakhouse said there wasn't room for us, he would buy the place on the spot and toss out all the other diners, just to clear us a table."

"No, I wouldn't," Adam says, but he shoots my sister a shit-eating grin. "I only did that once, anyway. And I didn't toss out *all* the diners, only the two at our special table."

We order an assortment of shareable dishes. Actually, we order one of each thing on the menu, from a plate of pacific oysters to the tiger prawn toast, the duck pancakes to the charcuterie, adding a platter of local Australian cheeses. When the food starts to arrive, our conversation slows down.

"These fries!" Adam says, which strikes me funny since there are so many more exotic morsels in front of us, such as gribiche sauce on toasted brioche and smoked stracciatella. Apparently, Morgan thinks this is hilarious, too. Or maybe she finished off her first glass of wine too quickly and is into her second one, because she does a true belly laugh that gets the rest of us laughing with her.

As we share the food, the conversation shifts from business to more personal territory. "How long have you been in cybersecurity, Morgan?" Adam asks, another parmesan-and-truffle fry in his hand.

"About six years professionally, but I've been coding since I was a kid. My dad taught computer science at MIT."

Clover perks up. "Parents have such influence, don't they? Our dad is obsessed with quality control for the chocolates. He passed that on to Luke."

"I wouldn't call it obsession," I interject. "More like attention to detail."

"Please," Clover says. "You once made them stop an entire production line because the caramel centers were a shade too dark."

Morgan looks at me with genuine interest. "Really?"

I shrug, feeling strangely exposed. "Consistency matters. Our customers expect a certain experience."

"That's what I love about my brother," Clover says, "his passion. Though it didn't always serve him well in New York."

I shoot her a warning glance, but she ignores it. I'm sure she's talking about my very public and stupidly passionate wooing of Isla Devereux.

"What happened in New York?" Morgan asks, evidently curious.

"Nothing interesting," I say quickly. "Just corporate shenanigans. I'm thinking of dessert. Anyone else?"

"Basil and Lark were both working here," Clover begins while ignoring my attempt to change the subject and pissing me off by using the name I shed when I was old enough to realize I had a middle one. I'm starting to fear she's had too many cocktails.

"But my brother was being groomed to take over the New York office when our dad retired," my sister explains. "He was on track, had even moved back to the Big Apple, until he suddenly decided Australia was more his speed, after all. Lark landed there, so to speak, and he came back here."

"Circumstances changed," I say. Lark suddenly *needed* to be in New York because of some guy who'd captured her interest, and I respected that. We kept our reasons for switching places to ourselves. Weirdly, I should've stayed in the States for exactly the same reason that my sister did. For love. I guess I chose Lark's happiness over my own.

There's an awkward pause because I don't elaborate. I know Clover is considering whether to mention Isla and our brief engagement that ended when she refused to move to Australia with me. I silently plead with my sister to drop it.

Adam, sensing tension, steers the conversation elsewhere with surprising tact. "Tell Morgan how you crashed your new truck into your grandfather's irrigation system, putting the entire vineyard at risk," he says to me. "One of my favorites."

Relief floods through me. "That's ancient history," I protest, despite being grateful for the shift. "And the crash is pretty much the whole thrilling story. But I really loved that truck."

"He was sixteen," Clover says, nodding at Morgan. "Thought he could impress some girl by doing donuts in the field."

Morgan's eyes widen. "No way." She looks at me with what seems like genuine delight. "Mr. Perfect CEO was a teenage troublemaker?"

"I'm far from perfect," I admit, finding it easier to discuss youthful misadventures than failed relationships. "And I paid for that idiocy by spending the entire summer replacing pipes, even those I hadn't broken but were simply old. But every spare minute that Gramps gave me, I used to restore my truck."

Morgan looks delighted, which sends intense signals to my groin. I want to see that expression on her face later. But I note she's switched from white wine to some fruity cocktail that's bound to give her a headache by 5 a.m. I wonder if I'll be there to give her some aspirin and a big glass of water.

"Luke was always headstrong," Clover adds. "Our sister Lark is the same way. They're both all-in once they decide on something."

Morgan's gaze meets mine for a brief, electric moment, solemn and sober, before she looks away. "That must have been quite a summer," she says, her voice softer than before.

"It was," I confirm, memories flooding back. "I learned more that summer about how the vineyard operated than I ever wanted to know. But it also made me appreciate the land. There's something about Australia that gets under your skin."

"Is that why you stayed?" Morgan asks. "Or rather, why you came back?"

"Partly," I nod, thinking of Lark's tear-stained, grateful face once I agreed to take over the Sydney division. In the end, she didn't stay with the guy who cost me my fiancée. Morgan doesn't need to know any of that. "But also, because it felt right at the time." I don't explain that the breakup with Isla cemented my decision to make Australia my home. It stung when she chose New York over me, but

I guess I didn't love her enough to let her dictate where I lived. Enough said.

"Going from managing this office together with Lark to being halfway around the world was hard on you," Clover says, her expression softening, then turns to Morgan. "My younger siblings have always been close."

I shift uncomfortably at the maudlin turn our conversation has taken. Probably Clover is punch drunk from the jet lag on top of the alcohol. "Dad wanted to retire," I point out. "It had to be one of us, or hire outside the company. Unless *you* were going to give up graphic design to become a candy-maker." I stare Clover down, silently telling her to change the topic again and shift it off of me entirely.

Taking the hint, she leans back and yawns politely behind her hand. "The pool here is amazing." While she describes the subterranean spa under the hotel—"the pool is heated to the perfect temperature, and overhead, there's a painted night sky, like a celestial ceiling, with soft lighting that makes it look almost real"—I turn my gaze to Morgan again. When I see her eyelids grow heavy, I feel the need to take care of her.

"We should go," I say, hopefully not too abruptly. "Work in the morning. I guess it's too late to see Ivy anyway."

"Better when she's fresh," Clover agrees, "and she's sound asleep right now."

"I hope," Adam says.

Morgan yawns less politely than my sister did, and I can see she is well and truly buzzed.

"I thought we'd be the ones to cave early," Adam adds, amused at how my crack cyber security expert is leaning back, head sort of cocked to the side.

"We didn't get much sleep last night," Morgan announces, as she hands me her second empty cocktail glass without even looking my way, like we're a couple!

Shit and double shit! I sit there like an idiot for a full three seconds, holding the glass, my eyes undoubtedly as wide as my sister's and my mouth open like a fucking carp.

Adam grins and rises to his feet. "In that case, we all better get to bed."

12

Morgan

Pain jackhammers through my skull, and I'm instantly certain I'm dying. I don't mean the slow-dying we're all doing every day. I mean actively dying. Viscerally dying, due to a sudden onset brain aneurism. It has to be that. Or a malignant tumor.

Nobody could naturally have this much pain. But after my body floods with anxiety and my pulse races, bringing more intense throbbing behind my eyelids, I recall it's self-inflicted. No one to blame but myself.

Evil sugar-laden cocktails and a runaway mouth. I actually told Clover and Adam that Luke and I "didn't get much sleep last night." *Why is that memory clear as crystal?* My only consolation is that I never have to see them again. Never have to face Clover now she knows her brother thoroughly screwed me all night long.

I roll over, carefully, enduring an enormous wave of nausea and discover that I barely managed to get undressed before passing out. I'm in my bed—alone—still wearing my dress, now a wrinkled disaster.

Fragments of the rest of the evening drift back. Clover and Adam's knowing smiles. Luke's shocked expression. Being bundled into his car, then his gentle hands guiding me upstairs to my door. After he settled me on the sofa, I think I came on to him. I grabbed his arm and tried to drag him down beside me. All I wanted was his lips on mine. Well, that wasn't all I wanted from him.

Everything after that is a blank. I don't even recall how I got from the sofa to the bed, or him leaving. And I certainly don't remember taking off my sandals, which are neatly placed side by side at the foot of my bed. Another moment of mortification.

My phone buzzes, and I wince as I reach for it. A text from Luke:

Good morning. How are you feeling?

Blunt, to the point. Not pretending I wasn't bombed out of my mind, which only makes me feel worse. Such a gentleman. Now and last night.

Like death

Should I bring up last night's comment? I can't. I have to throw up first. Knowing I can't make it to the bathroom, I lean over the side of the bed and . . . It's a miracle. The small trash bin, gray of course, that's usually beside the toilet, is on the floor, next to me. Luke must have put it there, because I'll bet my last bitcoin there's no fairy godmother for the drunk and stupid.

I wretch, then heave. It's not pretty. At least I manage to hold my hair back. Of all times not to have it in a pony tail. When my stomach is empty, I actually feel a bit better, but I need headache relief. *What did I bring from Boston?*

Still, I don't move. I'm feeling wretched and wishing Luke were here. No, not Luke! How embarrassing would that be? I want my mother or one of my sisters. Probably Pru, since she's nearly a full-fledged doctor. Taking a deep breath, I roll to my other side as my phone buzzes again.

Do you want me to come take care of you?

I don't know what to say since I do and I don't. He adds:

I should have stayed over. On the couch. And made sure you were OK.

Now I feel guilty that Luke is so worried. He should be pitying me, maybe scorning me, but not treating me like glass. It was my own damn fault.

Sorry I spilled the beans. Do you think Clover and Adam think I meant something other than what it sounded like?

His response comes quickly:

All she said was "Been there. Next time, stick to wine."

Next time? There can be no next time. Not for any of what happened in the past forty-eight hours. I respond with an emoji of a person whose head is exploding.

Glancing at my phone, I curse. Already 8:30. I'm late for work, and he must be texting me from his office. I'm not worried about my boss firing me, but I don't want to look like a slacker.

I'll be in soon.

He replies:

No rush. Drink water.

Forcing myself to move, I stagger to the bathroom with the trash can, gritting my teeth against the throbbing ache in my head. After cleaning out the bin, I get in the shower, where hot water and the scent of my floral shampoo do little to ease either my physical discomfort or my embarrassment. I'm not a heavy drinker, and I know better than to mix wine and cocktails, at least to that degree. I can't recall the last time I drained so many glasses of any fruity concoction. *Yes, I do*. In college.

The sweetness ensures my temples keep up their intense drumming. I open the closet and can't seem to focus on anything. After too many minutes spent just staring, I settle on taupe slacks and a simple periwinkle blue blouse, nothing that requires much thought or coordination.

In the living room, I see a half-full glass of water on the table by the couch and remember Luke bringing it to me. I think I passed out before I could finish it. Even worse, I think he carried me to my bedroom. Dead weight, so sexy. *Not!*

Now, I drink two full glasses of tap water, eat nothing because I just can't face food, and then find only a lint-covered aspirin in the bottom of my purse. I take the humble, fuzzy little white pill like it's the most important medicine in the whole world.

Sunglasses are a necessity, even if it was overcast, which it's not. Not a drop of rain since I arrived in Sydney. By the time I reach the office, two long, jarring blocks away, it's after nine-thirty. Jack Thompson's disapproving glare greets me the moment I step into the IT suite.

"Nice of you to show up, Ms. Anders," he says, loudly enough for the other two staff members to hear. Also loudly enough that I might vomit over his shoes. "Bit of a big night on the turps, eh?"

If he only knew. "Not feeling well," I mumble, heading straight for my desk without removing my sunglasses. I don't work for him, and he can shove his attitude up his ass.

"Apparently not," he says, following me, getting on my last frayed nerve. "Mr. Henley has asked for you. Twice."

"If you leave me alone for a second," I say quietly, because even my own voice hurts my head, but as seriously as I can to make him back the hell off, "I'll let him know I'm here."

"No worries. I already sorted that out." Jack hovers, clearly enjoying my discomfort. "As soon as I spotted you wobbling through the foyer like a drunken roo! Didn't you have a meal with his sister and her hubby last night?"

Before I can respond with a kung fu blow that will snap his head back, Zoe rolls her chair over. "You look like a busted thong at Bondi beach!" she says, sounding genuinely concerned. "Reckon you've caught what my mum calls *the lurgy*."

Sounds about how I feel, but I ask anyway. "What's the lurgy?"

"Covers anything flu-like," she says.

"Could be," I lie, grateful for the cover story. Her sympathetic smile makes me feel even more pathetic.

"Can I grab you anything?" she asks.

I start to shake my head, then think better of such a brain-rattling movement.

"No, thanks." I'm unable to contemplate swallowing more than water, and I have a bottle with me.

Zoe shrugs. "Hope you're on the mend soon." She pushes off and zooms back to her desk on incredibly noisy caster wheels. Brad, the other IT person, who has almost zero personality beyond the occasional fist pump when his rugby team wins, ignores me entirely.

Reluctantly, I remove my sunglasses, wincing as the office lighting stabs my retinas. Quickly, I slide on my blue-light blocking glasses, and find they help a little. At least, I should be able to look at my laptop screen.

Yesterday, despite the interruption of meeting Clover and Adam, I made progress in the cyber investigation. It wasn't easy to explain during dinner, but I've narrowed down the potential sources of the breach to a handful of access points. Someone is creating shadow transactions that look legitimate, so real in fact, that shipments are going out to fulfill the orders, keeping customers happy, but the payments are not coming to Henley Confectionery. The thief is smart.

I've only just picked up where I left off when a familiar voice cuts through my concentration.

"Ms. Anders."

Looking up, I find Luke standing at my desk, impeccably dressed in a blue suit that makes his golden-brown eyes even more striking. In one hand, he holds a large cup and straw, and in the other, a bottle labeled Panadol, which I hope are painkillers. My hero and my tormentor rolled into one devastatingly handsome package.

"Mr. Henley," I manage, my voice raspier than intended.

"I thought you might need these." He sets the cold drink and pills on my desk. "Triple shot. Cream. No sugar."

Perfect, I think, reaching for it. Then he adds, "With protein powder, spinach, and banana."

I hesitate. "*Um* . . . Thank you?"

He smiles. "Trust me. It's a coffee protein shake. It'll give you the needed boost of caffeine to ease your headache, while also replenishing essential amino acids and vitamins."

The gesture is thoughtful enough to make my eyes sting with gratitude, or maybe that's just the hangover. Then I realize. "That's not from the break room."

"No. As soon as Jack said you were in the building, I sent Dan to the best coffee bar in Sydney. You're going to love it."

"I thought his name was Dave," I mumble.

Luke starts to laugh, but I hold up my hand. "Not so loud, please."

Jack emerges from his office, eyebrows raised at the scene. "Everything all right, Mr. Henley?"

"Fine, Jack," Luke says smoothly, not looking at him. "Just checking on our consultant's progress." He winks at me, then adds, "If you're feeling up to it, I'd like your preliminary report this afternoon. Say, three o'clock in my office?"

"Of course," I agree, popping two pills and washing them down with a sip of the thick, creamy shake. The rich flavor and smooth, chilled consistency are exactly what I need, although my stomach protests slightly.

Luke lingers a moment too long. "Drink plenty of water today," he adds quietly. With my lips still around the straw and our gazes locked, I silently draw my water bottle out of my satchel and put it on my desk. He nods. "See you later."

As soon as he's gone, Zoe calls out from across the room, "The big boss is fetching your coffee? Strewth!"

When did she start using a megaphone?

"It's nothing," I dismiss, but it's clearly a *wow* in any company on any planet. "He just wants results on this security audit."

"*Mmm-hmm,*" she hums skeptically. "That explains the personal pharmacy service."

I change the subject quickly. "Did you have time to create a spreadsheet of the shipping records? And more importantly, the companywide logins with timestamps? I'm tracking a pattern."

"On your server," she confirms, mercifully dropping the topic of Luke's attention. "Give us a shout if you need a hand with anything else, yeah?"

I certainly won't shout, but I thank her. As the painkillers and the caffeine start to work their magic, I make a breakthrough over the next couple of hours. The amount of missing revenue adds up to a particular subset of shipments sent from the factory I toured. But these orders are not initiating on the Henley website. What's more, the order anomalies always occur during a certain few hours of the early evening.

Zoe's data tells me they don't occur every day. It will take a lot of digging to sort out which shipments are from orders coming through a shadow channel.

"I'm getting closer," I say out loud.

"To what?"

So busy cross-referencing employee schedules with access logs, I didn't notice Noah enter the IT suite. When I look up, he says, "You're lookin' a bit crook! Had a rough one last night?"

"Something like that," I mutter. "What can I do for you?"

He leans his hands against my desk. "Just checking in. Haven't seen much of you lately."

I shake my head, immediately regretting the movement. "I've been busy with work."

"All work and no play makes Morgan a dull sheila," he teases. "How 'bout we grab a feed? Bit of fresh air might do you good."

Normally, I'd find an excuse, but a break from the office after two hours of data scraping is precisely what I'm craving. Plus, I've finally regained my appetite.

"A short walk and a quick bite to eat," I agree.

He smiles. "Ace! I know a bloody good sanga joint down the street."

"Sanga?"

"A sandwich, love."

Standing, I'm relieved to find the room no longer spinning. *Progress.* Sunglasses in place and purse slung over my shoulder, I leave with Noah. Sydney's 80-degree temp—*in February!*—and breezy ocean air does help clear my head.

"It's probably 30 degrees back home," I tell him. "Gray sky, heavy with snow that's about to fall on the already packed snow on the ground."

He shudders. "About as appealing as a mozzie bite on my backside."

That about sums it up, I think. "Winter isn't all bad," I say, deciding to defend New England. "I love to ski. And a roaring fire is best when there's snow outside."

He nods. "I guess you'll be back to your Boston weather soon enough. How's the gig treating ya?"

"How's my job?" I ask, stalling. There's so little I can talk about.

He nods.

"It's good," is all I tell him before he launches into office gossip about people I barely know. Noah is quite a talker, requiring minimal input from me, the perfect companion after a hangover. More than that, it's a relief not to feel nervous tension and overwhelming desire. Today especially, I fully appreciate utter neutrality.

"Anyway, why are you looking like a stunned mullet?" he asks a couple minutes into the walk. "Too many tinnies at the pub last night?"

I'm catching onto his slang, although I don't ask what a mullet is, stunned or otherwise. "Worse than a few cans of beer. I drank wine chased by cocktails at the Langham with Lu—" I cut myself off. "With Mr. Henley's sister and brother-in-law."

Noah whistles. "Crikey! You're meeting the rellies already? Must be fair dinkum serious!"

Noah's laugh follows us in to the lunch place, a hole-in-the-wall that I can tell will be great by its general vibe and mouth-watering aromas. But his remark makes my cheeks heat up as I approach the counter. So much for being relaxed.

"It's not like that," I protest, not sure why I'm explaining myself to him. The only person I need to have a talk with is ten thousand miles away. "Mr. Henley's sister wanted to meet me because I'm working on the security audit. That's all."

"Makes sense," he says, his expression dead-pan. "That's why the boss rocked up with a cuppa and some headache tablets for you this morning."

I startle. "Does everyone in the office know about that?"

"Glass walls, remember? Bloody impossible to keep anything on the down-low in that joint. And that Zoe has got eyes like a hawk. She doesn't miss a bloody thing," he adds with a shrug.

I guess I'm sharing work space with the office gossip.

Great. Now the entire company probably thinks I'm sleeping with the CEO. Which I am—*or was*—but that's beside the point. In five minutes, we're eating sandwiches at an outside table, leaving the topic of my personal life behind.

"You got any plans for the weekend?" Noah asks out of the blue. "There's this ripper coastal walk from Bondi to Coogee beach. Bloody perfect for a Saturday walkabout."

"I don't know," I hesitate. "I might need to work." Once I get close to cracking a cyber case like this, I become hyper-focused.

"I'm a gem of a tour guide," he says. "Besides, if you slog through the weekend and wrap it up, you'll be headin' off without checking out the best spots! What're ya gonna tell your mates when they ask what your favorite thing was in Sydney?"

No worries there. My favorite thing in Sydney is on the top floor of the Henley Confectionery office building. But I won't be telling anyone back home. Regardless, Noah's persistence makes sense. I'm well ahead of my three-month contract, anyway. Getting away from the office and from Luke might restore my sanity.

"I'll think about it," I promise.

Back at my desk, I feel completely normal again. The last of the dull throbbing has relinquished its grip, and I'm determined to make progress before my meeting with Luke. For the next two hours, I lose myself in data. The pattern is becoming clearer. What's more, I'm starting to narrow down potential suspects, based on when certain employees are logged in.

By 2:45, I'm ready to meet with Luke. My pulse quickens as I grab my laptop and then stop by the break room for a cup of fortifying coffee. Despite my resolve not to cross any lines again, the thought of being alone with him in his office sends a flutter of anticipation through me. The elevator ride to the executive floor gives me very little time to compose myself. But hopefully enough.

When I walk through Luke's open door, he's reading something on his screen. Seeing me, he gets to his feet, shrinking the room to the size of a closet. His jacket is on the back of his chair and his shirtsleeves are rolled up. This time, he's wearing a platinum watch with a black band.

Sure, go all GQ on me!

"You look better," he says.

"I *feel* better," I admit. "Thanks for being my Florence Nightingale this morning. And last night, too. I really appreciate the positioning of that trash bin."

He winces, but says, "No worries."

But I'm not done thanking him. "I'm also grateful for how you, you know, put me to bed."

His smile is like a thousand watts. "I wasn't sure whether you'd be angry that I didn't take you up on your offer on the sofa."

"Oh, jeez! I thought I remembered propositioning you, but I hoped I was dreaming."

"Propositioned is a polite word for what you asked me to do to you."

I wish the floor would open beneath me.

"Don't look like that, Morgan. If you hadn't been bombed out of your mind, it would have been my absolute pleasure to comply. Anyway, you were snoring before I could take advantage and ravish you."

He's teasing me now, so I smile. "OK, well, thanks. Let's put that all behind us."

"Agreed." When he gestures to the casual sitting area rather than one of the stiff leather chairs facing his desk, I nearly mutiny. Then reconsider. It's a test. If I can't even sit beside the man on a sofa without jumping his bones—or asking him to jump mine like I recall doing last night—then I might as well go home.

In any case, Luke doesn't crowd me. Instead, we both angle our bodies toward one another. When I breathe deeply, I catch a delicious whiff of his cologne. My lady-bits tingle, as my brain recalls the familiar sexy scent while he was deep inside of me. *Shit!*

I open the laptop to get myself focused on business.

"Before we start," he says, "I want to apologize for last night at the restaurant."

I blink in surprise. "*You're* apologizing to *me*? I'm the one who made that ridiculous comment about both of us not getting sleep."

A smile tugs at his lips. "Which I found rather endearing, actually."

"*Mortifying* is the word I'd use," I counter. "Your sister probably thinks I'm—"

"She likes you," Luke interrupts. "Both she and Adam do. My apology is for putting you into a situation that made you uncomfortable, because I selfishly wanted to spend time with you and have my family get to know you. By the way, they're heading to my grandparents' ranch this weekend and suggested I bring you along."

The invitation catches me off guard. "That's a terrible idea," I say bluntly. For one thing, I never want to see them again after what a fool I made of myself, not to mention dealing with their knowing looks.

Luke glances away toward the window, and I can't tell what he's thinking, until he looks back at me. "You're right," he says, which gives me a pinch of pain because I would, in fact, love to meet his grandparents and see where he spent his youth. But we both know it's totally inappropriate.

Glad I don't have to fight with him, I try to articulate my reasons without sounding overly dramatic. "We're trying to maintain a professional relationship. Spending a weekend together at your family's ranch doesn't exactly fit that objective."

Luke leans forward, his elbows on his knees. "Is that what we're doing? Maintaining a professional relationship?"

The question hangs in the air between us, loaded with implication. The part of me that would happily fail at that goal wants him again so much, it truly makes it hard to be in his company without reaching out to touch him.

As if reading my mind, he leans closer, and I try not to hope he's about to kiss me. *Try and fail.* I want him so much, I part my lips and wait.

13

Luke

I want to taste her so badly, I nearly kiss her. Seeing her pupils dilate, realizing Morgan is as ready as I am, she's irresistible. Reaching out to grasp her pretty chin and hold her still, at the last second, I drop my hand. Instead, I gently rap my knuckles on the laptop case.

"Any progress?" I ask briskly, knowing she can see right through me.

To her credit, she accepts the brusque pivot and puts her game-face on. "Yes, as a matter of fact. Let me bring you up to speed."

For the next twenty minutes, she walks me through her discoveries, including how the shipped orders in question, those whose revenue has been diverted, never have any custom additions but are limited to the pre-assorted selections of boxed chocolates. That's important because no custom orders means no one is calling a customer service number with questions or problems.

After what Clover said, basically accusing me of being a neanderthal who only likes to play with equipment, I listen attentively, ask questions that show I have as firm an understanding of business operations as I do the production side of our company.

"Based on access logs and the timing of the transactions," Morgan tells me, "I'm starting to narrow it down. About half a dozen people so far."

I'm surprised by this. "Already? Who?"

She pulls up the list. "A couple are utterly unfamiliar to me," she admits. "Of course, you'll know all of them."

I do, but two stand out, Jack Thompson and Daniel Kunz, my assistant. "Jack's been with us for years, and Dan is so . . . innocuous. I find it hard to believe—"

"I'm not accusing anyone yet," she clarifies quickly. "These are simply people who were logged in during the time of the known orders entering the shipping queue. I had to create a quick program to cross-reference each employee's login with the exact hours of the orders, bearing in mind I haven't identified every single shadow order yet. Now, I'm going to focus on the cyber fingerprints of the people on this list."

I'm sure my expression reveals how impressed I am. "You created a custom program for this particular problem?"

She shrugs, but is obviously pleased I noticed. "I guess we hired the right person." But then I recall something that happened today.

"This stays between us. I don't want anyone getting wind of your investigation. No need to tell Noah Matthews about any of this on your next lunch break. Unless it's too late."

When Morgan bristles, I wish I'd kept my mouth shut. "Of course," she says, snapping her laptop closed and putting it onto the coffee table in front of us. "It goes without saying, and without question, that I don't speak about my real job here."

Again, I wish I hadn't brought Matthews up. Now Morgan knows I was keeping tabs on her. *Dammit!* I was irked at seeing her stroll out the door with my sales manager at lunchtime. A silence settles between us. Our security discussion is complete, but I'm not ready to end our meeting.

Our gazes are locked in yet another silent battle. I know what I want to happen next. Fiery desire has been stoking my blood since the moment she entered my office. Actually, since this morning, when she looked up at me with that silly straw pursed between her perfectly lush lips.

"So," I say to recover from my stupidity, "about this weekend."

Her blue eyes widen. "I thought you agreed it would blur the lines," she says.

The lines my body wants to erase and cross this very instant. Leaning back, I cross my arms to keep from reaching for her. "I said you're right about it being a terrible idea for a number of reasons, mostly how it will probably drive me insane. But I didn't say I agreed you shouldn't come."

"Why?" she asks.

I'm watching her mouth, wanting to kiss her, knowing I will. It's inevitable. "Why what?"

"Why *me?*" she asks. "Just because I tackled you?"

I can't help smiling. "I admit you got my attention." *How can I explain how she's gotten under my skin?* I can't even understand it myself. Perhaps she feels the same. "Don't you agree it felt right when we . . . didn't get a lot of sleep?" I try to put it delicately, but still her cheeks turn pink. I love how she blushes despite being such a passionate woman and a tiger in bed.

"But I'm the worst possible choice for you to pursue," she says. "I have a boyfriend who has asked me to marry him, and I'm only here for a short time."

Then she straightens. "Unless that's what makes me so appealing. Nothing like having a juicy fling with someone you know can't get attached to you because I'll be leaving. Is that what you want? Hot monkey sex with no strings? And you don't care if it shreds my conscience along the way."

"Hold up," I protest, uncrossing my arms. "First of all, hot monkey sex! What the hell does that even mean?" I don't wait for an answer. "Your being here for a short while is the worst thing about you." When I think of how quickly I pursued her, I add, "It has ruined my usual smooth romancing game, speeding it up to nonexistent."

She makes a face at my little joke. "What about professional versus—"

My control snaps. Morgan hasn't even finished the same tired old mantra before I lean forward and crush her mouth beneath mine. She softens, tilting her head so we fit better. I glide my fingers into her hair, cradling her head just beneath her ponytail, and deepen the kiss, rewarded as she sinks against me.

When I demand entrance with my tongue, she parts her lips, and I thrust inside her mouth. I've needed to penetrate her—anywhere—since I left her bed.

Morgan's hands grab my shirt. I swear I can smell our mutual lust as our bodies heat. Our kiss becomes a full-on make-out session. I'm tempted to use the couch we're on.

Gliding my hand from her hair, I palm her lush breast. Her nipple peaks instantly, and she moans into my mouth. I need to close the privacy blinds. But she suddenly stiffens and rises to her feet.

Clutching her laptop like a shield, she slips away from me. In the space of a heartbeat, she dashes out of my office but hearing the elevator ding, she takes a turn into the conference room.

Chasing after her, I reach the elevator as the doors open and Charlotte steps out. We nod and smile, and I try to block her view of an entire glass enclosed meeting room that takes up the space between my office and hers at the other end of the floor. Luckily, she has her hands full with a cup of coffee and a bakery bag from around the corner. Sometimes I wonder how my entire staff isn't chronically overweight.

"Nearly quitting time," my VP says, as if we're hourly workers who don't spend innumerable extra hours per week.

"Roger that," I reply, a term I never use, earning a frown from her before she salutes with her coffee cup and heads along the wide hall to her office. Then I turn around. Behind me, Morgan has disappeared. Entering the conference room, I flip the switch sending the vertical blinds swinging closed before I shut the door. Slowly, she rises from where she ducked behind the table.

"It's not like you shouldn't be up here," I remind her. "You could have simply opened your laptop and looked as innocent as apple pie."

She sends me a sheepish look. "I panicked. You had me all confused." Her expression is conflicted, and I feel like a heel. Running a hand through my hair, I let out an uptight breath.

"I thought you wanted me to kiss you."

"I did," Morgan confesses. "I do," she adds more softly, but I hear her. With that invitation, I move closer until she puts up her hand. "But I can't, *Mr. Henley.*"

I want to yell with frustration. I know all the reasons she doesn't think we can start anything, but that doesn't make me want her any less. "Don't." The formality stings. "Don't pretend we're just boss and employee. Not after everything."

"That's exactly what we should be."

"Why? Because of Ethan?" The name tastes bitter on my tongue.

She lifts her chin. "Because I'm temporary. Because I'm here to do a job. Because—"

"Because you're scared?"

Her eyes flash. "I'm not scared."

I step closer, close enough to smell her perfume, to see the slight tremor in her hands. "Aren't you? Because I think you feel exactly what I feel, and it terrifies you."

"Luke . . ." It comes out as a whisper.

"Tell me I'm wrong." Another step closer. "Tell me you don't think about that night in your apartment. Tell me you don't feel this pull between us."

She backs up until she hits the conference table. "It doesn't matter what I feel."

"It matters to me." I brace my hands on the table, caging her between my arms. "Everything about you matters to me."

For a moment, I think she'll be the one to kiss me. Her eyes drop to my mouth, and her tongue darts out to wet her lips. Then her phone buzzes in her pocket, and the spell breaks.

"I can't do this," she says, ducking under my arm. "I won't."

"Maybe you should talk to Ethan and call it quits."

Her chin lifts, and I know I've said the wrong thing. "You are so arrogant," she says. "I can't believe you just said that. You don't know anything about him. In fact, you know very little about me."

"And yet I want you more than any woman I've ever met."

She rolls her eyes, which isn't very complimentary where I'm concerned. I guess she doesn't believe me.

"I know that sounds like a line, but it's not. And I want to learn everything about you, if you'll let me. What's more, it's important to me that you find out about me, too. Come with me this weekend. Meet my grandparents. If nothing else, you'll experience a real working Australian ranch. We have a vineyard, too."

Morgan puffs up her cheeks and then blows out the air, seeming exasperated. "I don't know."

"You do know. You're a data analyst among other incredible things. How can you make any decision about us or your life back home if you don't gather data?"

Finally, she smiles. "You're good, Henley."

"I'll sweeten the deal," I add. "I'll make sure Jim sends a couple pounds of the chocolate macadamia clusters to the ranch."

"A couple pounds? A bit excessive, don't you think?"

"My grandparents will want to try them. We've never used macadamia nuts before. Too expensive for most people. Plus, Adam and Clover will want to try them. Maybe I better make it three pounds."

Morgan is shaking her head, which I don't like since I thought I'd already closed the deal. "What are you thinking?"

"I can't spend the weekend with your sister and Adam," she says with a whine to her voice. "Not after what I said. Maybe Clover will spill the beans to your grandparents. What will they think?"

I close the gap and take her in my arms, not much caring if she does put her hand up again to ward me off. But she doesn't. She tenses, and that's all. She doesn't push me away.

"Nan and Gramps will adore you," I promise, "and I can guarantee Clover won't tell them anything. Besides, if my granddad found out you've so much as let me kiss you, he'll think me an extraordinarily lucky man. He has an eye for beauty and brains, just like me."

Her hands rest on my chest, and she's keeping her gaze level with my shirt button that she's fiddling with. "You're not making it easy to turn you down."

"That's my intention." And if she keeps playing with my clothing, I'll have to tear it off and haul her against my bare skin.

"I do have another invitation," she says, cutting through my barbarian thoughts. "I'm supposed to walk from Bondi to Coogee Beach with Noah and have lunch."

The surge of jealousy is ridiculous. I know she's so mixed up about her guy back home, there's no way she's interested in Matthews. The only man who's going to make her feel conflicted and guilty is me, and that's a fact. Still, my tone is snappy when I respond.

"You'll go to Coogee Beach with me. It's a nice walk. I'll take you one evening next week."

She looks up at me finally, her deep blue eyes so distressed, I almost want to let her go. *Almost.* But this weekend, I intend to convince her to give us a try. A real relationship that transcends her departure date. We should proceed as if that's not happening and see how we get on.

"Please come," I say again, running my thumb across her gorgeously full lower lip.

Morgan sighs as if she carries all the cares in the world on her pretty shoulders, and I would do anything to lighten her load. Which is why I say something really stupid.

"What if I vow that I won't make any moves on you while we're there. Platonic fun in one of the prettiest places I know." *God, what did I just say?* The ranch will be hell on earth, and I'll be tortured in that hell like the worst sinner.

Her gaze becomes thoughtful. Then she frowns, looks at my mouth, glances away, battling silently. Finally, she nods. "OK, I'll come. But only if you'll totally behave."

I let her go, watching her practically run from the room. Back in my office, I find her covered cup of coffee, still hot when I touch it.

Just like my feelings for her, still burning hot no matter how hard I try to cool them.

14

Morgan

The sprawling landscape of the Hunter Valley unfolds beyond the car windows, a stark contrast to Sydney's urban bustle. We've driven north for two hours, arriving in Pokolbin. Rolling hills covered in neat rows of grapevines stretch to the horizon, bathed in late afternoon sunlight. It's breathtakingly beautiful—and intimidatingly permanent.

Luke drives with one hand on the wheel, the other gesturing occasionally as he points out landmarks, which don't stop when we're on Henley property.

"My grandfather planted those vines thirty years ago," he says, indicating a hillside to our right. "And over there is where I crashed the truck into the irrigation system." His smile is self-deprecating, and I laugh despite my nerves.

The driveway to the Henley property is long and winding, lined with eucalyptus trees that create dappled shadows across the gravel. My head is on a swivel as on one side, there are sheep in a fenced field and multiple barns.

On the other, there's a paddock with horses that raise their heads when we pass. As we crest a hill, the main house comes into view, and I can't help but gasp.

"That's not the same place from your office painting," I protest. It's a sprawling, single-story structure with wide, vine-covered verandas and a sparkling-blue pool peeking out from behind. The terracotta roof appears to be ablaze, as the glazed tiles reflect the setting sun. There are extra buildings dotted around, all with the same red roofs. Rustic *yet* luxurious, it manages to look both welcoming and imposing. Suddenly, I'm scared shitless.

"Talk about curb appeal," I say, wiping my palms on my denim skirt. "So, this is the Henley homestead."

"Home, original candy headquarters, and heart of the family," Luke confirms. "My grandfather built it himself, with some help. The ranch house was much smaller—as you saw in the painting. And the kitchen from the photo in the factory samples room has grown quite a bit, too. They expanded everything once the confectionery business grew. The wine-making is just a pet project, though. It's only sold locally, which drives the price of a single bottle way up. Gramps is a smart business man, for sure."

"What about the *ranching* part of the ranch?" I ask. "All those cute sheep we just passed."

Luke laughs. "Gramps keeps them for tax purposes. That flock is all mutton now if you tried to dine on one." He parks under a carport near the front entrance, where Clover and Adam are seated on the porch, in the shade. They get up as I climb out of the Batmobile.

Clover, wearing a coral-colored bikini top and matching sarong skirt with her hair wet and slicked back, bounds down the steps in stylish flip-flops to embrace me. Some of my tension eases, since she's greeting me as if we're old friends rather than recent acquaintances.

Certainly not like I'm the employee who got drunk and spilled my guts in public before actually spilling my guts. Thank goodness I did that in private.

"You came!" she exclaims. "I wasn't sure Luke could convince you." Clover doesn't sound as though she thinks her brother's hooked up with a skank.

"It didn't take much convincing," Luke says before I can respond. "Not when I promised chocolate-covered macadamia nuts. I hope they arrived."

He shakes Adam's hand and kisses his sister's cheek. Then, his fingers splay across the small of my back as he guides me past them, up the three steps to the veranda and into the house. The casual touch radiates warmth through me. Maybe this will be OK, after all.

The interior of the house is a blend of comfortable charm and modern luxury. Polished hardwood floors gleam beneath my feet, and the high ceilings create an airy atmosphere. The first thing I see in the front hall are family photos lining the walls. I spot Luke as a teenager, grinning beside what must be the *ute* he told me about, a fire-engine red pickup truck. Other family photos show his parents, with Clover and him and his other sister, Lark.

"Basil!" A warm voice calls out, before a tall woman in her seventies emerges from around the corner. She's wearing an apron over shorts and a pretty light-blue cotton shirt, her silvery-gray hair swept into a messy bun.

"Nan," Luke says, stepping forward to hug her tightly while she kisses his cheek and tousles his hair. When he steps back, for a moment, he's transformed into a young boy. Then he shakes it off. "This is Morgan Anders."

Eleanor Henley's keen blue eyes assess me quickly before her face breaks into a genuine smile. "G'day, love. Welcome to our place. We've heard heaps about ya."

I shoot Luke a questioning look—*What exactly has he told them?* Before I can do more than say, "Hi, nice to meet you," a strapping older man with Luke's build appears behind his wife.

Patrick Henley has the same commanding presence as his grandson, though his hair is white and his face weathered from years in the sun. And then there are the eyes, which

I've come to think of as Henley gold, since Clover's are the same topaz-color as her brother. Now I see where they both get them from.

"So, you're the sheila who put our boy on his back," Patrick says with a hearty laugh. "About time someone took him down a peg."

I feel my face heat. I hadn't realized he'd told anyone about the night we met. "I'm never going to live that down, am I?"

"Not likely," Luke murmurs close to my ear, making me shiver.

A timer goes off somewhere in the interior. "That'll be my rolls," Eleanor says. "You made good time from Sydney on a Friday arvo. Tucker's nearly ready. Oi Luke, grab Morgan's gear and show her to the sleepout on the right. Then both of you come back for some coldies. Clover, love, are you ever gonna get out of that cossie?"

Fortunately, Adam looks as befuddled as I feel. At her husband's perplexed expression, Clover translates. "You made good time from Sydney on a Friday night. Dinner's almost ready. Luke, get Morgan's bag and show her to the bunkhouse on the right. Then both of you come back for drinks." She nods at her grandmother, who's smiling, blue eyes laughing. "Then Nan asked me if I was ever going to take off my bathing suit?"

"I'll help her out of it," Adam says, making Luke laugh, but Patrick narrows his eyes.

"That's my granddaughter," he reminds the tall, dark-haired billionaire.

Adam looks chagrinned until Eleanor bursts out laughing. "Don't you worry, mate. Pat's just havin' a laugh. Now, off you go, everyone, or I'll end up burnin' tonight's tucker!"

The "sleepout," or as Clover called it, the "bunkhouse" turns out to be a charming single-bedroom cottage, just past the turquoise-blue pool. I imagine the other structure on the left is similar.

When I enter, I doubt it ever housed dusty ranch hands, not with a floral-covered sofa and chair on a cream-colored, braided-wool area rug. I can see through an open door that the queen bed also has a floral duvet.

Luke takes my weekend bag all the way into the bedroom, setting it on top of an oak dresser before reemerging. He leans against the doorframe, and I'm very aware that we're alone. With. A. Bed.

"This is lovely," I say, turning away from him. I don't want to sit, not after the drive, but I'm not sure what to do with myself.

"Think of it as your private sanctuary, except for when you have to use the outhouse." That makes me look at him directly, probably with an expression of horror. He smiles. "Just kidding. The bathroom has been fully modernized." He jerks his thumb over his shoulder to the bedroom. "It's in there."

I wonder if he's brought other women to stay here. Dismissing it as none of my business, I ask, "Where are you staying?"

"In my old room." He approaches me, causing me to step aside quickly and let him pass. "Come here, Morgan."

I join him at the open door, and again, Luke rests his broad hand on my back, as if he can't help touching me when I'm close. I can feel his heat like a brand through my cotton shirt. "Those are my windows, right there." He points to a room diagonally across from mine, with the pool and a large patio between us.

"It looks inviting," I say. "I mean the pool, *not* your room. Obviously, I didn't mean your room." I finish my blather with a small laugh.

He keeps his gaze straight ahead as lights come on automatically around the pool and all around the ranch house. I know how electricity and timers work, but still, I smile at the wonderful fairytale aspect of the pretty lamps.

"We can take a swim after dinner, if Clover doesn't hog the water."

"Even if she does, I'm up for a swim." Much better in fact if *all* the other adults are in the pool as chaperones.

Luke nods, still looking outside. His fingers stroke up and down my back, causing tremors in my muscles and tingling between my legs.

"More fun alone," he muses.

I shake my head. "You promised to behave."

"Already regretting that promise." His voice is husky, and I have to keep my gaze trained on the horses standing with their heads over the post-and-rail fencing. I don't want to do something stupid like turn and lean into him, glide my fingers into his hair, and draw him down for a kiss. *Nope. Better not do any of that.*

"OK, cowboy," I say, moving out from under his touch. "I think I'll wash my face and brush my hair before I sit down to dinner with your family." Then I pause. "Should I change?"

"Yes," he says. "Most definitely. If you're not wearing an evening gown, Nan won't let you eat with us."

"*Ha ha.* You're really a jokester when you're not at work, aren't you?"

He fixes me with those golden-brown eyes and smiles, a sexy little grin that makes my insides flip. *How did I get so lucky as to be here with him?*

$♥$♥$♥$

Dinner is a relaxed and lively affair at the same time. Before we eat, I'm given a tour, learning how this ranch house grew from a few rooms to the current sprawl. The kitchen that I saw in the factory photo has been remodeled to make even the most persnickety chef happy.

The main living area is big and open, suitable for a country that is both of those things, with a stone fireplace for the cold months of May through August. And nothing is gray. Eleanor has decorated in cream and tan, with pops of saffron, red, and bright blue. It's a happy looking home.

I meet Adam and Clover's little Ivy, with her head of very dark curls and her father's intense slate-gray eyes, and their nanny, Meg, a widow in her sixties who had time on her hands and a love for looking after children. Overseen by Clover, Ivy eats early. Noodles, pieces of boiled chicken, and freshly shelled peas, which she throws with surprising accuracy at whomever passes by.

Luke and Adam manage to catch most of the peas. Eventually, Meg whisks Ivy away from the kitchen island to the far end of the house.

"I chucked the Bonvier mob down that way," Eleanor explains to me, "so we won't wake up the little tacker if we get a bit too loud and carry on like a bunch of galahs."

"More likely so Ivy won't wake *you* up, Nan," Clover says. "Bright and early with the sun. Every damn day." She and Adam click their wine glasses together in parental solidarity and drink the Henley's Reserve, oak aged chardonnay. I have a glass of it, too, and am taking miniscule sips. No repeat performance of drunken Morgan tonight.

Eventually, we gather at a long dining table under three lighting fixtures of hammered copper. They're industrial and beautiful. I'm told the natural, deep-red table is a massive slab of Jarrah heartwood, native to Australia. With jade green place settings, it's like being seated at a piece of ancient art. Eleanor asks her husband to dim the overhead lights as she puts a match to four thick candlesticks along the table's center. The flickering reflection gleaming on the rich Jarrah is stunning and feels primal.

Soon, Patrick regales me with tales of Luke's childhood misadventures. Apparently, he had more than Lark and Clover put together.

"Remember when ya got bucked off and wouldn't get back in the saddle till Jazzy egged ya on, mate?" Patrick says to Luke. I feel him tense beside me. "That sheila saved ya months of being a proper scaredy-cat and me having to crack the whip to get ya ridin' again."

"Reckon she'll pop 'round tomorrow for a feed," Eleanor says. "Told her you were headin' up this way. If we're lucky, she'll rock up with one of her ripper banoffee pies."

"Jasmine practically grew up here," Clover explains, catching my eye. "Her family owns the neighboring property."

I take another sip of the excellent Henley wine, trying to ignore the knot forming in my stomach. Of course there would be a *Jasmine*—beautiful name, probably a beautiful woman. Someone who belongs in Luke's world, with roots here, who will stay forever.

"Morgan's from Boston," Luke says, smoothly changing the subject. "She's been telling me about sailing on the Charles River."

"Your mob's all there?" Eleanor asks, her shrewd eyes studying me.

"My mob?"

"Your family," Eleanor clarifies.

I nod. "My grandparents were from Germany. My parents own a bookshop in Cambridge. In Massachusetts, I mean, not the UK. And my two sisters live nearby. Kate, who's a teacher, and Pru, whose an internal medicine resident at Mass General. We're close."

"Must be tough, bein' way out in woop woop," she says gently.

Luckily, I guess what she means, and the kindness in her voice nearly undoes me. "It is," I admit. "But sometimes you have to . . . to explore your options." Luke's hand finds mine under the table, giving it a squeeze. I probably shouldn't add the truth, but I do.

"I'm only here for a short while anyway." With that, he gives my fingers one more gentle grasp before withdrawing his hand.

After a long dinner, stretching past midnight, making swimming out of the question, at least for me, I escape to the back deck. I need air and a break from trying to understand his grandparents. Adam and I spent a lot of time wide-eyed, exchanging confused looks.

But night sky and stars are universal. I look up and realize I'm wrong. The Southern Hemisphere stars are different, creating unfamiliar patterns in the velvet sky. Talk about *woop woop*, I feel as though I've traveled to an alternate universe. Then I hear footsteps behind me, knowing it's Luke before he speaks.

$♥$♥$♥$

Luke

Morgan slipped outside while we were all talking about the brilliance of chocolate-covered macadamia clusters. On the back veranda, she's silhouetted against the railing, her rich caramel-brown hair illuminated almost to copper by the soft yellow lamplight. My promise to keep my distance seems impossible now, watching her out here alone, vulnerable.

"Stop brooding," I say, moving to stand beside her.

Morgan turns, and I can see the conflict in her eyes. "I'm not brooding, *Basil.*"

"Don't tell me you didn't know my first name," I say. She had access to all company records and must have seen it.

"I knew it," she agrees, "but I didn't know how to pronounce it."

I shrug. "Now you do, but since I hate it, most people respect my wishes and don't use it."

"I guess that doesn't apply to grandparents," she says. "Anyway, I wasn't brooding, merely thinking."

"About Ethan?" The guy might as well be right here on the ranch since he's always in her thoughts.

"About everything." She gestures to the sprawling property. "This is *your* world," she reminds me, "and it's beautiful. But it's not mine."

I step closer. "It could be."

She laughs softly, but there's no humor in it. "Luke, you can't just—"

"Can't just what? Want you? Too late." I'm close enough now to catch the scent of her shampoo, floral and fresh, that makes me want to bury my face in her hair. "You can fit here in my world. I think you do already."

"Your grandparents mentioned someone named Jasmine. A lot," I point out. "How come you never told me about her?"

"She's in my past," I say firmly, not wanting to talk about someone who had an important place when I was a teenager but not since. "Like Anong."

Morgan told me a little more about Ethan on the drive up here, and asked me about my own love life. Anong was the most recent long-term lover, so I mentioned her. I haven't told her about Isla yet. One ex at a time seemed prudent. But Jasmine never even entered my thoughts.

"You know what? Neither of them made me feel like this."

Morgan turns to face me fully, her blue eyes luminous in the white moonlight. "Like what?"

Instead of answering, I cup her face in my hands and kiss her. She tastes like the wine we had with dinner. My family's wine, bold, creamy, complex. When she parts her lips, I deepen the kiss, pulling her against me. Her hands slide up my chest to my shoulders, and I know I should stop, remembering my vow, but I can't.

"Come with me," I murmur against her mouth.

"Where?"

"My room. Your room. The Batmobile. It doesn't matter."

She hesitates, and I press my advantage, trailing kisses down her neck. "No one will know."

"Your sister will know," Morgan protests weakly, even as she tilts her head to give me better access. "She already suspects."

"Clover won't say anything." My hands slip to her waist, fingers finding skin where her shirt has ridden up. "I need you. You need me, too."

Morgan shivers, and I think I've won, but then she steps back, breaking contact. "You promised," she says, her voice shaky. "You promised we'd keep things platonic this weekend."

"I was an idiot. Delusional. Unrealistic. Insane." I reach for her again, but she dodges.

"No, you were right the first time." She wraps her arms around herself. "We need to know if there's more between us than just physical attraction."

"I already know that," I confess.

She groans. "I'm sorry, Luke, but I need to figure out what I want without your hands on me, making me crazy. Because your touch has become like a drug."

Running my fingers through my hair in frustration, I know she's right, but that doesn't make it any easier. The moonlight catches her face, and she looks so beautiful and vulnerable, I'm rattled by how much I want her.

"Fine," I say. "Tell me something about yourself that you haven't already." *Because I want to learn everything.*

She relaxes slightly, leaning back against the railing. "I'm not that complicated. You know about my parents and my sisters. That Katie is engaged to—"

"Keith, an investment banker whose family came over on the Mayflower," I recall.

Morgan smiles. "You listened."

"To everything you say, sweetheart."

"*Hm.* OK, did I tell you we have Sunday dinner together every week when I'm home. Except Pru often can't make it because of hospital duty."

I digest this nugget of information. "And that's what you want? To go back to that life?" I don't mention *the boyfriend*, as to me, Ethan is incidental.

"I don't know anymore." Her voice catches. "I thought so when things made sense. Before I met you."

I reach for her again, but she holds up a warning hand. "Luke, please. I'm weak when it comes to you, and I need space to think."

"All right." I force myself to step back. "But know this—I'm not giving up. Whatever's between us, it's worth exploring, don't you think?"

She looks at me for a long moment, and I can see the struggle in her eyes. Finally, she nods. "Goodnight, Luke."

I watch her walk away, three steps off the veranda, and then across the stone terrace before she rounds the edge of the pool toward the guest cottage. My body aches to follow her, but I keep my feet planted firmly on the stained wooden deck. Tomorrow, I'll show her more of the property, help her see how she could belong here, a transplanted daughter of Boston, living a great life in Australia. By my side.

But tonight, I'll keep my promise. Even if it kills me.

Because Morgan Anders is worth waiting for.

15

Morgan

The morning sun filters through gauzy curtains, and I remain on the cool sheets, thinking about my family. My sister Katie's text from half an hour earlier still burns on my phone screen:

Has Ethan heard from you? He keeps calling Mom.

Guilt churns in my stomach while I watch Luke through the window, his tall frame moving with practiced ease as he helps Patrick with chores. They're feeding the horses that live in the paddock nearest the house. Luke takes the time to stroke his large strong hand along the neck of each horse who comes near him. Some get an extra rub down their nose.

He belongs here—the way he handles them. He's probably an expert sheep herder or whatever the heck you do with them. And he told me last night he loves to be here for "crush," which I learned is when they harvest the grapes at the peak of ripeness and put them through the entire process of turning them into wine. Sorting, crushing, de-stemming, pressing, and putting the wine into barrels. He does it all.

"Everyone works together for long days, even eating lunch in the fields," he said, sounding wistful.

Now, I'm content to lie here and watch how naturally he moves across the paddock with hay on a big pitchfork. Everything about him screams Australian rancher-turned-CEO, right down to his perfectly worn boots. Just supposing we were to make a go of it, I try to imagine myself this far away from home for the majority of my life, with only short visits back to Boston. And it hurts.

I can so easily picture Mom preparing dinner for the one night a week we still gather together, the scent of rosemary and roasting chicken welcoming me in. I would miss that and my squabbling sisters. My chest aches at the thought, and it seems harder to breathe. So much for contentment.

I'm not going to go back to sleep, and the time is wrong to call Ethan, so I shower and dress and head to the main house. Peeking my head into the kitchen, I jump when Eleanor's warm voice comes from behind me.

"Go on in, dear. Got the billy on for a cuppa. Just took one to Clover's nanny. What a bonza sheila! And a widow at her age, poor thing."

I settle myself on a stool at the kitchen island. "Thank you, Mrs. Henley."

"Just call me Eleanor, righto?" She pours me a cup of tea and gestures to the cutting board that holds something resembling an overly large scone. At my expression, she says, "That there's a damper. Bloody ripper of a bush bread, that is. Chucked some walnuts and raisins in this beauty. Pat and Baz already smashed one between 'em before they shot through."

She cuts me what can only be described as a massive wedge, puts it on a plate, and slides it over. Then she places jam and butter within reach. "And here's honey for your cuppa." She indicates an earthenware pot with a wide cork.

Without waiting, she pours milk on top of my amber tea. "The only proper way to knock it back," she proclaims.

Well, I guess so.

"When Clover and her good-lookin' bloke get their rears up, I'll whip up a ripper brekkie. The fellas should be back in by then."

"Ripper brekkie," I muse aloud. "Really good breakfast?"

"You got it! A big cooked one with all the works to fill your belly and put a smile on your dial!"

I nod, enjoying watching her move around her gorgeous kitchen with its double-oven and stainless steel everything. "I love the backsplash," I tell her. Most of it is made up of off-white tiles of varying sizes, but they're interspersed with gorgeous, colorful painted figures.

Eleanor smiles. "I painted the accent tiles myself and had 'em fired locally."

"They're lovely." As I eat delicious bread and sip tea, I look at all her designs, and then I see the bird. Luke's bird, from his tattoo. "What kind of bird is that?"

Since she has more than one bird tile, I get up, walk around the island and point to it.

"A kookaburra. You've heard of 'em?"

"I think so."

"Some reckon their call sounds like human laughter, but that's a load of rubbish. They sound like bloody monkeys, fair dinkum. I'm gonna have a crack at teaching Ivy that tune every little ankle-biter learns."

Clover enters with Adam, who has Ivy in his arms. "Go ahead, Nan," she says, taking a seat at the island. "Sing it now."

"Not before brekkie," Eleanor says.

"Sing," Ivy demands imperiously, clapping her pudgy hands. "Sing."

I stand back, watching this adorable family dynamic. Adam has taken a seat beside his wife, keeping his daughter on his lap. He looks bemused, turning my way with a wink of greeting.

"Very well," Eleanor says and begins softly. "Kookaburra sits on the old gum tree."

Clover joins in, "Merry, merry king of the bush is he."

They sing together, "Laugh, kookaburra. Laugh, kookaburra. Gay your life must be." Ivy claps her hands again.

"There are two more verses, but that's more than enough for now," Eleanor says.

"What brought this on?" Clover asks, pouring Adam some tea. He looks a little disgruntled, glancing around for coffee, no doubt. Clover gives him a look, and he sighs and sips the tea.

"Morgan noticed my tiles," Eleanor says. "She was keen on that one."

"Was she?" Clover asks raising an eyebrow as she looks at me, and I know she knows that I've seen it on her brother. Nothing gets past this woman.

"What do your mob reckon about you being on the other side of the globe, after living in each other's pockets your whole life?" Eleanor asks, as she gives Clover, Adam, and even little Ivy hunks of damper.

"Nan," Clover says softly. I guess she thinks her grandmother is prying, but I don't mind. Besides I'm not sure I know what she's asking.

"My family's very supportive of me spreading my wings a little." I think about what my parents said. "Mostly because it's temporary, and they know the plan is for me to be back home soon." In fact, it would break their hearts in a way, although they have two other daughters living nearby. There I go again, seeing both sides and feeling like I'm somehow on both ends of a teeter-totter at the same damn time.

Eleanor's knowing smile makes me squirm. "Sometimes the best stuff in life just happens on its own."

Isn't that the truth? If anyone had told me I'd be falling in love with a guy I just met and more deeply than I've loved the man I've been with for three years, I would've laughed.

Eleanor sets about frying and sautéing, as well as brewing a pot of coffee, not letting Clover or me help in any way. And just as she takes the last rasher of bacon from the pan, Patrick and Luke come in.

Along with Adam, they eat a massive meal of every breakfast food known to man, including extras I'd never had with eggs, like baked beans and grilled tomatoes. Clover, Eleanor, and I have smaller helpings, but still, I'm stuffed by the time Patrick sets down his coffee cup and says to me, "Fancy giving us a hand with the chores. Baz was tellin' me you're keen on station life."

My cheeks heat. I'd made one comment about wanting to learn more about the ranch, and now I'm supposed to be Cowgirl Morgan? But I can't say no to Pat's earnest expression, although I do send Luke a small grimace.

Outside, his grin is both welcoming and mischievous. "Ready for your first lesson in ranch work?"

He leads me to the stables, where the earthy smell of hay and horses fills my nostrils. A massive bay horse snorts as we approach its stall, and I jump back.

"This is Thunder," Luke says, patting the horse's neck. "He's gentle as a lamb."

Somehow, I doubt that. Luke goes into the stall and puts a halter on the horse before leading it out and tying the end of the rope to a metal ring. Thunder, who I can now see is more than a tad dirty, towers over me. When Luke hands me a soft, oval rubber thing, I stare at it like it might bite.

"What do I . . . ?"

"Here." He steps behind me, his chest warm against my back. "It's called a curry comb. It cleans his coat. Thunder likes to roll in mud puddles. When he can't find one, he knocks the water pail over in the field and makes one."

Guiding my hand in circular motions along the horse's flank, Luke's warm breath is on my ear, making me shiver. "Like this," he says.

I'm enjoying Luke's arms around me and starting to feel confident when Thunder shifts, and I stumble backward, stepping hard on Luke's foot. Luckily, I'm wearing sneakers. "Sorry," I mutter.

"No worries, but I think you have the hang of it." Luke leaves me, but stays close, going in and out of each stall, filling up water buckets and dragging out dirty straw while the horses are in the paddock. Except for the massive beast giving me side-eye.

At first, I'm scared to continue, but then I manage to rub him gently, in one spot, on one side, because I'm nervous about going around him.

After a few more minutes of terror alone with Thunder, the horse whinnies and raises its head and snuffles so I can see his teeth—absolutely terrifying. Shrieking, I drop the rubber comb thingy, and run right toward Luke. Fortunately, he's not holding the pitchfork at that moment. When I collide with his strong body, his arms come around me instantly.

"I guess we're not having a riding lesson today," he quips, his chin resting atop my head.

"Nope," I say. Suddenly, I hope he'll kiss me, despite his promise of a platonic weekend. After working already for hours, he smells good, all man-scented sweat that's pure Luke. Tilting my head up to look at him, I give him all the signs, looking at his mouth, then into his golden-brown eyes.

For a second, his hands stroke my back before he pushes me away with an audible groan.

"Let me turn Thunder out into the field, and then we'll take the UTV to feed the sheep."

Fine. I deserved to be denied. It's what I wanted, after all. But the next chore doesn't go any better. In fact, it's worse. The sheep crowd around me, bleating and pushing.

They're not soft and sweet. They're strong and persistent and ill-mannered, freaking me out until I trip over my own feet and land in what I desperately hope is only a muddy run-off from their water trough.

Luke helps me up, clearly suppressing a big smile. "Maybe we should stick to the vegetable garden or check out the vineyard," he suggests. "Nothing more with animals today."

Looking down at my filthy clothes, I can't help laughing and don't mind when he joins in. This isn't my world, and we both know it, but I'm doing my best. I'm a city girl who can hack into a secure network but can't feed sheep with grace. Before I can tell him I'd love to take a stroll through the vineyard, the rumble of tires on gravel announces a visitor. We watch a black Range Rover go past us.

"Come on," Luke says, sounding subdued. "Nan will want us back up at the house."

"Who is that?" I ask following him to the UTV.

"Jasmine," Luke says, his tone purposefully neutral, making me suspicious.

Great! We drive in a cloud of her dust toward the house. He says nothing more for a few seconds, then adds, "Gramps and Nan are so fond of her, I think, because she steps in as honorary grandkid when Lark, Clover, and I aren't around."

Really? Is that why he believes she's here. I don't know ranching, but I know my fellow females. I'm sure Jasmine has ulterior motives to playing granddaughter. Like keeping herself in the running as granddaughter-in-law!

We park behind her vehicle, and she climbs out— reddish-gold hair to her waist, tall, slender, fit, and tanned. Leaning back in, she shows off her ass in tight jeans before emerging with a covered basket. Then in pretty red leather boots, that I know Clover will adore, she approaches our vehicle.

My stomach drops as I watch Luke's face. He got an eyeful of her rear, and now he's studying her front curves, climbing out of the UTV as Jasmine approaches.

"Hang on," she says when he leans in to hug her. Setting the basket on the driver's seat, she flicks me the barest of appraising glances, before sliding her arms around his waist in a familiar way. She's probably done it a hundred times.

While letting him give her a bear-hug that lasts a beat too long, she says something in his ear that makes Luke throw his head back laughing.

Feeling like an intruder watching their easy intimacy, I jump out the passenger side and hurry toward the house.

"Morgan," he calls after me.

"Gotta get cleaned up," I call over my shoulder.

Once inside, I glance back through the window, seeing Luke try to peek in her basket. She slaps his hand.

"Banoffee pie, of course!" Jasmine's voice carries across the yard, her Australian accent rich and musical. "Wouldn't dare show my mug without it, Baz."

Baz! I guess it's not used only by his grandparents. When I hear someone clear his throat, I turn to see Adam, Clover, and Eleanor, all three, watching me.

"The station's done you in proper," Eleanor says.

"I guess so." I slide my sneakers off so I can carry them through the house to the back. "I'm just going to . . ." *What exactly?* Shower? Hide? Hitchhike my way out of here?

"Wash up," Clover suggests. "If you didn't bring enough clothes, let me know."

"She *always* overpacks," Adam says, "especially footwear." Clover slaps his shoulder in the same familiar way that Jasmine slapped Luke's hand.

Nodding, desperate not to be a muddy mess when I meet her face to face, I dash out the back door toward the guest house. The bathroom mirror tells me it's worse than I thought, dirt from head to toe. I could use one of those curry combs Thunder enjoyed.

After a quick shower, I reapply mascara, going motionless when I catch sight of my reflection. I look haunted, nervous, uncertain. That's not who I am, but it is when I'm somewhere I don't belong.

"What are you doing here, Morgan?" I ask myself, shaking out my wet hair and deciding to stop with the primping. Luke needs someone like Jasmine—someone who understands his world, who can ride horses and bake pies and speak the language of ranching and all things Aussie. He left New York City behind because he couldn't stay away from this land that he loves. He'll realize how unsuitable I am soon enough, and all the styling and makeup won't change a thing.

Lunch is excruciating. After I reappear, I'm formally introduced to Jasmine Walker, who plasters on a big smile and offers her hand. She squeezes mine so hard—*must be all her ranch work that's given her such strength*—she brings tears to my eyes. And then, this fiery-haired princess who has been here many times and knows her established place in this home, rules over the meal.

Her stories about *Baz* and his youthful mishaps are meant for me, warning me off of a guy she wants. A guy she's had, if her intimate way of touching Luke's arm and smiling at him are any indication.

With each tale, Jasmine underlines how deep their connection runs. And honestly, I don't blame her. If he were mine, I would fight for him, too.

Clover tries to include me and Adam in the conversation. He seems unbothered, but I feel increasingly like an outsider. Because I am and because Jasmine makes it clear that I'm merely a guest, while she's practically family.

"Remember that time you took a tumble off Starlight?" Jasmine touches Luke's arm. *Again.* "You were trying to impress me, like a real bonza rider."

"As I recall," Luke says, his eyes finding mine across the table, "I was trying to prove I could jump the fence. Had nothing to do with impressing anyone."

"Sure, sure." Jasmine winks at me. "Whatever you say, mate. But there's no doubt you were bein' a show-off drongo when you went hoonin' 'round in the ute. Fair dinkum, you copped it sweet when Gramps made you repair the whole bloody lot of pipes!"

Of course! Jasmine is the reason Luke did donuts and crashed his truck into the vineyard's irrigation system.

I try not to hate her, but she seems so perfect. Right down to her pie, which is eventually carried out as though it's made of gold. We all get a generous slice, and it is impossibly delicious. A buttery biscuit crust is topped with layers of banana, caramel, and whipped cream. And crowning it are chocolate shavings. My jealousy and loathing grow as I shovel it into my mouth.

"Dear God," Adam says. "Brennan's bananas foster has nothing on this. I'll take another slice, please." Luke joins him in a second helping, and Jasmine basks in the men's praise, lapping it up the way they're lapping at the cream.

I'm one of the first to push away from the table. "I think I'll take a walk."

"I'll join you," Luke says.

"No, please. Stay. Enjoy your pie and your old friend." By that time, Jasmine is tugging at his arm to keep him beside her. It'll probably fall off when she's done with him. I stroll around the property, mostly staying on the gravel road after Pat gives me a brief warning of the various snakes.

Tiger snakes and death adders? Really? After about a half hour, I sit on the veranda with Clover and little Ivy.

"This is really all I want to do," Luke's sister says. "Bake in the Aussie warmth and relax."

"Sounds like a good idea," I agree, thinking of the cold winter we both left behind in Boston. But if doing nothing is so great, then why is Jasmine behaving like a circus performer?

We watch as she shows off her riding skills, helping exercise horses that haven't had enough lately, according to Pat. Luke joins her, perfectly at home. They make a striking pair against the backdrop of the Australian countryside. This is plainly his world, and I'm just visiting.

Adam joins us with two baskets and a list of fruit and veggies to pick from Eleanor's bursting garden. I actually have a really good time with these two as we hunt for cherry tomatoes, cukes, green beans, and bell peppers. With Adam carrying Ivy on his back and holding a watermelon and a cantaloupe, and Clover and I each holding a basket of salad fixings and veggie sides for dinner, we head back to the ranch house, drop off our fresh produce, and decide to take a swim.

By late afternoon, we've been floating and paddling for ages, long enough for Ivy to swim, go in for a nap, and come back out again. When I hear Jasmine's voice in the house, I hope she's coming out to say goodbye. Instead, she appears poolside in the skimpiest turquoise bikini this side of the French Riviera.

Or maybe Eleanor lent her a few postage stamps.

"Strewth, lucky I remembered to chuck a cossie in my bag," she says, drawing everyone's attention to her bathing suit. *As if we hadn't noticed it!*

Even Clover, who looks like a supermodel in her red-and-white striped swimsuit, does a double-take. "Down boy," she says to Adam, whose gaze is momentarily glued to Jasmine's figure, as the red-head strides to the diving board and enters the pool like a sleek dolphin.

Suddenly, with my pale bod in a black tankini, I feel like an orca. I'm Shamu in the shallow end. Luke comes out of the house with a tray of beers and a sippy cup for Ivy, who's floating in a clever contraption with a built-in umbrella. He matches Jasmine, being the sculpted male version of supermodel hotness.

Damn! Even his swim trunks are the same shade of turquoise. Their simpatico rapport is starting to become sickening. Luke occupies himself by giving his niece a ride back and forth across the pool, sending me friendly smiles whenever he catches me watching him. The kookaburra tattoo almost seems to flutter its wings when he moves his arm through the water, a trick of light and liquid. Jasmine stays close to him, jabbering like a monkey about what's going on at her parents' ranch, occasionally asking his opinion in a fawning way. Or maybe I'm just imagining that.

After I've stayed in the pool a polite amount of time, I climb out and take one of the lounge chairs, positioned under an umbrella. It's difficult, but I try to ignore Jasmine's incessant diarrhea of the mouth. Even chatty Noah has nothing on her.

When dusk settles, naturally Eleanor invites Jasmine to stay for dinner—*since she's still here!* The meal is a replay of lunch, but without the pie. Somehow, Luke extricates himself from his old friend long enough to drop into the chair beside me, but Jasmine snags the seat on his other side, sliding into it just as Clover is about to. It looked like they were playing musical chairs, and Jasmine won. Maybe she always wins.

He's not yours, I remind myself for the hundredth time today.

"How often do you come up to the ranch?" I ask Luke, suddenly thinking that perhaps Jaz and Baz hook up monthly or even weekly.

"Not often enough," his grandfather says. "It's been at least two months."

"Busy at work, Gramps," Luke replies. "More so since the whole cyber theft started happening. Plus, I had that time sink of a meeting in Singapore. Well worth it, though. Anyway, Morgan's nearly cracked the case."

I startle as all eyes turn to me. "Not quite cracked," I begin when Jasmine jumps in.

"When are you headin' off?" she asks me. "Back to Boston, I mean." *Possessive bitch!*

"That's a little up in the air," I explain. "If I solve the crime, then I can go home early." I'm keenly aware of Luke's face turned toward mine.

"Am I wrong to hope you don't solve it too quickly?" he asks. Heat spreads up my neck. I can't believe he said that in front of his family . . . and Jasmine.

Clover laughs. "I'm impressed, Morgan. There aren't many people whose company my brother would choose over the welfare of the family business."

Speechless, but feeling pretty good, especially when Luke presses his leg against mine, I duck my head and stab at the garden-fresh salad on my plate. Yes, I send a cherry tomato skittering off onto the table, leaving a trail of oily dressing, but I don't care. I laugh, and everyone joins in. Except for Jasmine, who is a little less spunky and bright for the rest of the meal. Still, she has one last trick up her sleeve when she finally declares she's going home.

Hallelujah!

"Good to meet you, Morgan." I don't let her shake my hand just in case she wants to break a few fingers. "Sorry I won't catch ya later, but I reckon you'll sort out that drama with security and be flyin' back to your homeland before you know it." Then Jasmine wraps her hands around Luke's arm again—*poor sore arm!* "Walk me out, Baz."

"Such a nice girl," Eleanor says, "but if I was her nan, I wouldn't let her out of the house in that cossie she wore earlier."

Everyone laughs but me. I don't know her well enough to be joining in. Besides, I've got my gaze on the carport where Luke and Jasmine are illuminated by the lights that dot the property.

They talk a little. She moves closer. He shakes his head. She goes motionless before reaching up to stroke his face. He captures her hand under his. He's still talking when she goes up on tiptoe and crushes her mouth to his. When his hands go to her shoulders, I finally look away.

"Who's up for a last swim?" Clover asks.

Without the red-headed mermaid in the teeny-weeny bikini, I'm all for it. Reaching for my glass of Henley wine, I drain it. "Why not?"

16

Morgan

I change into my swimsuit again. It's still a little damp and cools my irritation along with my irrational thoughts. *Luke is not mine,* I remind myself yet again. I also take a few moments to text Ethan. Despite knowing Luke is not the one for me—or rather, that I'm not right for him—I'm ready to tell Ethan the hard truth. *I can't marry him.* Of course, I don't say that in my text.

I'll call you as soon as the timing matches up for both of us. Need to talk.

When I exit the guest house, Clover and Adam are already paddling around, laughing softly, and I hesitate, not wanting to interrupt their romantic time. Not now that Ivy's gone to bed.

Adam spots me first. "Come on in," he says.

"The water's lovely," Clover adds. "And I brought adult beverages." Sure enough, there's a tray with four snifters of amber liquid. It seems she's expecting her brother to join us. "No fruity cocktails," she promises.

Feeling welcome, I walk down the pool steps. "It feels warmer," I say.

"It is. Gramps has the heaters set to start churning after two, so it's a few degrees hotter by dinner."

"Heaters? Plural?" I ask, accepting a drink.

Adam nods. "It takes a lot of BTUs to heat this much water." He gazes fondly at his wife. "But they'd do anything for my pool-loving princess."

Still, there's no sign of Luke. *Did he go somewhere with Jasmine?* Maybe he decided to make a return visit to her family's ranch. *Not my business*, I tell myself, sipping the smooth brandy before setting it on the pool deck. Then I stretch out in the dead-man position, letting myself float while staring at the emerging stars.

"Room for one more?" Luke is at the pool's edge, and my breath catches at the welcome sight of him, shirtless in board shorts, a different pair from earlier. Without waiting for an answer, he dives in, surfacing near me with droplets running down his chest.

"You were avoiding me today," he says softly, since we're out of earshot of his sibling and her husband.

"I've been giving you space to catch up with an old *friend.*" The word comes out accusatory, like I have a right to care they've been lovers. Maybe they still are.

His eyes darken. "Morgan—"

"She's perfect for you, you know." The words tumble out before I can stop them. "Jasmine knows your world, your family. She probably knows how to take care of sheep and crush grapes, for that matter."

Luke's hands find my waist under the water. "I don't want perfect. I want you."

"Gee, thanks," I say, trying to escape him, floundering around in the deep end, but I can't dislodge his hands.

"Mrs. Bonvier." The nanny has appeared. She looks flustered.

"Is Ivy all right?" Adam asks, while Clover is already climbing out of the pool.

"Don't be alarmed," Meg says. "She's just overly tired from the exciting day. But she wants her mama tonight."

As Clover wraps a towel around herself, Adam gets out of the pool. "You don't have to come," she tells him.

"I don't want to be a third fish," he says, drying off and picking up two of the drinks. Neither Luke nor I protest when he follows Meg and Clover into the house.

As soon as they're gone, Luke tugs me into the shallows until we can both touch the bottom.

"So," I say. "Jasmine."

"Has gone home," he says. "And we're still here."

"Right. You were just explaining how, now that Miss Perfect Pie has left, you're ready to slum it with me."

Luke laughs hard until I sweep my hand over the pool's surface, spraying him with water. Shaking his head, he slicks his hair back, looking even sexier. "I said nothing like that."

"Last I saw, you two were sucking face by the Range Rover," I point out. "Now you're making moves on me. What's the deal, Basil?"

"*She* kissed *me*, not the other way around, no matter what you think you saw." His hands go to my waist again, and he draws me close. Right up against his wet, hard body. "I should dunk you for that mean-spirited splash, by the way."

I lift my chin. "I'll take you down with me. We may be in water, but I still have moves."

His eyes widen, then he grins. "I love your moves. I'd rather kiss you anyway."

That's all the warning I get before Luke claims my mouth under his. Just like that, I'm lost. My body is humming with need that I can't bear to deny again. It's been too long since the last time he satisfied this sizzling arc of desire that connects us.

All the tension of the day evaporates as his mouth moves from my lips down my neck, nibbling a path. I want him nibbling other parts of me. When I wrap my legs around his waist, Luke backs us toward the tiled edge, our kisses growing ever more desperate.

Aware that there are lights all around the pool area, I wonder if his grandparents might glance out and see our bad behavior.

"Guest house," I gasp between kisses. "Now!"

He lifts me out of the pool, sitting my butt on the deck before scrambling out himself. Then we run, barely making it inside before his hands are everywhere, leaving trails of fire across my wet skin.

Soaked bathing suits hit the floor, and I waste valuable time, picking them up and tossing them onto the shower floor. I'd hate to be the guest that ruins the carpet or the hardwood. And then he encircles me and tumbles me backward onto the bed.

Luke

I watch Morgan's eyelids flutter closed as I take her nipple into my mouth, sucking and biting gently until she starts to writhe under me. I want to go slowly, but when she moans and sinks her fingers into my hair, it's hard to do anything but nudge her legs apart and settle between them. Sliding my hand between our damp bodies, I make sure she's as far gone as I am and discover she's slippery with need.

"You're ready for me," I say, not asking, but she nods as her eyes open, deep blue and sensual.

"*Mm-hm*," she agrees. "Please, Luke."

Hearing her say my name in her breathy voice is an aphrodisiac I don't need. Already rock hard and throbbing painfully against her opening, I slip my cock into her slick, wet pussy. Her walls clench around me tightly, embracing my rigid shaft as I slide deep inside.

A soft moan escapes her lips, and she grips my shoulders. When I start to move, Morgan's back arches, thrusting her full breasts up toward me. She is a caramel-haired goddess, and I'm the luckiest man alive.

Bracing my arms on either side of her head, I worship her nipples while plunging in long, steady movements, my muscles shuddering as I strive to keep control. Her legs lock around my waist, helping her hips to mirror mine. Burying my face in the nape of her neck, I inhale her hair's fragrant scent, which the saltwater pool didn't strip away. The tension coils deep in my core with each roll of my hips.

Grunting softly, I pick up the pace, our bodies gliding together smoothly. The sounds of our coupling fill the room, wet skin slapping against wet skin as I sink deeper. Morgan's thighs quiver against my sides. And then she freezes, digging her fingers into my shoulders. At first, I think she's climaxing already.

"Condom!" she half yells, half groans.

"Dammit!" I pull out fast, looking around wildly, as if one will suddenly fall from the ceiling fan. And then I remember. Although it might piss Morgan off, I think she'll forgive me. Stalking out of the room, like a naked madman, I go to the small couch, praying no one has cleaned under the seat cushion in this rarely used guest house.

Tossing it aside, I nearly weep with relief when I see a strip of four golden packets, tucked there from an earlier encounter that, as I recall, never panned out.

I'm sheathed and back before Morgan has time to rethink what we're doing. *Thank God!* But with one hand, she has started to draw the bedspread over her gorgeous nudity.

"Nope," I say, tugging off the covers, revealing every perfect inch again, as well as the sexy view of her other hand stroking herself. "I'll get you back there," I promise, gliding deep into her pussy like I'm going home. It's not the same feeling with a rubber, but it's so fucking good, I can't complain.

In just a few thrusts, she's panting once more, lips parted, eyes closed. "Please, Luke," she moans. "I need . . . I need . . ."

Reaching between us, I rub circles over her swollen clit—quick, steady, firm strokes—until she arches her neck, a beautiful smooth column that compels me to lean down and kiss it. Hungry, open-mouthed kisses on her scorching skin. She gasps, her walls spasming wildly around my shaft. Clenching even tighter, she comes undone, nails digging into my back, her climax long and loud with mewing cries that sends me quickly after her.

Pistoning harder, chasing my own release, I grunt deeply and come in a mind-blowing, spiraling climax that drains me dry. Morgan cries out again with my last powerful thrusts before I'm utterly depleted. The aftershocks leave me trembling in her embrace before I roll to the side.

"Morgan," I murmur, capturing her hand and bringing it up to my lips to thank her, while I'm still breathing hard, staring at the ceiling.

When I turn my head to look into her eyes, I know we've just crossed another invisible line. Myriad thoughts swirl behind her gaze. There's something new, something fragile and raw, simmering between us now. And the after-bliss hasn't even begun to fade away.

Tracing patterns on her smooth shoulder, I fear she's retreating again. The whole day has been a mess, starting with Morgan's fall into the sheep's runoff and Jasmine's long visit. Every attempt I'd made to fix things had only made them worse. Until I gave up trying, got in the pool, and kissed her. It seems to be the magic potion between us.

"Stop thinking so hard," I murmur, pressing my lips to her temple. Her skin is no longer damp from the pool but moist from our hot and exuberant sex.

"I can't help it." She rolls to face me, those clear blue eyes searching mine. "This is so difficult, Luke."

"Only if we make it difficult." But even as I say it, I know she's right. The strong, sweet fragrance of the night-blooming moonflowers and frangipani, both of which Nan has always insisted are associated with love and devotion, waft through the window screens covering us with a thick floral veil. But it can't shield us from reality—Morgan has a life waiting in Boston, one that she wants, and I have responsibilities here that I can't walk away from.

"You know who's not a difficult choice for you," she says in a whisper. "Jasmine."

Sighing, I prop myself up on an elbow. Of all the issues surrounding us, Jasmine is not one of them, not one Morgan should be worried about, anyway. "Jasmine and I hung out in our tweens and teens. We even played around a bit as we both discovered the opposite sex. We had opportunity and proximity. That's all."

"But she's beautiful," Morgan protests. "And the pie."

I can't help laughing. "There are a lot of beautiful women in the world. I just had hot monkey sex with one of them. And there are a lot who are great bakers. A connection that grabs you straight off the mark and won't let go, that's special. The thing with Jasmine was mere convenience, never anything serious, at least not for me."

Morgan opens her mouth and I interrupt her. "I know what you're going to say. Yes, she's always wanted more, but I've been clear about where we stand."

"She knows everything about you." Her voice is small, and she glances away. "Your history, your family, this place."

"Sweetheart, you know things about me that Jasmine never will." I catch her chin, making her look at me. "You know I wear a grungy hoodie for a long flight." We both smile in the dim light. "And you know how to take me down. Not just physically, but with a look or a word or the way you bite your lower lip." She bites it to prove me right, and my groin tightens. "You know how I take my coffee in the break room. You know how to move when I'm inside you. You probably know that those sexy little sounds you make when you're climaxing send me into the stratosphere."

She blushes. Her hair is tousled, her lips are extra red, even swollen, and she looks satiated. I feel a surge of possessive pride. I did that to her, given this amazing woman such overwhelming pleasure. And I want to take her all over again. Stroking her thigh, I feel her shiver. "You doing okay over there?"

Morgan takes a deep breath, and I see that she's trying to let everything go apart from this moment. "It's hard to complain when you're an excellent lover." She stretches languidly. "Although I might accuse you of playing dirty, distracting me from serious reality with your . . . talents."

"Serious reality?" I roll onto my back. "Like the cyber thief who's conning my company out of thousands of dollars? Or maybe the boyfriend you're stringing along back in Boston?"

I regret those words, but I'm not happy that her phone has pinged more than once while we were in the middle of an unbelievably good fuck. Actually, a great one.

Morgan winces. "*Wow*. Way to ruin the moment, Casanova."

"You brought up reality." I shrug. "I know it's complicated for you, but I want you to know this isn't a game for me, either. Hell, you're the most complicated woman I've ever been with."

"And did screwing my lights out help to simplify matters?" I can hear the smile in her voice, and turn my face to her again. She grins impishly.

"Among other things." I tug her against me again and kiss her nose. "The simple truth is I want to know everything about you, even the parts you're still keeping secret. I'm already imagining waking up every morning wishing you were next to me, even though I know you're leaving. Mostly, I spend time wondering if I can make you stay," I admit.

Morgan searches my face. "That's a dangerous thing to wonder, Luke. I can't stay, even if I wanted to. A lot of things would have to fall into place for that to happen."

"Making things fall into place," I echo. "I can sure as hell try."

"You're really serious about this?"

"Deadly. I can't believe you sound surprised."

Morgan doesn't look convinced. "We barely know each other, Baz!"

Reaching around her, I pinch her ass, making her yelp, but she adds, "Even if by some miracle, I could stay, there's no guarantee it would work. Look at Ethan and me."

I consider for about half a second. "You've never said it, but I don't believe you and Ethan have this kind of chemistry." I stroke her hip. "And I don't care how long it takes, I'm going to memorize every detail about you until I do know you inside and out."

"There you go, playing dirty again," she accuses, but she threads her fingers into my hair and brings me closer, fitting her luscious lips to mine. We kiss with a growing fervor that makes it clear she isn't really complaining.

Lost in her taste, her heat, I let myself believe that somehow, we'll find a way forward. That I'll make her see we're worth taking a chance on, even if it means uprooting her entire world.

But that's a battle for another day. Tonight, I have Morgan in my arms, and I'm determined to make the most of every moment. The night dissolves into a blur of passion and need. True to my declaration about memorizing every detail, I go down on her with my tongue and teeth, lapping up the sweetness between her legs and sucking her clit until she comes. Grateful for the extra condoms, I'm balls deep in her pussy twice more before dawn.

$♥$♥$♥$

I wake up later than I usually do on the ranch, since I take over the chores when I'm here. Morgan's fingers are lightly tracing the outline of my heart, which makes me smile.

"I have to call Ethan."

My happiness vanishes along with my smile. His name is like ice water. On the other hand, after last night, I'm no longer worried that he has any real claim on her at all.

"What will you tell him?"

"The truth. That I can't marry him." She touches my face. "That would be true even if you weren't in the picture. I needed to get far from him to be able to hear the little voice in my head and to see he and I were wrong for one another." Morgan's sigh is long and heart-wrenching. "But you *are* in the picture, right here in my bed, and that makes it harder to tell him."

I kiss her then, pouring everything I can't say into it. Using up the last condom, we have sex again, slower this time, as if we can stop time itself by staying tangled together in this idyllic guesthouse. Afterward, while she showers, I watch the ceiling fan, thinking about the drive back to Sydney later. Everything will be different now—we can't go back to pretending this is simply a fling. I've fallen for her, hard and fast, in a way I never have with anyone else.

The question is, will it be enough to make her stay? I think of Anong and the pull of her homeland. I remember Isla's expression, looking none-too-pleased with me, when I told her I wasn't staying in New York and asked her to come to Australia?

With Morgan, the stakes are higher than they've ever been because I don't want a future without her in it. Will *I* be enough for her to change her entire life? Because the thought of letting her go back to Boston has become more impossible with each passing day.

17

Morgan

On Monday morning, when I see the flowers on my desk, my grin grows as big as my whole face. Knowing who sent them, I quickly suppress it, even though Brad and Zoe aren't at their desks to witness me floating on a cloud of carnal satisfaction.

The heady fragrance envelops me the closer I get. Definitely not from Noah this time. These aren't sweet, cheerful carnations. These are two dozen, blood-red roses, as lush and seductive as the sex between Luke and me. And I don't know how I feel about them.

On the one hand, *yes!* Luke is everything I've ever wanted in a man. On the other hand, I didn't let him into my apartment yesterday evening when we got home because it felt wrong. We weren't able to keep our hands and mouths off each other at his grandparents' house despite our best intentions. And as we approached my apartment building, he asked what I wanted for dinner and whether I had any beers or wine inside. Luke assumed too much, that I was his for the taking. *Again.*

Which is why I sent him on his way. Not even a kiss goodbye, because one kiss and I would have let him upstairs. My entire psyche hasn't changed in two days. I haven't become easygoing and free-spirited. I still need to analyze the hell out of what's happening, and I can't do that with his magnificent body literally in my face, or his funny personality making me laugh.

Removing my lightweight jacket, I stow my purse before allowing myself to look for a card. Luke probably sent the flowers anonymously anyway. Not because Henley Confectionery Company has a rule against fraternizing between employees, but to spare my feelings if someone else saw the card. No one, particularly a contracted employee, wants her co-workers to think she's a tramp who's banging the boss.

After I sink into my chair, open my laptop, and set my water bottle beside it, I draw the vase toward me, slowly and deliberately. Burying my nose in the flowers and drawing in a big breath, I'm knocked back by the dense fragrance. *The bouquet of the bouquet.* Perhaps the most fragrant roses I've ever received in my life. Finally, I swivel the vase around until I find a card on a stick hidden deep on the other side.

Why are my hands shaking? I hope I'm not foolish enough to expect a declaration of love from Luke. I'm good in bed, but not that good. I glance at the card.

I love you more each minute,

My heart races for a second, until I keep reading.

And I'm counting the days until you're home, Love, Ethan,

Well, fuck me for a loser! My emotions flicker from guilt to sadness to anger and back again. There's only one reason Ethan is giving me the full-court press after I told him I wasn't sure about us and needed to be away from him for a quarter of a year. He's bullying me. Not the first time, either.

For the most part, he is a nice guy, who at times has got caught up in work to the point that he missed my birthday, but then he more than made up for it. But he also picked out our apartment and put a security deposit on it when I wanted to live in a different neighborhood. He even chose our first "together" furniture purchase of a living room suite by himself, while I was deep in a coding session at work.

"Just wanted to make it easy for you," he said when I dared to get annoyed.

I shove the card deep into my purse and then nearly shove the gorgeous flowers off my desk with spite. But I'm not that childish. Plus, some of my anger is fueled by remorse. Maybe Ethan really is counting down the days. It doesn't help when Brad comes in, followed five minutes later by Zoe, who goes apeshit over the roses.

"Looks like someone's either been heaps good or very, very cheeky," she quips.

My face probably wears a sickly, shameful rendition of my earlier happy smile.

About an hour later, I receive a text.

Was anything delivered?

The other thing about Ethan is he loves to get credit when he does good, and he gets super defensive when he does bad, which is why I usually let that stuff go, like the missed birthday or when he once forgot to pick me up at the airport. I've learned it's just easier that way. I text back.

Yes. They're lovely. Thank you.

He texts back:

That's it? I'm surprised you didn't text me right away.

Before I can respond, Ethan adds:

TBH, I expected a call.

And he deserves one.

I'm at work. I'll call you later.

The cloak of black, ugly shame that has settled over me is all my own doing. I fully intended to call Ethan after Luke dropped me home last night, but when I'd finally worked out what I was going to say and gotten up my nerve, the time difference made it impossible. It's not something you wake someone up at five in the morning to do.

"Hi, Ethan. Not only don't I want to marry you, I've been screwing another guy who has completely captured my heart." Yah, that's not going to happen. I've been feeling tight and tense in the pit of my stomach ever since I left the ranch and for the entire drive back. I'm just not cut out for fooling around and cheating.

When my phone falls silent and there aren't any more texts, I get back to work. Previously, I'd been auto-searching for "Henley Confectionery," "Henley Chocolates," and "Henley Candy" once every five minutes during the hours when the phantom orders have been placed. All these names should redirect to the official Henley website. Friday afternoon, I set my work laptop to run a URL search for any websites featuring "Henley Cand," to pick up sites that might be using the word *candies* instead.

Checking in my developer's sandbox, I gasp. Right there on my screen is the shadow website I've been searching for—HenleyCandee.com. HenleyCandys.com and Henley Candees.com redirect there, too. Very smart, indeed.

"Gotcha," I whisper, spending the next hour diving into the shadow site, tracking IP addresses, and examining the code structure. Whoever built this knows their stuff—it's a near-perfect clone of the legitimate Henley website but with subtle payment routing differences.

I'm so engrossed that I barely notice when Jack Thompson looms over my desk. From habit, I click the Escape button with a macro programmed to hide my work.

"Monday meeting in fifteen minutes," he announces, his eyes flicking to the roses with obvious curiosity. I'd already seen the regular meeting reminder. "All the bigwigs and top dogs," he adds, "and your name's on the list. No drama if you can't make it, seeing as you're not really—"

"I'll be there," I reply without looking up, not giving him the satisfaction of asking about the flowers.

My email notification chimes just as I'm closing my laptop. It's from Sawyer in HR—a mandatory team-building retreat in the Blue Mountains, Wednesday through Friday. Three days and two nights trapped with coworkers in the wilderness, trying to manufacture camaraderie through trust falls and motivational speeches. *No thanks.* That's bad enough, without being close to Luke while having to hide my feelings, feelings I'm still wrestling with.

After knowing this man for a month, do I love him enough to move to Australia? That's a big ask.

Fifteen minutes later, I see Luke for the first time today as I enter the conference room. He's leaning against the wall in a charcoal suit that makes my mouth water, looking every bit the confident CEO who spent the weekend making me scream his name. Our eyes lock for a brief second before I deliberately choose a seat next to Noah.

"Heard about the retreat?" he whispers as I settle in beside him.

"Just got the email," I murmur back. "Sounds intense." Luckily, I don't have to go. Not my real workplace, not my real team.

"Nah, it's actually not too shabby," he says. "Last year, we mucked about in kayaks and stacked ourselves into this ripper human pyramid. Reckon we'll have a crack at zip-lining this time round. Either way, it's three workdays off and all on the company's dollar. Been stuck in this joint pulling too many late ones. Bloody oath, I'm keen for some time in the bush."

I'm deciphering this and thinking that I didn't see that Noah had pulled any "late ones" in Zoe's time logs. About to ask him, I hesitate when Luke clears his throat, snagging my attention. Sure enough, he's frowning at us, undoubtedly for too much talking.

Charlotte begins the weekly Monday presentation, but I can feel Luke's gaze remaining on me. The meeting doesn't drag. It's kind of like their upcoming team-building, simply a way for the employees to connect and make sure everyone's in the loop for whatever lies ahead. Short project updates and quarterly projections only take up about half an hour.

I don't know why I was invited because no one asks me anything, and all I can think about are Luke's hands on my body and Ethan's roses on my desk—physical manifestations of my impossible situation.

When the meeting ends, Luke casually mentions he needs my input on a security matter. As others file out, Noah squeezes my shoulder.

"Chuck a spot for ya on the bus on Wednesday?" he asks with a hopeful smile.

It doesn't seem like the time to explain my aversion to going. I'll tell Noah later that I plan on remaining in Sydney. Besides, I'm too close to figuring out who the cyber thief is.

"Sure," I reply, perhaps too brightly, feeling Luke's energy shift behind me.

Once we're alone, he closes the door with a soft click.

"How's my favorite goat herder," he asks.

I can't help smiling. "She's working hard."

"The flowers on your desk?"

Just like that, I'm frowning. "How did you know I received flowers?"

For some reason, this powerful CEO in his bespoke suit seems sheepish. "Security cam."

He's been spying on me. *Damn.* Even though I sometimes have to do that for my job, I don't like it when it happens to me. Not one bit.

$♥$♥$♥$

Luke

"**S**tandard procedure," I say, watching the emotions flicker across her face. "I wasn't specifically watching you."

When she raises an eyebrow, I tell her the truth. "Perhaps for a few moments, I was specifically watching you."

I checked the security feed to the IT suite this morning, because I needed to know what she was thinking. After she shut me down at her apartment door last night, I've been in a tailspin of confusion.

"Your admirer has expensive taste," I say, trying to keep my tone light despite the jealousy coiling in my gut. "Noah seems to be stepping up his game from carnations."

She huffs and crosses her arms. "They're not from Noah."

"Oh." My relief is short-lived as realization dawns. "Boston, then?"

Morgan's silence is all the confirmation I need. *Ethan.* The shadow between us, the reason she keeps pulling away. She nods, looking miserable.

"Have you—?" I start, but she cuts me off.

"I haven't called him yet. The time difference makes it complicated."

"Right. The time difference." I can't keep the edge from my voice. Maybe she's putting it off because she's not sure she wants to burn that bridge yet. "Nothing to do with what happened at my grandparents' place."

Her cheeks flush. "Don't push me. I'm calling him in my own good time."

"You're running out of it, Morgan. We both are." I step closer, close enough to smell her familiar floral scent without touching her. "I don't want to be the man you're cheating with. I want to be the man you choose."

She sways toward me imperceptibly before catching herself. "I found the shadow website."

The abrupt shift to business catches me off guard. Professional Morgan, walls up, defenses armed. I admire her ability to *compartmentalize*, as she once said, even as it frustrates me.

But this is amazing news. "Show me."

For the next twenty minutes, we focus on her discovery—HenleyCandee.com, a clever misspelling that's been siphoning orders and money. I'm impressed by her work, and part of me is grateful for the reprieve from the emotional tension between us.

But when she leans close to point at something on her laptop screen, her hair brushes my cheek, and I'm lost again. I want to hold her against me, lock the door, and remind her body what her mind seems determined to forget.

Forcing myself to focus on the screen, which represents the money bleeding from my family's company, I try to ignore the way everything about Morgan, even her shampoo fragrance invades my senses or how her fingers tap the keyboard with a rhythm that's becoming as familiar to me as my own heartbeat.

"You've done brilliant work here," I say, straightening. "Lark will probably want to face-time to thank you. I know the board will be impressed."

She steps back, creating distance between us. "Thank you."

The professional courtesy in her voice only makes me want to break through it more. I face her directly.

"About the retreat—"

"I'm not going," she interrupts, crossing her arms. "It's for permanent employees. I'm just consulting."

I raise an eyebrow. "That's not true. The retreat includes *all* current staff, including consultants."

"I can make better use of my time here in the office. I'm close to identifying who created this shadow site."

"You have today and tomorrow to continue, and then that work will be waiting when you return. You still have weeks left in your contract." For which I'm beyond grateful. "Besides, the team-building exercises might actually be useful for you."

"Useful?" Her eyes narrow skeptically.

"You'll get to observe potential suspects in a less-guarded environment. People reveal themselves differently outside the office." I can see her considering this, her analytical mind turning over the possibilities. I press my advantage.

"What's more, staying here alone while everyone's away might raise questions. Remember, my employees think you're doing a straightforward audit of our systems. People will wonder why you're so eager to avoid social interaction with them."

"I'm not avoiding social interaction," she protests, but there's uncertainty in her voice.

"Aren't you?" I step closer, close enough that if I reached out, I could touch her. "Or are you just avoiding me?"

Her eyes flash. "Not everything is about you, Luke."

"No, but this is." I soften my tone, not wanting to push her too far. "Look, I'm not asking for anything more than your presence at a company function. You're being paid to integrate with my employees, to understand how we operate. This retreat is part of your contract."

I can see the moment she realizes I'm pulling rank—her spine stiffens and her expression cools. I hate using my position as leverage, but I'm desperate to keep her within arm's reach while she sorts through her feelings. After all, I might need to do something drastic if her resolve to dump Ethan starts to waver.

"Fine, I'll go," she says as if I gave her a choice. The only choosing I want her to do is me.

"Great. How about dinner tonight? There's a—"

She holds up her hand. "No."

"No?"

"No," she repeats, her voice firm but soft. "I need space, Luke. *Without* your . . . sex appeal messing with my mind."

I want to argue. More than that, I want a repeat of how our bodies fit together, how her laughter sounds against my chest when we're tangled in the sheets. But I recognize the determined set of her jaw.

"All right," I concede, stepping back to give her the physical space that mirrors what she's asking for emotionally. "I understand. But Wednesday—"

"I'll be there," she interrupts, already gathering her laptop. "For work. But we won't see each other until then, not outside of this building."

Morgan slides past me, careful not to let our bodies touch. The door closes behind her with a soft click, leaving me alone with my thoughts. Sinking back into a chair, every instinct in my body wants to follow her, to drag her into an empty closet, if that's the only place available, and kiss her until she admits we have something special here. But that's exactly the kind of behavior that sent her retreating in the first place.

The flowers from Boston complicate things. They're a physical reminder of the life waiting for her back home, even if not with Ethan—a life I'm asking her to reconsider and reject after knowing me for mere weeks. When I put it that way, even I can see how overwhelming it must seem. But the way she responds to me isn't merely physical. There's something deeper between us, something worth fighting for. I need to be patient enough to let her come to that conclusion herself.

I spend—or waste, as I see it—the rest of Monday and all of Tuesday keeping my distance, watching from afar as she works diligently, occasionally conferring with Jack Thompson and his team. She's professional to a fault, never looking my way when I pass by the IT department, although I feel her awareness like a physical touch.

By Wednesday morning, as my employees board the luxury coaches bound for the Blue Mountains, and the rustic Cloudridge Resort, I'm practically vibrating with pent-up energy.

Just when I'm starting to think she's a no-show, Morgan finally arrives, looking sexy in casual hiking clothes that highlight her athletic frame and a touristy version of the wide-brimmed Akubra hat. Traditionally made from rabbit-fur felt, this one looks like tightly woven straw, and its headband proclaims "Down Under and Loving It."

I can't help smiling at her get-up. She's smartened up since the ranch, however, wearing authentic tan Blundstone boots instead of sneakers. At least three-quarters of the people on the two coaches are wearing Blunnies, too. Even me.

True to what I overheard, she takes the seat Noah saved for her, near the center of the bus. I settle into my seat at the front. The privileged position of CEO does nothing to improve my mood when I turn to chat with Charlotte or Jeff and catch glimpses of Morgan laughing at something Noah says.

The journey to our lodge in the heart of the Blue Mountains takes about two hours, the cityscape gradually giving way to eucalyptus forests casting dappled shadows across the winding road. I pretend to review quarterly projections on my tablet, but my attention keeps drifting back to Morgan. She's animated now, explaining something to Noah with those expressive hands that I know can be both gentle and demanding. The way they seared a path as she stroked my body, over my abs, and finally down to tease my cock. I swallow. Team building will be an extra *hard* challenge for me this year.

When we arrive at Cloudridge, northeast of Katoomba, the staff efficiency almost makes up for my sour mood. They usher us into a stone-and-timber main lodge with floor-to-ceiling windows that frame panoramic mountain views. Sawyer, our HR director, distributes cabin assignments, while the resort coordinator, Jackie, explains the schedule, giving everyone the option for a paper copy or one sent to their phones.

"Your first team challenge begins in one hour," she announces. "Everybody, please grab a bottle." Jackie gestures to the table full of cases of water. "If you're not already wearing appropriate outdoor gear, please change and meet at the north trail on time."

I scan the list in my hand. The C-suite execs get private cabins—a perk I'm especially grateful for today. As everyone disperses, I catch Morgan's eye across the room. She holds my gaze for a heartbeat too long before turning away to follow Noah toward the guest cabins.

The first challenge is a scavenger hunt designed to force cross-departmental cooperation. I watch with growing irritation as teams are assigned, and Morgan ends up with Zoe from IT, who is also one of her cabin mates, Jeff from accounting, a couple women from sales, and Ben, our CMO and the sole executive on their team. My team consists of Lacey from marketing, and four junior staff I barely know. I guess this is my opportunity to learn all about them, which normally, I would be enthusiastic to do.

Today, not so much. I'd trade the rest of my team away to be with Morgan.

"The objective is simple," the facilitator explains. "Each team must locate five markers hidden throughout the property. At each marker, you'll find a puzzle piece and a team challenge. Complete all five, and use your puzzle pieces to solve the final riddle."

Morgan's team takes off immediately down a path into the forest, and I watch her cute ass until she disappears. My team takes a different route at a more measured pace, with Lacey chattering about a marketing idea she has for selling chocolates in sand pails. Despite thinking of the melted mess that could be, I nod absently, my thoughts on spotting my sexy cyber expert through the gum trees.

Twenty minutes later, as we locate the third marker, I hear someone yell. It sounds painful and has all of us running in the same direction.

18

Morgan

"It's Jeff!" someone calls out as we converge on the source of the now blistering string of curses.

I push through the eucalyptus undergrowth, branches snapping back at my face as I hurry forward. Jeff, who's on my team but had been racing ahead like he wanted to win all by himself, is sitting on the ground, clutching his ankle. His face is contorted in pain.

"What happened?" I ask, kneeling beside him.

"Stepped wrong on that bloody rock and I went arse over tits," he says, nodding toward a jagged stone half-hidden in the leaf litter. Then he groans. "Heard a right nasty pop, too."

Luke arrives with his team moments later, immediately taking charge. "Let me see," he says, crouching down beside his accounting director. His fingers probe the ankle with gentle authority, and I'm struck by how naturally leadership comes to him. "It's swelling already. Probably a sprain, but could be worse."

"Can you put weight on it?" Ben asks, offering his hand to help Jeff up.

Jeff tries and immediately sinks back down with a hiss. "No chance."

"We need to get you back to the lodge," Luke says, looking around at the assembled teams. "I'll call Jackie."

While Luke calls for assistance, Zoe digs through her backpack and produces a first aid kit. "Be prepared," she says, and I recognize the motto from my sister Katie's time as a Girl Scout. "Hey, Morgan, can you get his boot off?"

Noah is crouching nearby, taking it all in. "Crikey, mate! There's your drama right there," he tells Jeff. "Ya went and chucked on your runners instead of your Blunnies, ya drongo!"

I do as Zoe asks, removing Jeff's running shoe while he swears loudly in my ear, and then I sit back with Noah as Zoe wraps up the swelling ankle.

"This'll keep it steady, mate," she says, "until we can get you to a proper doc."

"Zoe knows her first aid," Noah says, giving her a high five.

"Strewth, didn't spend seven years in Girl Guides for nothing," she says, just as Luke returns.

"Should have some help in a minute," he promises. Sure enough, Jackie soon zips to the scene in a UTV like I rode in with Luke to feed those cursed sheep. The sight of it takes me right back to the ranch . . . and the guest house.

Luke and Ben position themselves on either side of Jeff, with his arms over their shoulders. They raise him off the ground and load him into the utility vehicle. Before Jackie drives off with the pale-faced Jeff, she says, "Teams, gather your members and proceed with the scavenger hunt."

"Are you kidding?" I blurt out before I can stop myself. "One of our teammates is injured." He was also the most gung-ho of our group.

The coordinator looks unmoved. "This is precisely why team-bonding exercises are valuable. Learning to adapt to changing circumstances is essential in business."

I bite my tongue, but Luke catches my expression and winks. I guess Stacy is right. Just like in life, you have to adapt.

"Drink some water, everyone," Luke announces with quiet authority. "Take a minute or two, and then let's get this over with."

As the teams disperse, Noah falls into step beside me.

"Crikey, that was a bit intense," he says, running a hand through his sun-bleached short curls. "But Zoe and you were ace with that first aid. Proper little lifesavers."

"Thanks, but it was all Zoe." I'm distracted, watching Luke speak with his own team members. His shoulders are slowly releasing the tension of the past few minutes. "You better get back to your group," I tell Noah.

"Cheers, see ya, mate."

After Luke's team wins—making me wonder if whatever team he's on will always win because the man is just so supremely capable—we eat a cold lunch of sandwiches and my favorite LLB to wash them down. We were told to sit with people who weren't on our first team, so I sat with Noah and some Henley employees whom I've never interacted with before. It was fun because people were simply happy to be in such a gorgeous setting.

The afternoon activity is again at the retreat because they want to keep us off the coaches until tomorrow. We start with new teams for a more skilled challenge. Paint-ball. This time, we're three large "armies," dressed in blue, red, or yellow raincoats. We have to protect ourselves but also our team members, providing cover as we make our way to the designated goal. Points for reaching it first, but also for having the most surviving team members. This is intended to keep anyone from racing to the end and leaving his or her teammates to be slaughtered.

Luke is in blue and I'm wearing yellow, although I lose track of him quickly. I swear it's non-stop laughter for most of us for an hour and a half until the red team sends up a red flare indicating a member has reached the appointed goal. The remaining teams keep scrambling, squeezing the trigger and firing at will, trying to be second. The blue flare goes up next.

Well, shit! Ultimately, the red team loses to the blue team because they had half as many members left when they reached the goal, which turns out to be a box of Henley chocolates. When our CEO tosses back his head covering, raising his paint gun in victory, a cheer goes up. Then we all start firing at him. He takes it in stride.

At last, as the sun starts to set, we're given our beverage of choice. Most grab a Great Northern Super Crisp, which I learn is the Australians' favorite beer. We're in large groups on blankets, chairs, and even on logs, as Sarah from marketing is when she starts screaming.

"Funnel-web," she shrieks. "I've been bitten."

"Are you sure?" more than one person asks.

"Dammit," Luke says, jumping up from a neighboring circle. Our fearless leader has to take charge again.

"That's a type of spider, right?" I ask the person next to me. Learning that it is, I hang back, letting others handle it. *Not my favorite animal on the planet.*

Luckily, the bite turns out to be from a huntsman—scary but not deadly, I'm told. Still, Sarah opts to return to the lodge for monitoring. And having just learned there are deadly spiders hanging around, I consider sleeping on the bus.

"They're dropping like flies," I say to Zoe, as we finish our beers. She nods with round eyes.

"I hope this'll be the last bloody time I gotta deal with this drongo business."

I'm surprised by her remark. "Don't you have a team-building retreat each year?"

She shrugs, then shoots me a friendly grin. "I reckon I won't be slogging away at this joint forever."

Next on the agenda is . . . blissfully *nothing* apart from hot showers followed by dinner *indoors* in the lodge's huge function room. Luke is seated at a round table of eight on the opposite end of the room, and I'm starting to realize I needn't have worried about our close proximity. But then, it's bonfire time.

Although multiple fires are lit around the perimeter, we sit in clusters, mainly focused on the flames of the largest bonfire in the center of a clearing. To my amazement, Luke plops down beside me. I glance around, but realize no one suspects we've been boinking just because the CEO decides to sit with the consultant.

"Hey," he says. "Having fun?"

"Sprained ankles and spiders," I quip. "What's not to love?"

"At least neither happened to you. I'm enjoying myself."

"You and your team won twice," I point out.

Luke leans down, mouth close to my ear, making a shiver dance down my spine even before I feel his breath against my neck. "Maybe we can team up tonight," he says.

Just like that, my pulse starts to race, and my body begins tingling. My nipples harden in anticipation, and I'm damp between my legs—all in the space of mere seconds. Luke has some powerful mojo.

I don't answer. I can't. My tongue feels thick in my mouth. Instead, I turn my attention to Charlotte, the VP, who is sharing a story about her recent trip to Denmark where she visited Copenhagen's Human Library to "borrow" a person for thirty minutes and learn about their life.

"What I could do with you in half an hour would shock my VP," Luke says quietly. "No talking needed."

I think I actually gulp loudly and definitely feel my panties getting wetter.

Others take turns, sharing something. Not personal, but about something interesting they know that others might not. Some don't speak at all.

When the person in front of me finishes, I don't mind speaking up. I tell the Henley employees about the Bridegroom Oak in the Dodauer forest, a true story passed down from my German ancestors through my dad's mom to her daughter-in-law, my mother, then to me and my sisters.

"While the tree is over five hundred years old and has more than one myth attached to it, the most famous is the one from the late 1880s about the daughter of a forester and a . . ." I falter as I realize why I've been thinking of it.

"A what?" someone calls out. "A frog or a prince?"

I can't help my nervous laugh before I say, "A chocolate maker's son from Leipzig."

Whistling and catcalls fill the night air, followed by general laughter. "Better get ya rear end to that tree, Mr. Henley," some wise-ass calls out. Luke lifts a hand and gives a little wave, which makes everyone start laughing even harder.

I explain how the young couple left their love letters in a hole in the tree trunk as a way to communicate. Eventually, after her father gave in, they were married at the tree in 1891.

"The cool thing is," I continue, "letters are still delivered to the tree by the German mail system. There's even a ladder to help people get to the knothole, which has obviously grown higher in the past hundred and fifty years. It's a romantic, hopeful spot, if you think about it, but also, I'm sure, one of disappointment."

I stop talking abruptly, with the emotions hitting too close to home. Everyone claps and someone else starts speaking. I can't look at Luke, but I can feel his gaze on me.

When I go to bed an hour later, I set my alarm for 6 a.m. My surprisingly comfy twin bed gives me a restful night, even while sharing a cabin with three other women, one of whom snores like a leaf-blower. Braving the chill morning air, using my phone as a flashlight although the sun is coming up, I make my way to the lodge where there will be a good signal and privacy.

"Now or never," I say to myself, dialing Ethan's cell. I nearly hang up before he answers. Maybe I should wait until the weekend, but he's been waiting for a call since I got the flowers on Monday. At least, right now, at 4 p.m., I know he's leaving his office. He'll be in his car, secluded, heading home. If I wait any longer, I'll be in the middle of breakfast or a team challenge.

"Morgan," his voice is achingly familiar. "I was starting to think you'd fallen off the face of the earth."

"I'm sorry about not calling sooner," I say, my heart pounding. "The time difference makes it tricky."

"I don't care. I'm just happy to hear your voice now. Did you like the flowers?" His voice is warm, hopeful.

"They were beautiful, Ethan, but . . ." I close my eyes, steeling myself. I don't want to waste time chit-chatting. I want to rip the Band-Aid off. "We need to talk."

"About the wedding? Look, I know you needed time to think, but three months is excessive. Come home early. We can start planning—"

"No," I interrupt, more firmly than I intended. "That's not what I want to talk about. I . . ." My throat tightens. "I can't marry you."

The silence that follows is deafening. When he speaks again, his voice has changed, becoming harder. "Is this about the guy you're seeing?"

My blood runs cold. "What?"

"Please. Katie mentioned you seemed different in your last video call. Happier. And you've been dodging my calls."

"I haven't been dodging—"

"Stop lying!" The sharp edge to his voice makes me flinch. "If you could face-time with your sister, you could have found time to call me. If you'd wanted to. You're throwing away three years for what? Some Australian fling?"

I'm momentarily shocked by his awareness that my happiness must mean something, and that something is bad for him.

"It's not about anyone else," I say, even though it partly is, only in that Luke has shown me what's been missing. When I left Boston, all I knew was that Ethan's and my relationship felt unsatisfying. Solid, perhaps, but I had nagging doubts and a hollowness that I couldn't ignore any longer, not when faced with a marriage proposal.

"It's about us, Ethan. About how we want different things."

"Do we?" he demands. "Like what?"

I shouldn't have gone down that road, trying to take the easy way out with generalizations, so as not to get personal and hurt him. I so don't want to cause him unnecessary pain.

"Forget that," I say, because I think we both want a happy relationship and children. "It's more about how you make decisions for us *without* consulting me. Remember the apartment or . . . or the couch and chairs." Those reasons sound so lame.

He laughs bitterly. "That's what this is about? Ancient history?"

I try to clarify. "It's about patterns, Ethan. About how you bulldoze through my concerns and call it *taking care of me*."

"Because I love you!" His voice breaks. "Everything I do is because I love you."

"I know," I whisper, tears starting to fall. "But love shouldn't feel like control or be suffocating."

"You're making a mistake," he says, his voice becoming eerily calm. "You're confused, Morgan. When you come home—"

"I'm not coming home," I say. Then second-guess myself, because I do still want to go home. "I mean, I am, I think. But not to you. I'm sorry, Ethan. I truly am."

"You'll regret this," he says quietly. "When this fling ends and you realize what you've thrown away—"

I end the call, my hands shaking. Leaning against the lodge's wooden wall, I let the tears fall freely. It causes me a lot more pain than I expected, this ending of something that was such a huge part of my life. I slide down the wall until I'm sitting on the wide-plank wooden deck, wrapping my arms around my knees.

"Morgan?"

I freeze at the sound of Luke's voice. Of course he'd be up early, probably planning to get in a run or create a new chocolate flavor or something equally responsible. I quickly wipe my eyes with the backs of my hands, but it's useless—he's already seen me crying.

"Hey," I manage, trying to sound normal and failing miserably.

He crouches down beside me, close enough that I can smell his soap-clean scent.

"What happened?"

"I called Ethan." My voice cracks on his name. "I ended it."

Luke's hand hovers near my shoulder, but he doesn't touch me. "Are you OK?"

"No," I admit, then let out a watery laugh. "Yes. I don't know." I press the heels of my hands against my eyes. "It was harder than I expected. And I hurt him." Then I lower my hands and look at him. His gorgeous golden-topaz eyes are filled with concern. "Ethan knew about you. Not specifically *you*, but he guessed there was someone. Because he found out from my sister that I seemed happy." My voice breaks on the last word.

"Morgan—" He reaches for my hand.

"Don't." I scramble to my feet, needing space. "I can't. I just need some time to process this." If I think this hurts, I dread how I'll feel on the long, lonely flight back to the States.

"Let me help," Luke says. The genuine caring in his voice makes my chest ache. "We could talk, or just—"

"No." I back away, shaking my head. "I did this for *me*, not for you or us or . . . I need to be alone right now."

Before he can respond, I turn and flee toward the walking trail, away from Luke, away from the mess I've made of everything. Because, as much as I'm drawn to him, I don't see Australia as my future. Falling in love with him, knowing how bad it's going to suck when we're apart, that's definitely the biggest mess I've ever made.

The sun is barely up, casting long shadows through the trees, but I welcome the solitude of the early morning. I need to get my head straight before the day's activities begin, before I have to face everyone and pretend I haven't just blown up my entire life.

Behind me, I hear Luke call my name once more, but he doesn't follow. For that, at least, I'm grateful.

19

Luke

I watch the sunrise paint the Blue Mountains in amber hues, my mind on Morgan and her phone call this morning. After a short coach ride, our group assembles for an early hike, and I position myself at the front with our coordinator, despite every fiber of my being wanting to be next to the woman who's hurting. And partly because of me.

The navy fleece I'm wearing suddenly feels too warm, and I know I'm crazy but I think I can catch her scent on the breeze. I look around to see how far from me Morgan is.

"Today's about experiencing the natural beauty of the area," Stacy announces, "while maintaining your team connections through partner activities."

There's one partner activity I would dearly love to participate in. I look for Morgan again. She's placed herself in the middle of the group, but I track her movements often enough to notice when Noah Matthews sidles up next to her, monopolizing her attention. Probably, he's giving her facts about the Three Sisters rock formation we're walking toward.

Although my awareness of her never wavers, I focus on the path ahead, leading our group toward Echo Point Lookout, where we'll get the best view of the iconic sandstone shaped by a million years of Mother Nature, as well as seeing a stunning panorama of the Jamison Valley.

While everyone clusters around the viewing point with their phones, I seize my chance. Finding Morgan slightly apart from the others, I approach.

"How are you holding up?" I keep my voice low, intimate.

"I'm fine." When I raise my eyebrow, knowing better, she sighs. "Really. You were right, you know. I came to Australia already knowing things weren't great with Ethan. This just"—she makes a vague gesture with her hand between us—"made it impossible to ignore anymore."

I can't resist touching her, letting my fingers brush against hers. "I hate how you think this"—I make the same gesture—"is tainted by timing. I don't think it is."

"Luke—"

"Morgan!" Matthews' voice grates on my nerves. "Come have a gander at this ripper view!"

My jaw clenches at his jolly Aussie persona, but I step back and watch her rejoin the group. Throughout the day, I manage to create more intimate moments, stolen seconds where I can remind her that what we share is real and meaningful.

By evening, I sense a shift in her energy, maybe even an acquiescence that wasn't there before. At our final dinner, this one indoors, I maneuver myself to the chair beside hers by bumping junior staffers out of the way and giving Matthews such a glare, he pales and goes in the other direction.

Dropping into the seat, I wait until Morgan realizes it's me, holding my breath, wondering what my reception will be. When she sends me a genuine smile, I can't help pressing my thigh against hers under the table. The contact sends a charge through my body.

As the group starts dispersing toward the campfires on this extra warm evening, I lean in close enough to catch her scent. Then I risk being totally snubbed and denied.

"Come to my cabin in ten minutes," I whisper, hoping I don't sound as desperate as I feel.

Her breath catches. "That's risky," she whispers back, but I see the flush creeping up her neck. She didn't turn me down flat. I'll take that as a win.

"Worth it," I murmur, before casually going toward the campfire so everyone sees me. I walk through the crowd, chatting with employees, being friendly until I reach the gathering's outer edge. Then I disappear into the shadows and make my way toward my cabin, grateful tonight to be a Henley who doesn't have to share.

Not my sleeping space, and after her phone call to Ethan, not my woman.

Thirteen minutes later, after I'd grown certain she wasn't going to come, there's a soft knock. Yanking open the door, I find Morgan, her hair loose around her shoulders. She slips inside quickly, and I waste no time gathering her in my arms.

"I just came to . . . to talk," she protests while I nuzzle her neck.

"Sure you did." I crack a smile against her skin.

Feeling her sigh, Morgan finally relaxes. "I came because it's been a week since you held me," she confesses.

My heart squeezes at her honesty, and I kiss her until I'm hard as a stick of rock candy and her fingers are clutching at my T-shirt while she presses her hips to mine. Unfortunately, it's my turn to be totally honest.

"No condoms," I admit between kisses.

Morgan freezes and draws back slightly. Tilting her head, narrowing her gaze, she considers. At least she knows this wasn't premeditated and that I had fully intended to make it through the company retreat without jumping her gorgeous bones.

"Then we'll have to be creative," she says with a wicked smile that makes my groin feel hot and heavy.

In the dimly lit cabin, I lead her to the double bed, her hand tucked securely in mine. The atmosphere shifts, charged with an electric anticipation that only we can satisfy. I snuff out the single lamp and open the curtains to welcome the moonlight.

Instantly, it changes her eyes into fiery sapphires. Reaching out, gently cupping her cheek, my thumb traces her bottom lip. She leans into my touch, her breath hitching, and I thank my lucky stars she feels it too—this undeniable magnetism between us. Much more than sexual, although this second, that's uppermost in our minds.

"Arms up," I command, and she obeys, so I can tug her sweatshirt over her head. Then I trail my fingertips across her collarbone until I reach her bra strap and the sexy curves below that have been tantalizing me all day and night. Slowly, I slide the straps off her shoulders before unhooking the back. Palming her breasts, I rub her nipples with my thumbs, and she closes her eyes.

"Yes, please," she whispers.

My slow seduction speeds up. "Jeans off," I order her, while I shuck my own clothing faster than I ever have in my life. Even though I've seen her naked before, my breath catches at the sight of her—flawless, exquisite, and mine. All mine.

After yanking the blankets aside, what follows is one of the most erotic encounters of my life, as we explore each other with hands and mouths, finding new ways to give and receive pleasure. I start by urging her backward onto the bed, her honey-brown hair fanning out against the sheets. Our mouths fuse, hungry and fierce, tongues sliding, lips sucking. She moans, echoing my own increasingly desperate desire. We both need more.

Breaking away, I travel down her body, exploring the hollow of her neck, first with my fingertips that raise goosebumps on her creamy skin, then with my lips, my tongue, even my teeth. When I go lower and lavish attention on her breasts, her nipples harden into pebbles, drawing out a gasp from deep within her.

Continuing my descent, I nibble and lick her stomach and the curve of each hip, before settling between her thighs. Her scent is familiar, her arousal evident. Parting her legs gently, I expose her to me. Her pussy is pink, glistening with need, her clit already swollen and begging for my touch.

I lean in, flattening my tongue against her, licking her in one long, slow stroke. Her hips buck, another moan escapes her lips. I do it again, and again, her taste driving me wild. Focusing on her clit, circling it, sucking it, eventually I slide two fingers inside her. She's tight, warm, and so fucking wet. I curl my fingers, hitting that sweet spot, as I continue to ravish her with my tongue and lips.

Morgan's sexy sounds grow louder, her breathing ragged. She's close, I can feel it, in all her muscles, including her slick channel. Increasing my pace and pressure, I send her to the moon. Her orgasm rips through her, her body convulsing, her pussy clenching around my fingers. When she cries out my name, it's a sound so sweet, so satisfying, it makes my cock grow longer and thick, throbbing with need.

As she comes down from her high, I kiss her inner thighs, her stomach, making my way back up to her lips. She greets me eagerly, her taste still on my tongue, her hands roaming my body. Then she scoots out from under me, urging me onto my back before straddling my thighs. Her hands encircle my cock, and I groan at her touch.

I honestly cannot recall being so excited for a blowjob. She strokes me, her grip firm, her pace steady. When she backs up to rest between my thighs and leans down, her breath hot on my skin, I nearly come, I'm so damn ready.

Thank God I don't! Because when Morgan takes me between her lips, I close my eyes and see stars.

With a bob of her head, she feeds my cock deep into her mouth, until I can feel the back of her throat with my tip. Then she draws back, all the way, releasing me with a strong pop of suction. *Mercy!*

With my fingers clasping the sheets, like I have to hang on for dear life, I hiss out a breath. The sensations are overwhelming and utterly fantastic.

"Luke," Morgan whispers, and I open my eyes to see her watching me as she looks up along the length of my torso, her gaze intensely erotic. And then deliberately, slowly, while I'm captured by the view of her, mesmerized by her full breasts suspended over my crotch, she lowers her face to my steel erection and takes me into her mouth again. Then she works magic on me.

Her tongue swirls around my tip, her lips tighten around my shaft before rolling down my cock. She takes me deeper, her head bobbing, her hand pumping in sync with her mouth. The extra special delight of watching her tits bounce along with her movements brings my climax on fast as a freight train.

My orgasm builds, my body tenses. I try to hold back, to prolong this sweet torture, but she's too good. She sucks harder, her pace quickening, and I can't take it anymore. Can't hold off another instant. My entire body stiffens as my cock pulses, my release pouring into her mouth. She takes it all, sucking and swallowing every last drop, her eyes never leaving mine.

Exhausted, I throw my head back and groan with utter satisfaction. She climbs up over me, her face appearing above mine with a smirk. "Good?"

I laugh because she knows it was fucking amazing. "Incredible," I admit, just before she collapses onto my chest. Wrapping my arms around her, I hold her close, still feeling my heartbeat pounding between us.

In this moment, it's just us—no ghosts of past lovers, no greedy cyber thieves, no hundred-and-fifty people team-building.

A sharp knock at the door freezes us both.

"Mr. Henley?" It's Dan, my assistant. "Sorry to disturb you, but it's important."

Morgan's eyes go wide with panic. Glancing around, with nowhere to hide, she simply tosses the covers over her head while I yank on my jeans.

"Just a moment," I call out, trying to steady my breathing. Taking an extra second, I put on my T-shirt, too. Otherwise, it's too obvious. Then I open the door just enough to see Dan's pale face.

"I was about to head over to the showers," I say casually. "What's up?"

"Phone call at the lodge," he starts, then pauses, peering past me. I hope he can't see her foot sticking out at the end of the bed.

"What phone call?" I ask quickly to regain his attention.

"From Mrs. Henley, your granny." Dan has my full attention, and my heart is racing again for an entirely different reason. "She said it's important."

"Why didn't she call my cell?"

"Mrs. Henley said she tried. Service must have dropped out. But the landline at the lodge works fine."

"Let me get my shoes on, and I'll go over there." I close the door in his face, acutely aware of Morgan scrambling out from under the covers, naked as the day she was born. Hair mussed and her lips puffy.

"Did you hear?" I ask.

"Yes, hurry," she says. "I'll slip out after you leave. Please let me know what's going on."

The worry in her voice alarms me. To calm myself, I say, "Maybe it's just something about Clover needing the pool pump fixed or Ivy saying a full sentence."

Morgan nods, unsmiling. Cramming my feet into my Blunnies, not bothering with socks, I pause to kiss her. I gain a measure of courage and comfort when I do.

She has become *my person* really fast. "I probably won't see you until breakfast," I say and dash out the door.

20

Morgan

Pacing my apartment Saturday morning, I clutch my phone in my hand. Sleep was impossible after I slipped from Luke's cabin and returned to my own—worried but hopeful he'd let me know any minute that everything was all right. He never did.

The phone call, his absence at breakfast the next morning, followed by the discovery that he'd left the retreat the night before, all of it sits like a giant stone of apprehension in my stomach now that I'm back in Sydney.

No one would tell me anything beyond vague mentions of a "family emergency" and that the CEO left by private car shortly after midnight. I hadn't been included in any of it, and the exclusion stings worse than I want to admit. When my phone finally buzzes around noon, I nearly drop it in my haste to read the text, wishing he'd called instead.

Sorry for disappearing. Gramps had a mild stroke. At hospital now. He's stable.

Relief washes over me, followed immediately by concern. Even a mild stroke is nothing to shrug off. Besides, Eleanor and Pat treated me so kindly, and I know how much Luke loves them. I type quickly:

I'm so sorry. But glad to hear he's stable. Do you want me to come? Happy to help at the ranch or just be with you at the hospital.

The three dots appear, disappear, then reappear. Finally, I read:

Need to keep it to family for now. Clover's already here. And Nan has help at the ranch, including Adam.

I stare at his message, reading between the lines. I'm not family. I'm not even close enough to be included when things get difficult.

Let me know if there's anything I can do.

I set my phone down, feeling hollow. This is exactly why getting involved was a mistake. I'm leaving in a few weeks. I'm temporary. Australia was never meant to be permanent, and neither was Luke Henley.

The rest of the weekend passes in silence without any further message from him. For a change, I don't work. Instead, I take long walks around Sydney and go to the beach by myself. Noah texts me, but I don't want even his laidback presence. I need to be peaceful and satisfied with my own company.

By Sunday evening, however, I've gone from worried to hurt to annoyed. Two texts? *That's all I get?*

This is the mother-of-all karmic paybacks after how I treated Ethan. I realize that's the other reason my phone is so unusually silent. For the first time since I left Boston, I haven't had ten texts a day from him. I hope he's OK. I know if the situation were reversed, and he'd broken up with me over a quick phone call after avoiding me for weeks, I'd be devastated. I'm a shitty human being.

Monday morning brings a company-wide email from Luke's office:

To the Henley Confectionery Family,
Thank you for your patience and understanding during my brief absence. My grandfather suffered a mild stroke last week but is recovering well. The doctors are optimistic about his prognosis, and he's already asking when he can return home.

Business operations will continue as normal. Please direct any urgent matters to the appropriate department heads until my return.
Best regards,
B. Lucas Henley
Chief Executive Officer

I read it three times, each time feeling more distant from the man who had his face between my thighs just days ago. A company-wide email—impersonal, professional, cold. I hit refresh a couple times, as well as check my phone messages. Nothing personal to me alone.

Jack Thompson approaches my desk at lunchtime, and I am so not in the mood for his games. "How's the security audit going?" he asks. "Got a minute to update me?"

I force myself to be cordial despite how he has treated me. "Actually, I'll be finished sooner than my contract."

"Then you'll be leaving earlier than expected?" He needn't sound so gleeful. But I know he was worried he was the one being investigated for incompetence. The clever cyber theft could have happened under anyone's watch, and what the thief did was beyond the standard IT manager's purview. Although if I were in charge of the company's technology profile, it would not have happened.

"You run your department well, Jack," I tell him. "That will be in my report, but I'm also going to put in place some better cyber security measures that I'll need to walk you through. I'm sure you'll understand the process as soon as you lay eyes on it. It'll be up to you to make sure it runs correctly and keep it updated."

His eyes widen, and then he nods solemnly. I think I've finally made a conquest of this disapproving colleague, simply by showing him some good old-fashioned respect.

"I have a few more checks to run, but I hope by the end of this week, I can turn it all over to you."

When he moves away from my desk, I see Zoe looking over. She smiles. "Need anything else from me?"

"Nope," I say. "I'm good."

By all rights, the week should drag because of Luke's absence, but it flies by as I chase the shadow company and use all my skills to trace its origin and to keep it from popping up as it does with infuriating regularity. But its maddening consistency is also going to be its downfall. The fake Henley website shows on a schedule, run by time-based redirects and the server-side scripting capabilities of the thief.

Knowing when I can look for it gives me a start. If the individual has hired a hacker—a risky practice of sharing guilt and potentially being ratted out—then there could still be multiple people on my list. If the individual *is* the hacker, working alone, then the field is narrowed to one really tech-savvy person.

By Wednesday, I know the truth, having placed an order, tracked where my credit card charge went, and broken into the shadow website without the thief knowing it. Actually, two thieves. It's worse than I thought because I was stymied for a while by the data Zoe gave me. And it had been corrupted.

I'm ready to confiscate two company laptops, but I believe most of the evidence will be discovered in Noah's apartment and on Zoe's personal computer. I could easily finagle an invitation to the former, and maybe search Noah's place. I've got my martial arts training, and I'm sorely tempted.

On the other hand, that would be going above and beyond, like when I tackled Luke. And people have become violent over less money than Noah and Zoe have stolen. I still can't believe she was under my nose all along. Both of them actually. Obviously, they suspected why I was here and sought to get close to me.

The last two pieces of the puzzle were locating Noah's true time-stamped digital records of when he was online, and seeing a certain "ZGirlGuide" in the shadow site's admin list. If Noah hadn't mentioned his late nights, I probably wouldn't have compared Zoe's data to the server's.

With her "be prepared" motto, there's no way I'm confronting her myself. She can probably make all the evidence disappear in the blink of an eye. I make sure to screenshot and download everything. But with my sense of accomplishment, I also feel sadness. If Zoe can do this, and hide it so well, she could have done something great with her skills.

As for Noah, he had the knowledge of exactly what products were available any given week, only needing to work late to monitor the shadow site's transactions in real time—watching orders go through HenleyCandee.com while tweaking inventory and wiping system logs before the overnight audits ran. Zoe's code did the heavy lifting, but he was the one keeping it hidden.

Strange to think Luke was right all along about Noah. Speaking of which, I need to call the CEO. It's either him, or call Lark Henley. Either way, one of my employers ought to know immediately and start the proceedings to press charges.

Secluding myself in an empty conference room, I bring out my phone and call Luke's number. After three rings, a female voice answers.

"Hallo." *Who has Luke's phone?* Australian accent, so not Clover, but the tone doesn't sound gravelly enough to be his grandmother. One of the nurses, maybe?

"Hi, I'm trying to reach Luke Henley."

"Yeah, g'day—who's callin'?"

"Morgan Anders from . . . from Henley Confectionery. Is he available?"

"Morrr-gaaan." The voice turns syrupy sweet with recognition at the same time as I identify her. "It's Jasmine. Baz is with Gramps right now. They're talking with a physical therapist. Family comes before work, ya know?"

"Right, of course." I swallow hard. *Why is she answering his phone?* "Could you ask him to call me when he's free? I have something important to tell him."

"Of course, mate. Soon as I can get my hands on him." Jasmine's tone makes my skin crawl, not to mention her choice of wording. "Unless you're keen to spill the beans, and I can pass it on," she adds. "In case he's too flat out to squeeze in a yarn about business. We've all been run off our feet, going between the hospital and keeping the station ticking along. Bit of a mob effort, that."

The "we" isn't lost on me, nor the use of the word *mob*, meaning *family*, as I recall.

"It's confidential," I tell her, keeping my voice level. "Give him the message and tell him I wish the best for his grandfather. Thanks." I hang up before she can twist the knife any deeper.

He doesn't return the call, nor on Thursday. Sitting opposite Zoe, we're both playing nice. But fielding lunch offers from her and Noah is becoming tedious. I grimace each time I see the rubber duck on the edge of my desk.

When Noah offers to walk me home, I have to keep my cool so I don't tip him off. Later, I try to reach Lark Henley but get her voicemail. Leaving her a message about solving the cybercrime, I also tell her I hope her grandfather gets better soon.

Friday morning, I'm determined to finalize my report and present it to the VP, Charlotte Bauer, if I don't hear from Luke or Lark. I know it seems rash, even impulsive, but I'm also thinking this is my last day. I can zip a password protected file and turn everything over to both CEOs by email and then Charlotte can fill them in.

If I pack this weekend, I can be on a plane by Sunday afternoon. Who cares about the short-notice cost of a ticket? I'm not paying for it anyway.

This week without Luke's presence, without the push-and-pull of our attraction, without the tension, sexual and otherwise, I've realized there's nothing for me in Sydney. I don't want to put down roots here. I don't want to learn about their poisonous spiders, nor their snakes, for that matter. I don't want to be a stranger in a strange land where I know no one apart from a company of nice strangers and one man. One captivating man who all-too-easily shut me out the first time there was a test of what constituted his private life and what he wanted to share with me.

I'm in the break room, using the sleek coffee machine that now produces whatever I ask of it, when footsteps enter behind me. The hair on the back of my neck raises, and I know it's him. Turning, I find Luke standing there, looking exhausted. His suit is impeccably pressed as always, but shadows linger under his eyes.

"You're back," I say, my voice carefully neutral despite the fact that my heart is hammering in my chest. I want to throw myself into his arms and hold on tight. But I wanted that last week, too, and he distanced himself from me as if I was utterly unimportant, cutting me off from his personal pain as if I really were nothing more than a temporary employee he happened to have sex with.

"Just got in." He moves closer, lowering his voice. "Can we talk?"

I think about the two topics we might discuss. Our hidden affair or the business with Noah. "Here?" I ask. "Do you really want to talk here?"

"Right, not a good idea. Let me make some coffee," he says, "and then—"

"I've concluded my assignment, by the way," I state flatly. "Solved the crime."

Luke blinks, momentarily thrown by my businesslike tone, or maybe by what I've achieved. "That's incredible. So fast, too. But Morgan, about last week—"

I notice he didn't even ask who the thief is. "I've compiled all the evidence in a digital report. You'll find everything you need to confront *them* and take legal action."

"Morgan." He places the coffee he's just made on the counter and reaches for my hand, but I pull away, noticing someone glance in while walking by.

"Mr. Henley," I begin.

"Don't." he says. "Don't pretend we're just boss and employee. Not after everything."

I feel brave when I meet his golden topaz eyes without flinching. "That's exactly what we should've been all along."

"Look, I'm sorry about how things happened. Gramps had us all worried—"

"You don't owe me an explanation." I turn my back and head for the door. "I always wanted simply to do my job. It became tangled in something else." I gesture between us. "Getting caught up in your personal life, especially at your grandparents' ranch, that was a huge mistake," I explain while he remains silent, his jaw tense and his mouth in a flat line. "Now, I've finished, and I'm going home ASAP."

"Is that what this is about?" His face looks gaunt. "You're upset because I didn't ask you to come back to the ranch?" He sounds almost exasperated with me.

I can't believe we're having this discussion in the middle of the brightly lit break room. I hope I'm matching his stony expression, not letting my hurt show.

"No, Luke. I'm upset because I let myself believe we were already at a deeper level of caring about one another, but when I offered to be there for you, you shut me out completely. One text and a company-wide email in a week?

I had to hear from Jasmine how you two managed your 'mob effort.'"

He lets out a frustrated sigh. "When did you speak to Jasmine?" he asks. "Besides, she exaggerates."

"It doesn't matter now." I guess she didn't bother to give him my "important" message. "We both knew our situation was always temporary. I came to Australia to figure things out with Ethan and to help your company. I've done both, and I really want to go home. I learned this week that I don't want this." I gesture my hand between us, which makes him shake his head.

"That's not true, and you know it." His voice drops to a whisper. "What we have is real, Morgan. I wasn't trying to push you away—I was trying to protect my family during a crisis while dealing with my own fear. Gramps is everything to me."

"And I'm what? A distraction? You didn't see me as someone you could share your fear with or turn to." The words tumble out before I can stop them. "And honestly, I think that's for the best. Mr. Henley."

Something like irritation flashes across his face. "After what we've shared?"

I shrug, looking at it realistically. "A few enjoyable moments in bed? That's *all* we really shared."

Our deepest connections have been while we were naked, but I started to read too much into the affair. Maybe Luke has, too. Or perhaps he's pissed off that we won't have another few weeks of great sex.

I grab my coffee, needing to escape.

"Morgan, wait—"

"I'm going back to my desk to finalize the report and finish the documentation for your legal team today. Then I'll send you and Lark the zip file. Please read it at your earliest convenience and let me know if you have any questions. You can always email them to me at my Boston office next week."

With my heart hammering as I truly end this, I walk out without looking back.

But I don't go straight to my desk, I stride toward the bathroom, head up, shoulders back. Once inside, I lean against the sink, trying to steady my breathing. This is why I came to Australia—to gain clarity, to make decisions, to do an excellent job. And I should be pleased at doing all three.

When I get back to the States, Baz Henley will become just another memory—a good one, I hope, apart from this past week. And he'll also be a lesson learned about keeping my heart safe, especially when I'm half a world away from home.

21

Luke

The office feels empty without her. *Hell*, the entire city of Sydney seems like a wasteland. Every morning, I walk past IT on my way to the elevators and cannot stop myself from glancing through the glass at her former desk.

It's utterly empty, cleared of the few personal items she kept there—a small potted succulent, which I wonder if she was allowed to take on the airplane, a Boston Red Sox mouse pad, and that ridiculous rubber duck, stamped with "I ♥ Sydney." I squeezed it once and it quacked, making Morgan laugh.

God help me, I miss the sound of her laughter. And her voice. And her breathing when she sleeps.

The IT department has not yet reassigned her workspace, but I can't stop seeing her there, head bent over her keyboard, caramel-brown hair falling forward as she concentrated. Zoe's desk is also glaringly empty, and Jack is conducting interviews for a new IT person.

After reading Morgan's report and talking to Lark, we had the police take Noah and Zoe into custody. With Morgan's clearcut evidence, neither had any way to deny their guilt. Greedy bastards. Noah wasn't content with his generous sales manager salary, so he started stealing right and left. And Zoe wanted to prove she was smarter than the rest of us. Just because she could. Turns out, she wasn't smarter than Morgan, who found their joint bank account in the Cayman Islands.

In the end, I was right about the sneaky prick, and Morgan was wrong about him being merely a friendly guy. But even this victory feels hollow without her here to roll her eyes at me. Besides, Zoe had been an asset to the company and had a bright future, so that's a damn shame.

"Mr. Henley?" My assistant's voice draws me from my thoughts. "Your sister Clover is on line one."

I grab the phone, grateful that she and Adam extended their stay another week, but now they've gone home, the entire Australian continent seems even lonelier.

"How's Gramps?" she asks.

I smile, knowing she could call Nan for a better update, but Clover has an ulterior motive which she'll bring up any second. "You know I'm not staying there right now, but Nan said he's better every day. The PT and OT both say he's made remarkable progress."

"Good, Good," Clover says. "But that's not the only reason I'm calling."

Don't I know it. Leaning back in my obscenely expensive chair, I stare at the Sydney skyline through my office windows. "Really? I never would have guessed."

"I take it you haven't spoken to Morgan," she says.

"Nope. There's no point."

"How about simply to hear her voice because you really, really like her?"

"What's there to say?" I ask. Besides, hearing her voice, knowing I can't touch her, will probably make it worse.

"You're an idiot, you know that?"

"Thanks for the support, sis."

"I'm serious, Basil Henley." I cringe at her tone. "You pushed her away when she tried to be there for you, and now you're moping around like a kicked puppy. Go after her."

"It's not that simple." *Or is it?* The thought has been haunting me for weeks.

"Actually, it is. You're just making it complicated because you're scared."

Complicated was Morgan's favorite word to describe us. But I'm not letting my big sis accuse me of being scared. That's absurd.

"I'm about to hang up on you, but I want you to know two things. You're wrong, and I love you."

Her advice follows me through the rest of the day. By the next day, I can't focus on work any longer. Telling everyone who needs to know that I'm going to the ranch, I drive into the Hunter Valley. Even though Morgan was only here once, I loved bringing her with me and wish more than anything that she was in the passenger seat of my Batmobile, as she called it. The familiar scent of eucalyptus greets me as I park.

Finding my grandparents on the back veranda, Gramps is in his favorite chair pushing at a blanket that Nan seems insistent on putting over him.

"Back off, woman. I'm not some posh invalid," he gripes. "Those bloody nursemaids are aggro enough without you carrying on."

Nan sees me first and jumps to her feet. "There's my favorite grandson, you little ripper." She kisses my cheek.

"I'm your only grandson," I remind her, but she waves this off.

"Too right, that's why you're my favorite." She studies my face. "You look knackered, love. Getting any kip?"

"I'm fine." I don't tell her how many sleepless nights I've had lately while ruminating over Morgan. But Gramps is already shaking his head.

"You've been *off your face* since that Yank sheila left." His voice still sounds different to me from what it was before the stroke, some might say quieter, even weaker. But the doctors say he has almost fully recovered, and his mind is sharp as ever. "That bonza one who knocked you on your arse."

"Strewth, Pat!" Nan scolds, but there's a smile in her voice.

Sinking into a chair beside them, I watch the sunset paint the valley in shades of gold. Morgan loved this view. She was always taking pictures of the Australian sky, marveling at how different the sunset and the stars looked here.

"I stuffed up," I admit, using my grandmother's favorite term for "screwed up."

"Too right, you did," Gramps agrees readily. "But you can sort it."

"Morgan wants to live in Boston. Her whole family is there."

Eleanor touches my arm. "And most of our mob is in New York now, includin' your folks. What's your point?"

"The company—"

"Can be run from anywhere," Gramps interrupts. "We've got heaps of talented people here. And there's always video calls and planes when ya need to be hands on." He leans forward, fixing me with the topaz-gold eyes he passed on to my father and to me and Clover. "When I met your nan, her family wanted her to stay in Melbourne. But she chose love, didn't she?"

"You moved to Hunter Valley for him?" I joke, looking at Nan, imagining the young lovers in the photograph at the factory.

"Best bloody decision I ever made." She squeezes Gramps' hand. "But it was *my* choice. No one made it for me."

"Morgan makes ya rapt as anything," Gramps says simply. "I saw it that weekend she was 'ere. You were different with her—strewth, more yourself."

I reflect on those days at the ranch, how natural it felt to share my world with her. How right she seemed in it, despite her protests about being temporary.

"What if she's settled and enjoying her life as it is?" What I really mean is, *what if she wasn't as in to me as I thought?* She's so fucking fine, so smart and sexy, there are probably a hundred guys lined up around the block to ask her out. Maybe Clover is right about my being just a little afraid. "Morgan probably hasn't been sitting around waiting for me."

"Never took you to be a few stubbies short of a six-pack," Gramps said.

"Don't be harsh, Pat," Nan says, before looking at me. "Then at least you'll know," Eleanor says. "But you've got to give it a burl. A fair go and all. Love isn't about playing it safe. It's more like a dog's dinner."

I stand up, decision made. "I need to go to Boston."

"Finally," Gramps mutters, adjusting himself in his chair with a knowing smile. "Now that's the grandson I know. Go get 'er. If you cock it up, come back with a case of Coopers and we'll get absolutely hammered. None of that Great Northern rubbish, mind you."

"Pat!" Nan exclaims, but her expression is full of love.

Then, thinking it through, I sit again. "I want to stay with you two for a few days first, get my head on straight."

Nan nods. "Just like when your gramps and I used to sit in that kitchen and dream up the next choccy creation."

I can't help frowning at her words. "Not sure I follow you."

"We had to come up with the right blend of sweet and salty, and sometimes, we had to chuck in a few nuts."

That makes me laugh until I lean my head back and almost want to cry. There's so much distance between me and Morgan, and what feels like a billion obstacles.

With utter seriousness, Gramps says, "Stone the flamin' crows, truer words were never spoke, nor better advice."

God, I love these two.

$♥$♥$♥$

Morgan

Boston wraps around me like a familiar blanket, but something feels off. Maybe it's the New England spring chill after Sydney's summer, or maybe it's the hollow space in my chest, an ache that never goes away.

"Earth to Morgan." Katie waves her hand in front of my face. We're sitting in our parents' kitchen, and I've been staring at my coffee for who knows how long. "That's the third time you've zoned out. What's going on with you?"

"Nothing." I force a smile. "Just jet lag."

"For a month?" Pru looks up from her tablet, which displays some medical text, like always. This one has graphic images of the body's internal organs. With dark circles under her eyes matching mine, she agreed to meet me and Katie at our parents' house between hospital shifts. "That's not jet lag," Pru adds. "That's depression."

"I'm not depressed." But even I can hear the lack of conviction in my voice. "I got the promotion, remember? Head of Cyber Security for Wayland Tech. Dream job."

"Yeah, and you haven't smiled once about it," Katie points out. She slices a second piece of Mom's heavenly *Schwarzwälder Kirschtorte*—Black Forest cake, in the States— and places it on the licked-clean plate in front of me. She does the same for herself and for Pru.

"Come on, spill. What really happened in Australia? And don't say *nothing* again. You've been different since you came back."

Stalling, I dig my fork into the four layers of soft chocolate cake and slide the bite into my mouth. To avoid answering, I savor the chocolate and the kirsch and the cream. Luke's dark chocolate bars would make excellent shavings on top, but it's hard to improve on the way Mom has made it all my life. My sisters wait me out. They've had years of practice at doing exactly that. Finally, I set my fork down.

"What makes you think it's more than sadness from breaking up with Ethan?"

"*Duh!*" Katie says. "Because how sad could you be after finally getting rid of that turd?"

My mouth drops open, as I stare at Katie.

Pru nods. "You know she's right."

I shake my head. "What did you both see that I didn't see?"

"You saw it, but you ignored it," Katie says. "Come on, he was controlling and spoiled and—"

"And a classic bully," Pru finishes. "Dad made us watch you for bruises."

The blood drains from my face. "That's ridiculous. He never tried to hurt me."

"Physically," Pru says, "because you have a black belt. But mentally . . . ," she trails off.

I'm truly stunned. I guess I can't hide anything from my sisters, so I confess, "In Sydney, I met someone special. And I miss him."

"I knew it!" Katie nearly knocks over her coffee in excitement. "What's his name? What does he do?"

"It doesn't matter. It's over." I push the plate away, suddenly no longer tempted by Mom's baking. "Basil Lucas Henley," I add.

"Basil?" Katie snorts with laughter.

"He goes by Luke. He runs his family's company in Sydney. They have another branch in New York, run by his sister. Anyway, we . . . I mean, it was just for fun. We had a few good times, and that was it."

"The way you say his name tells me differently," Pru observes quietly. And yet people say I'm the analytical one. "What was it about him?"

Everything. The way he looked at me like I was the only person in the room. How he could make me laugh even when I was furious with him. The quiet strength he showed with his family, except when he shut me out.

"Morgan?" Katie prompts.

"It wouldn't have worked," I say firmly. "I missed you all too much. Different continents, different lives. I belong here."

"Do you?" Pru switches off her tablet, ready to get into a deeper discussion rather than focusing on work. "Because you don't seem thrilled to be back."

My phone buzzes, saving me from having to answer. Unknown number. My heart leaps before I can stop it, but when I answer, it's not Luke. A woman's warm voice, both slightly familiar and friendly, starts talking.

"Hey, cyber superwoman. It's Clover Bonvier." As if she needs to use her last name with a first name like that. "Got a minute for a chat?"

Taken off guard, I say, "Sure." Both my sisters perk up at my surprised tone. "Is everything okay? How's your grandfather?"

"He's doing much better. That's not why I'm calling." She pauses. "Have you heard from my idiot brother?"

"No." I keep my voice neutral. "And I'd prefer not to."

"Oh, shit. Really? He's miserable without you. Barely eating, working crazy hours, snapping at everyone."

"That's not my concern." But there's that familiar ache, even more painful at the thought of Luke suffering. "I'm not going back to Sydney, so this is all moot."

She pauses, then speaks from the heart. "I know he circled the wagons after Gramps' stroke, but Luke was scared. He doesn't like to lose control of anything."

"None of us do. But I would have been there for him." The words escape before I can stop them. "I wanted to be."

"I know. And he knows that now." Another pause. "He misses you, Morgan. More than he's ever missed anyone. I can promise you that."

I close my eyes, remembering the last time I saw him, how cold I'd been. "It's too late, Clover. I'm back home, I have a new position. My life is here." It's kind of a new beginning all around. Not just the job, but with my family's help, I found a second-floor apartment in South Boston within two weeks of returning, staying with my parents until I did, and letting Ethan keep our old place.

Looking at my sisters who are watching me with curious eyes, I take a fortifying breath. "If Luke hadn't shut me out, it might've taken me longer to realize what had to happen. But I didn't want to be a fish out of water. Sooner or later, I would have wanted to come home. And sooner was easier for both of us. This is where I belong."

"Is it?" she asks. "Because you sound about as happy as he does."

"Clover—" I start to protest.

"No, no, I hear you. Forget Luke for a minute, promise you won't be a stranger. We had fun at the ranch. Adam and I meant it when we said we'd like to have you over to our home. Beacon Hill, remember?"

"Yes, thank you. That would be nice." I leave it vague.

"No, I mean it, but we'll start with just the two of us. Drinks at six o'clock at Farmacia."

"Clover—"

"Aren't you free? Do you have a new boyfriend already?"

"No," I begin, not that it's her business. "In any case, that place has like ten seats and a waiting list a mile long." Ethan had always wanted to try the exclusive place down the street from Paul Revere's house.

"Nine seats and typically a sixty-day wait. But don't forget, I'm a—"

"Bonvier. I mean, a Henley. I mean . . ."

Clover starts laughing. "I'm a determined business woman. See you tomorrow night."

After we hang up, my sisters are staring at me. "What?" I ask.

"That was this Luke guy's sister?" Katie asks. "The one who lives in New York?"

I shake my head, then catch myself. "How did you know he has a sister who lives in New York?"

"Because you just told us," Pru says dryly. "The second HQ."

"Right." My thoughts are scattered, thinking of Luke being sad. It's a crappy feeling because there's nothing I can do about it, and he's on the other side of the planet. Then I draw the plate back toward me and eat a massive bite. Luke misses me. A little warmth trickles through my frozen center. "That was his *other* sister. She and her husband live here in Boston, and I met them while I was there."

"I guess you made your usual awesome Anders impression on all of them, but especially Luke."

"His grandparents are very nice, too," I say.

"Yes, I bet they're the reason you're so blue. Missing someone else's Oma and Opa," Katie says, using the words we call our German grandparents.

"Sounds like he must be in pretty rough shape for his sister to call and . . . What? Plead on his behalf? Did she ask you to go back to Sydney?"

"Stop," I order softly. First Clover and now them. "Just let it go. It doesn't matter how I feel about him or his family, or any of it. We live on opposite sides of the world. Nothing can change that."

But the fact that I wish something could is what keeps me up at night and hurts the most. I am so screwed.

22

Luke

Boston is crisp and clear in May, a stark contrast to Sydney's mid-autumn warmth. Standing in Clover's elegant Beacon Hill townhouse, I tug on the sleeves of my lightweight cotton sweater for the fifth time, then push them up my forearms again. I'm out of sorts and unusually apprehensive, despite my sister's insistence that showing up as a surprise guest at her dinner party is a good idea.

Clover leaves Adam's side and glides over on four-inch-heels, bringing me another glass of wine. I can drink before, during, and even after this party because I'm staying in one of the guest rooms in their massive townhouse on Beacon Hill. Adam doesn't do anything by halves, and there's even a basketball hoop with a quarter-court surrounding it on the top floor.

"You're fidgeting again," she says, not loudly enough that any of the guests can hear.

Not that I'm interested in the guests who're already here. I'm waiting for one in particular, and I can barely keep from jumping out of my own skin. *Why is Morgan late?*

But grateful for the refill, all I say to my older sister is, "I don't fidget."

"You absolutely do when you're nervous." She picks an invisible piece of lint from my sweater. "And you've been checking your watch every thirty seconds since the doorbell first rang. Did you know only about thirty-two percent of people still wear watches daily? Although not usually in our age group."

I sigh at her marketing-speak, but she's a trained graphic designer with her own advertising business. I saw her latest mock-ups in her home office upstairs are for a watch company. Personally, I find a watch easier than dragging out my phone especially when I'm eager for a beautiful woman to show up.

"I'm just jet-lagged," I mutter, though we both know it's a lie. I've been in the States for a week, spending time with our parents and Lark in New York, before coming to Boston. Adam and Clover returned from Russell and Bunny Henley's big anniversary party four days ago, and I followed this morning.

Her knowing smile makes me want to disappear into my wine glass. "Just remember what we discussed. No ambushing her, no grand declarations in front of everyone."

"I'm not stupid."

"The jury's still out on that one." She squeezes my arm affectionately. "Morgan should be here any minute."

My stomach tightens. "She has no clue I'm here?"

"None." Clover's a sweetheart for arranging this, but her conspiratorial expression wouldn't fool anyone. She winks and drifts away to greet new arrivals. The doorbell chimes again, and my heart leaps into my throat, but it's just another couple—friends of Adam and Clover. I try to focus on their conversation about Boston's real estate market, but my mind keeps wandering back to Morgan. *Will she be happy to see me?*

"Oh, good," she exclaims, waving to Adam's younger brother and his wife, who entered without ringing the bell. "Do you want to chat with Philip and Eloise, take your mind off . . . ," but she trails off seeing my expression. "Never mind. Just hang in there. She'll be here soon."

Seven minutes later—not that I'm counting—the doorbell chimes again. I hear Morgan's laughter before I see her, that rich, melodious sound that's haunted my dreams for weeks. And then she steps into view, and everything else fades away.

She's wearing a sapphire-blue dress that highlights her blue eyes, her honey-streaked brown hair falling in loose waves past her shoulders. She looks vibrant, alive—and she's not alone. My heart stutters, then plummets. She's followed inside by a tall, swarthy-skinned man wearing a confident smile that I instantly want to smash off his face. His hand rests possessively at the small of her back. My own hands clench into fists.

"Morgan!" Clover greets her enthusiastically, even pulling her into an embrace. How close of a friend has my sister become with my . . . ? *Damn.* What *is* Morgan to me? My once and future lover? "I'm so glad you could make it," my sister continues. "And you must be her lucky date."

Date! Did Clover know Morgan was bringing a plus-one and neglect to tell me? I watch Morgan, relaxed and engaging, receiving a kiss on the cheek from Adam.

"This is Dominic Russo," she says, her voice warm and sexy, even when saying some other man's name. "He owns Bellissimo in the North End. Dom, this is Clover Bonvier."

Dom? I don't like him or his name, and I bet Nan is a better cook. I can only hope his "noodle" is soft.

"A pleasure," Russo says with a charming smile and a hint of an Italian accent. "Morgan handled a cyber issue for me."

My sister is an excellent hostess. Morgan may have thrown her by bringing a plus-one, but Clover recovers. "Oh my God, my husband and I love your restaurant. Adam, this is the owner of Bellissimo."

Adam shakes the man's hand, and takes the newcomers' drink orders. Or at least, he gives them to one of the servers circulating through the ground floor rooms. Then he introduces the latest couple to those around them. Morgan is shaking hands with the real estate mogul, Marcus Parisi and his wife, Lindsey, when her eyes casually scan the guests beyond them.

When her gaze finds me, her lovely face registers utter shock. After all, I'm supposed to be ten thousand miles from this party. Her lips part slightly and her spine straightens. When I nod in recognition, she nods back at me before turning her attention to something Mrs. Parisi is saying.

After waiting and watching in agony for a few excruciating minutes, I force myself to take in a deep breath and plaster on a placid expression when Morgan and this Russo restaurateur finally come my way. Her gaze meets mine again, longer this time, a complex mixture of emotions flickering across her lovely face.

Time to step up. With that, I move forward.

"Morgan, it's good to see you."

"Luke," she replies, her voice deliberately neutral. At least she didn't call me Mr. Henley. "What a surprise."

"I was in New York for family stuff," I explain, as if that answers why I'm standing before her without warning. "Thought I'd visit Clover while I was stateside."

Her date extends his hand. "Dominic Russo."

"Luke Henley," I reply, shaking it.

"*Ah*, the Australian boss." He nods knowingly. "Morgan mentioned she did some consulting work for your company."

My jaw tightens at the reduction of our relationship to "consulting work," but I manage to nod accordingly. "She did brilliant work. Your business is lucky to have her."

"I feel very lucky to have her *in my life*," Russo replies smoothly, his hand finding Morgan's and clasping it. I swear I see red for the first time ever.

Adam appears with a server in tow, who's holding their drinks on a tray, breaking the tension. "Negroni for the Italian chef," my brother-in-law says, handing Russo a glass. "And a gin and tonic with lime for the lady." Morgan takes it from him.

"Perfect timing," she replies, her fingers encircling the glass with visible relief. I believe I see her hand tremble before she takes a long sip, and I know she's as unsettled as I am.

More guests arrive, and Adam leaves us, but with the awkward tension between us, Morgan's date excuses them both and steers her out toward the back patio. I'm swept into a conversation about Australian wine with a sommelier friend of Clover's, but my attention keeps drifting through the open doors to Morgan under the exterior heat lamps.

She seems to be listening intently to a conversation, but I notice how her eyes occasionally flick in my direction. We are both equally aware of precisely where the other one is. And every moment that we're not connecting seems a wasted one.

At dinner, Russo is perfectly at ease, his arm draped casually across the back of her chair. Every time he leans in to whisper something that makes her smile, I feel a knot tighten in my chest and a caveman urge to stand, upend the table, and grab my woman.

It's a special kind of torture, watching another guy touch her so freely. And all I can think about is how great it was to have her at Nan and Gramp's table. Well, not all I can think about. Mostly I'm thinking about the night we spent together in the guest house.

"So, Luke," Adam says, while wine glasses are being refilled around the table, "how was the rest of your stay in the City after Clover and I came home?"

"The highlight was Mom and Dad's party," I answer, grateful for the distraction. "After you left, I had a meeting with Lark and just hung out for a couple days. That's it."

"Not quite all. My assistant loves society gossip." Adam winks at Clover with some inside joke, then focuses on me again. "Janice saw a photo of you in Page Six."

Shit! I start to get hot around my neck area, shooting a glance at Morgan. Yup, she's all ears.

"You were photographed with"—*Please no! Don't bring her up*—"your old fiancée. Clover had to tell me who she was, but you made a nice pair."

If I could reach past this nice woman, Lindsey Parisi, seated between me and the head of the table, I might try to knock my brother-in-law out to shut him up. The entire room full of guests seems to have fallen silent, as if I'm radiating my mortification. Morgan is staring directly at me while a cold sweat covers my back.

With my brain frozen, because I know this will result in trouble, I shake my head at my brother-in-law, hoping he gets the message to drop it.

"You and that stunning blonde. What was her name again?" Adam snaps his fingers, trying to remember. "Isla something?"

What can I do? Too late to have a private conversation with Morgan about my past, I fill in the blank.

"Devereux," I confirm through gritted teeth, feeling Morgan's gaze like a physical weight. I glance at Clover, willing her to gag her husband.

"Isla Devereux, that's right," Adam says, then catches Clover's warning glare. "Sorry, was that not—"

"It's ancient history," I say quickly, but the damage is done. Morgan's expression has closed off completely, her fingers tightly grasping her napkin.

Yet she's the first to speak. "I guess not so *ancient* if you were photographed . . . When? A few days ago?"

"An unexpected meeting," I say.

"You seem to have a lot of those," she quips, meaning tonight's surprise, no doubt.

"We all have a past," I point out, wanting to quickly neutralize any bad feelings over Isla, if possible.

"Some more hidden than others," she says. I realize the rest of the guests are quiet while they witness this volley of words from one side of the table to the other.

I'm almost grateful to Russo when he chooses this moment to lean in, his arm slipping around her shoulders. "Speaking of pasts, Morgan told me about her time in Sydney. The beaches sound incredible."

"They are," I confirm, unable to tear my eyes from a flashing pair of blue ones. "Though perhaps not as spectacular as the attractions in the Blue Mountains."

Morgan's cheeks flush slightly at my pointed remark—memories of our last encounter pass quickly between us.

"She didn't mention those," Russo says.

I just bet she didn't. I can't tell if he's oblivious to the tension, or trying to defuse it. He looks at her. "Maybe next time You're in Australia, I'll be with you. We can do a wine and foodie tour."

"I think I've seen quite enough Down Under," Morgan says before finally breaking our epic eye contact. She gives Russo a small smile. "Besides, I'd rather go with you to Italy."

Advantage Morgan, with that slice to my heart.

Clover, ever the perfect hostess, steers the conversation to safer waters. After dinner, I can tell Morgan is ready to bolt while others are enjoying the circulating dessert trays of Henley chocolates and petit fours.

After visibly recoiling from the selection of chocolates, she says something quietly to Russo, then heads along the hall toward the powder room. Without thinking, I follow, catching up before she closes the door.

Staring at one another in silence, Morgan frowns, but she doesn't object when I join her and close the door behind me. I guess she knows we have to talk, although this isn't the romantic setting I'd hoped for.

"What are you doing here, Luke? In Boston?"

"I came to see you."

"With no warning? After weeks and weeks of silence?" She crosses her arms, making her breasts plump up at the neckline of her clingy blue dress. "You ambush me at what was supposed to be a relaxing evening, and then I find out you were out on the town in New York with your ex-fiancée? One you never bothered to mention."

"I went to New York for my parents' anniversary party, just like Clover and Adam. Seeing Isla was accidental. We both showed up at the same time in the same high-profile place. *Hell*, I wouldn't have even been there, but Lark asked me to fill in."

Her silence is damning, and I know what she wants me to explain. Running a hand through my hair, I lean my hips against the marble sink. "I never told you about Isla because our engagement was years ago. I was young. Too young. And when you and I were in Australia, she was on a different continent. Anyway, Isla was and is irrelevant."

Morgan nods. "What happened to break you up?" Her tone is still cool but at least curious.

I know this won't go over well, but I tell her. "She didn't want to live in Australia."

Her face pales. "I see."

"No, you don't. I was overseeing Henley New York at the time. Isla's parents are New York royalty. She was fun and beautiful, and I fell hard."

A flash of hurt crosses her face before she masks it with a polite smile. "Why wouldn't you?"

I don't want to hurt her, but I might as well finish. "Lark wanted to come back to New York, and I was fine with returning full-time to Sydney. But Isla wanted the Big Apple more than she wanted me."

"And you wanted Sydney more than you wanted her," Morgan points out.

I smile. "Yes, exactly. It wasn't even close, but it stung a little for both of us. It was good to see her again and clear the air. But it's not like we—"

"It doesn't matter." She drops her arms to her sides. "You're free to see whomever you want."

"Clearly, so are you," I counter, unable to help myself. "How long have you been dating your Italian stallion?"

"That's none of your business." Her shoulders tense. "Just like your engagement wasn't mine, apparently."

"One's in the past. And the other is in my sister's living room."

Morgan's eyes flash with anger. "Knowing about Isla would have clued me in early."

"To what?" I ask, curling my fingers around the countertop on either side of my hips to keep from reaching for her.

"Location, location, location," she mutters. "That's your dealbreaker, isn't it?"

"Not fair," I say, wishing I couldn't smell her familiar floral scent. I'm like Pavlov's dog, and the fragrance is making my body react. My desire has ramped up since we came into this enclosed space, my cock is rock hard, and all I can think about is touching her.

"Fair would have been letting me comfort you when Patrick had his stroke. Fair would've been a goddamned phone call that first week since the last time we'd been together, I'd had my mouth around your dick. Fair would've been some message from you since then." Her voice trembles slightly. "What do you want from me, Luke?"

"I want . . ." The words catch in my throat. How do I tell her I've crossed an ocean because I can't work, eat, or sleep without thinking of her? "I want to know if you're happy."

Her expression softens for a moment. "New job. New apartment. Life is good."

"That doesn't answer my question."

"I don't owe you answers."

Morgan's right. She doesn't. We stand in tense silence, the air between us charged as usual. Her pulse flutters at her throat. I groan and give in to the scent tickling my libido.

Reaching for her, taking both her hands in mine, I drag Morgan closer until she's nestled between my thighs. She doesn't protest. Not even a little. Sliding my hands into her hair, glad that it's loose and flowing, I lean down and cover her mouth with mine.

God, it's good to be home.

23

Morgan

I should back away, give some small protest, but my body is humming the way it hasn't since the last time Luke touched me. I tilt my head one way, and he goes the other, and suddenly, I can't get close enough. I'm so hungry for him. Our mouths are moving, devouring one another, then we both open up for our tongues to glide and fence. If I did nothing else for the rest of my life, this would be enough. It's so freaking hot and intimate.

Pressing my hips to his erection, I feel myself gush with desire. If he put his hand under my dress and fingered me, I wouldn't stop him. In fact, I'd go off like a firework with a short fuse. His hands move to my ass, cradling it, lifting and tilting me so my mound is against his bulging fly.

For a few seconds, we're like teenagers as he rubs me up and down his cock. My pussy lips spread wide against my damp panties so my clit is now engaged and happy.

"I've missed you so much," Luke says against my mouth. I feel one of his hands doing what I was just imagining, sliding up my thigh.

"Please," I whisper, begging for his touch.

"Not here," he says, although his fingers have found and slid under my panties, making me gasp. He strokes my clit, and I have to bite my lip to keep from crying out. "Let me take you home tonight. Forget that guy."

Luke's words are like ice cold water. Extricating myself from his embrace, rather inelegantly, I stumble back, tugging at my clothing. Despite throbbing with need, when he pushes away from the sink, his pupils dilated with lust, I put my hands up. Breathing deeply, watching his stunned expression while he calms down, I can't believe what we almost did. Here in Adam and Clover's bathroom!

"I came with Dominic," I remind him, my voice shaking.

With frustration dripping from his tone, he says, "When you and I had hot monkey sex before, you were as good as engaged, so let's not let a little thing like dating that Russo guy stand in our way."

The blood drains from my head, even as I see his own face go pale. *Did Luke really just say that?* "Is that what you think of me? That I'm some kind of cheater who jumps from man to man?" My voice rises slightly. I can't help it.

"No, Morgan—" he begins, obviously regretting his hateful words.

"How dare you!" I say, a pretty weak retort. But I'm just getting started. "You hounded me, pressured me, wouldn't leave me alone until I caved."

"I know. I—"

"Then you have the nerve to throw it in my face." My voice is echoing in the tile bathroom.

"I didn't mean—"

"Of course you did. You meant to hurt me because I'm trying to be a decent human being here, not giving in to the *irresistible Baz Henley!*" Although I'm giving myself too much credit because I sure as hell was giving in.

"I'm sorry," he says. "I was completely out of line."

"When you had your fingers up my dress or when you insulted me?" I shoot back.

"Both," he says, his voice as loud as mine. "Dammit, Morgan! This is just so fucked up. I want you and you want me. Now I'm right here, and you're with some other guy."

I could put Luke out of his misery and let him know I've never slept with Dominic, but I'm not feeling particularly generous at this moment.

When he moves closer again, I don't give up my ground. I'd have trouble dropping Luke with a dragon tail kick in this dress, but I could do a quick thrusting punch to his throat that would keep him from saying anything vile to me for a few hours. But I can't hurt him like that, although I reconsider a few seconds later when he adds, "I would bet when you kiss Russo, you're thinking of me!"

Arrogant toad. He's correct, but still . . .

There's a knock at the bathroom door. We freeze, eyes wide, breathing hard and staring at one another. Finally, I clear my throat.

"Occupied," I say, trying to sound normal.

"No kidding," Clover retorts. Trying the handle and finding it unlocked, she pushes her way in. Luke's sister's expression is only partly concerned. The other part is exasperated, bordering on royally pissed off. "Your voices are carrying," she says. "Half the party can hear you. Luckily, not those on the patio where Adam steered your date."

I am beyond mortified. "Please, would you go get him? Tell him I'm waiting out by the car. And that I don't feel well, because I don't," I add, sparing Luke one last look. He's red-faced and tight-lipped.

Clover's glance goes between me and her brother, then back again. Finally, she says, "You realize Adam and I can never go to Dominic's restaurant again. He'd probably poison our food." Then she sighs. "Yes. I'll send him out."

"Thank you," I whisper, mortified, but grateful. Unable to meet Clover's eyes and determinedly avoiding Luke's gaze altogether, I squeeze past her and escape before either of the siblings can move.

$♥$♥$♥$

Luke's words hit too close to home last night. I *have*, in fact, thought about him the two times Dominic kissed me. I've fantasized about Luke while in bed, using my favorite pink vibrating toy. And I've even pictured him going down on me while stroking myself in the shower. I'm obsessed. But I'm also strong. I didn't cave and have bathroom sex. That's not enough, though, to let me keep stringing Dominic along, not for a fourth date. He deserves better.

He had to have known something happened between me and Luke, because when he dropped me home after my speedy exit from the Bonviers' party, I said I needed space. He agreed to give it to me.

Then there was the weird moment when I saw my "Welcome" mat had been turned upside down. Again. Realizing whoever did it would've had to gain access through the locked outer door, come through the small lobby, and then upstairs to my apartment, it gave me the heebie-jeebies.

Or it's an inside job from one of my neighbors. Maybe a kid's prank. But I don't think so. It's too subtle, along with the red paint I found on my mailbox and car door, like someone's sending me a message they know everything about me. A kid would just throw an egg.

I'll have to ask the building management if I can look at the security footage. But it's the weekend, so that'll have to wait. Stretching, I climb out of bed, feeling crummy. On the one hand, after all this time, I finally had what some might call closure with Luke. On the other hand, I found out he once was so in love, he asked a woman to marry him. I also ditched a great guy last night.

Under any other circumstances, Dominic would have been my dream man. Kind, considerate, a great cook, and good looking. And I sent him running.

"*Argh!* I'm crazy," I exclaim aloud, putting on my slippers before going into the kitchen, because the old wood floors are always cold. Turning on the coffee maker, I think of Luke. What a rat bastard, surprising me like that. And I'm not too fond of Clover, either. We met up once for drinks after her phone call, and she must have had the willpower of Sisyphus not to bring up Luke, but somehow, she held her tongue.

Another time, I went to her home for dinner, and it was just her, me, and Adam. After we laughed about what he'd said back in Sydney, that a foursome is better, we pulled Ivy's high chair up to the dining table. I had a pleasant evening. I was thinking Clover and I might become friends, if I could handle the torture of not asking about her brother.

And then she goes and blindsides me last night.

My phone rings, and I see *his* name. I can't deny a thrill goes through me. But I ignore it. *Nope.* Not going to happen. Sitting on the couch with my coffee, I try to read emails. It rings again. And again. No voicemail, though. Finally, I text Luke.

What?

Scarcely a second later, he replies:

Can I please come up and talk with you?

Rushing to the front window, I press my cheek tightly against the glass, trying to look down to the front step. I can't see from this angle until he suddenly steps back and looks up. I dodge to the side.

Too late. I saw you.

Go away.

Luke tries guilt next:

I came 10,000 miles so we could talk in person.

Not good enough. I text back:

I think you said enough last night.

This time, there's a short lag, then:

Too much wine.☹ You had that problem once. Remember?

What a gentleman, bringing up my drunken night in Sydney.

Go away.

Is Russo with you?

I can't believe he's asking me that.

Not your business.

I don't see his car.

What the hell!

How do you know what he drives?

I watched you leave my sister's last night.

I don't answer. He is sucking me into a discussion. When my phone falls silent, I count to ten, then look out the window again. Seeing nothing, I even slide the glass up and put my nose to the screen. No Luke. Good. I ignore the massive wave of disappointment that he gave up so quickly.

Plopping myself back down on my sofa, I drain the coffee. A few more minutes go by. My phone rings and I pounce, but it's not Luke. It's Clover. I hesitate, waver, and answer.

I speak first. "Your crazy brother is outside my apartment harassing me."

"My crazy brother is harassing me, too, asking me to beg you to let him in. Please, Morgan, what have you got to lose?"

My heart. "My mind," I snap.

"He's super sorry about everything," she adds, sounding distracted. "Yes, Ivy, in a minute, sweetums."

Clover would probably say anything to get Luke and I out of her hair.

"I don't know—" I start.

"Great. Perfect."

"Wait, are you talking to me?" I ask.

"Yes." Then, "Give that back to Mommy."

I know that's not directed at me. "Clover, I'm going to let you go now."

"Wait! Luke's gone someplace close to buy you bagels and muffins and breakfast wraps and donuts." She laughs. "Gee, I guess you two really don't know one another that well. Please let him in when he returns. Hugs. Byeeee." And she's gone.

I could actually kill right now for an egg-and-bacon wrap. And maybe a donut. I could also gleefully squeeze Clover Bonvier's neck for tricking me last night. On the other hand, I guess it couldn't hurt to talk to the man who swept me off my feet just as much as I did him. Who I've been crushing on for three months nonstop, pretty much from the moment I knocked him on his ass.

Plus, now there's the possibility of free food. When there's a knock at my door, I don't wonder too much about how Luke got into the locked lobby, I just open it.

Ethan! The look on his face is frightening, and I immediately try to shove the door closed, but he's too quick. First his foot stops it, then his shoulder makes it fly inward, nearly knocking me over. I'm off balance for only a second before I put the coffee table between us and face him. My phone is on the sofa, and in a split-second, I consider my chances. Probably not good. Ditto for trying to run down the hall to a lockable door.

"Enough of this nonsense, Morgan," he says. "You belong to me."

"I don't," I say, keeping my voice even, despite my heart racing like a rabbit. "You know no one *belongs* to anyone. Why are you here?" Does he want to kill me?

He shoves the low wooden table effortlessly to the side. "I just want you to remember how good we are together."

This must be a cosmic joke. Two men in twelve hours saying practically the same thing. One made my entire being melt with yearning, the other is terrifying me.

"This isn't helping. You're scaring me."

"Oh, no, baby," Ethan says, looking shocked. "Don't be scared. I just want to be the way we used to on a Saturday. Staying in bed late, having morning sex."

I think we did that once when he whined how I never stayed in bed on a weekend. I gave in, like I always did with him.

"Ethan, let's go have coffee at the Rusty Nail, like we used to. I'm hungry." I need to get him out of here and out into public.

"Why are your hands up like that? Do you think you can beat me in a fight?" He laughs, making me shiver. My hands went up automatically once I got my feet under me and faced him. This man whom I thought I knew has utterly snapped. All the worst aspects of him—needing to get his way, his desire to dominate, and how he always wants to win—are now on full display.

"Go strip off, Morgan, and get on the bed."

I don't let myself be shocked. Knowing the best defense is offense, I go into attack mode. With my elbow raised to the side, using a wide upward swing, I punch him in the temple. He can't block it. But my next blow with my other hand is to his chest and—*Fuck!* Unexpected pain radiates up my arm as my hand hits metal. *Is he wearing armor?*

Startled and suffering from the jarring effect, I back up while Ethan holds his head.

"Dammit! It hurts." He looks pissed off. I'm angry too, and my knuckles are throbbing. When I shake my hand out, he grins and lifts his shirt. He has a large metal sheet strapped with duct tape across his entire torso. I think it's a heavy gauge baking sheet.

"I came prepared," he says.

While he's talking, I move swiftly forward, jump, and give him a roundhouse kick to the knee. Of course, as with any kick, that leaves me vulnerable momentarily until I regain my balance. But he's staggering back and swearing, not worrying about me. I give his other knee the same treatment, and he goes down into a crouching position. That's perfect, allowing me to land blows on his head and my heel to his nose. Blood starts dripping.

"You are going to pay for that," he warns, but I'm feeling pretty confident.

"I'm going to keep beating the shit out of you," I say, starting to breathe hard, "with or without that cookie sheet, so I suggest you get out."

To my amazement, he crumples before me, head to the floor, and starts sobbing. "I've missed you so much. You were my world. And then you went away and changed. Then last night, you were with that Italian guy. Why are you torturing me?"

Ethan looks up, wiping his hand across his face, leaving blood and snot and tears on his palm.

Am I torturing him? Did I change? I tried to tell him before I left, but I should have been firmer. Grabbing a napkin from the coffee table, I approach him. He looks pathetic, and my heart is in pain for the man I once loved.

"Here," I say, keeping him at arm's length.

Lurching forward, his hand whips out and grabs my ankle, jerking my leg toward him and taking me down on my ass. *Wow!* He's more of a snake than I knew, but he should have thought this through.

As I easily pummel him with the balls of my feet, aiming for his head, my phone rings. *Luke!* In that tiny moment of distraction, Ethan jumps on me, his full weight pinning me to my own apartment floor. The damn metal sheet is brutal on my breasts and rib cage.

"You bitch," he says softly.

I can't stand looking up at his battered, bloodied face so I turn my head and realize the window is open.

"Luke. Help me!" I shriek as loudly as I can before Ethan puts his hand over my mouth.

"Morgan! I'm coming." I wonder how he'll get in the lobby door, but Ethan must have done something to the lock because barely seconds later, Luke is literally busting my door down. For a split second, I think about how I'll be responsible for that with my security deposit, and then Ethan is lifted off of me like he weighs no more than a child.

"Is this Ethan?" Luke asks, and he has him already jacked up against the wall by his throat. My ex-boyfriend's eyes are bulging, and he's flailing, trying to dislodge Luke's muscular forearm and failing.

"Yes. That's him." I'm reaching for my phone. "I'll call the police." Luke looks over and we lock gazes. He's making sure I'm ok. I nod.

"I don't know what you saw in him," he quips, and I can almost laugh despite the situation. When Luke lets up on Ethan a little so the man can breathe, he tells him, "You're lucky I got here and saved your ass. Looks like she was about to throw you out with the garbage."

The police come within minutes and take Ethan away in handcuffs. Only then do I realize I'm trembling. Luke's strong arms encircle me.

"I'm so impressed," he whispers against my hair. My tears begin to fall with the release of all the adrenaline and fear. A little while later, when I'm not feeling so shaky, I lift my head from his chest, "I thought you were bringing me donuts."

Luke starts to laugh, and I feel it through my whole body. Silently, I thank my parents for making me take classes to defend myself, and I thank Clover for bringing her brother back into my life.

"Hold on," he says and moves toward the door. "Are you good by yourself while I run downstairs?"

"Yes, I'm honestly not the wilting-flower kind of person."

"Yeah, I figured that." He's only gone for half a minute and returns holding a big white bag. "When you screamed, I dropped our breakfast in the bushes, but not too much harm done."

Luke takes care of everything, while I sit in a chair at my kitchen table and get over the lingering shock. He moves around like he owns the place, making fresh coffee, setting out squashed donuts and cold wraps onto plates. The muffins are a bit crumbly, but all-in-all, it's mostly salvaged. I feel tons better after eating too much.

"We have to go to the police department," he reminds me, "but I think they wouldn't mind if you showered and changed."

I'd completely forgotten I was in my long T-shirt that I sleep in and my pajama bottoms, although my slippers flew off during the epic battle.

"I hope I never start my day like that again," I say, finishing my second cup of coffee. "I think I may return to the dojo, though. I was a bit rusty."

"Looking at that asshole's face," Luke says, "I'd hate to see what you're like when you're in top form." He's doing everything right, not babying me, not asking me if I'm OK over and over. Just treating me like the capable person I am. And it works to get me over the scare and the shock. But maybe my body's still a little revved, because there's one thing on my mind.

"Shower time," I say. "Will you join me?"

24

Luke

The shower spray hits Morgan's back as I kiss her lips, then her sweet face, tasting a hint of salt from her earlier tears. Her fingers trace paths on my shoulders while my hands glide over her wet skin, checking for bruises. My blood is still up from finding Ethan on top of her, but she's not interested in being treated like a victim. Her mouth is as eagerly exploring as mine, making a hot path across my chest.

Gliding my hands over her full breasts, pausing only to pinch her nipples, I continue exploring, down her slippery skin and straight between her legs.

"Luke," she urges, closing her eyes, tilting her head back in response to my fingers parting her and sliding inside her tight pussy. She lets me play until she reaches out and grasps my cock with one hand. When her eyelids flutter open, her other hand slides behind my neck as she tugs me toward her. Our mouths fuse, demanding and fierce while we continue to stroke one another.

"I want you inside me," she whispers against my lips.

"Are you sure you're—"

"Luke, please."

I lift her, pressing her back against the tile wall, and she wraps her gorgeous, lithe legs around my waist. The warm water cascades over us as I enter her in one slow thrust. Her gasp of pleasure echoes off the bathroom walls. I start moving, finding a rhythm that has her tightening around my cock and her fingers pressing into my shoulders. We won't last long.

"God, I've missed you," I say, echoing my words from last night, only this time there's nothing between us. Not Russo, not the specter of Ethan, and . . . *dammit!* not a condom, either.

"No protection," I remind her, barely slowing my thrusts.

"I'm on the pill," she says, blinking her deep-blue eyes at me. "And I trust that you're clean."

I freeze, nearly asking why she is on birth control, but I really don't want to know. Not in this moment, when we're literally joined at our hips. I simply nod my gratitude and continue plundering her sweetness, going as deep as I can. She's strong enough to support herself with her legs, so I can free up one hand and slide it between us. I want to give attention to her clit. It's a hard, swollen pleasure bud that I intend to work until her body unfurls around me.

As soon as I touch it, she moans. "Yes, Luke. Don't stop!"

Increasing the pace of both my finger strokes and my ramrod cock, like it's part of a well-tuned piston engine, I feel my own release building. But I get her there first. When Morgan climaxes under the hot shower spray, she does it with a cry of passion, her magnificent body uncontrollably shuddering against mine. I follow right after, my head thrown back, roaring like a lion. I'm so goddamn happy to be back with her, experiencing this amazing sex with the only woman I ever want to bury my cock into again.

We stay like that for a beat or two, catching our breath, before I carefully set her down. Her legs are shaky, but she's smiling.

"I needed that," she says, matter-of-factly, like I just gave her a good piece of chocolate. I grin down at her, unable to imagine being any happier. When she reaches for the shampoo, I take it from her hands.

"Let me." Working the lather through her hair, I can't help but think how right this is. I want to take care of her, cherish her, love her, and fuck her lights out for the rest of my life.

$♥$♥$♥$

At the police station, Morgan is calm and composed while she gives her statement. I'm proud of how she handles everything, answering questions clearly and precisely. When the detective asks about earlier incidents, she mentions an incident with her doormat and some red paint, things she hadn't told me about. My jaw clenches, but I keep quiet. This isn't about me.

"You should have reported those incidents," the detective says, but Morgan just shrugs.

"I wasn't sure it was him until today."

When we leave, it's already afternoon. "Hungry?" I ask.

"Starving. But I don't want to go anywhere fancy. Just somewhere we can relax."

We end up at a small diner in her new neighborhood. Morgan orders sausage and pancakes—"Comfort food," she says—while I get a turkey club. And strangely, we talk like we're on a first date. When we were in Australia, it seemed like my upbringing and my family dominated our discussions. She tells me about the dream job she came home to and more about growing up in Boston. Morgan has a unique outlook on so many issues, I find myself falling even more in love with her.

After our late lunch, we walk through the Public Gardens, stopping to watch the swan boats, although neither of us is in the mood to get on one. I know Morgan's feeling a little raw, and I feel the need to protect her, so we stroll past the line of tourists.

Doing nothing at all except being with her is exactly what I want on this balmy spring day. No one would know what she went through this morning, looking perfect in a cream-colored sweater and dark jeans. Her hair is down the way I like it, all streaked with sunlight. I want to freeze this moment, but I also want to move forward and start a life with her.

"Come back to Sydney with me," I say suddenly.

She slowly releases my hand she's been grasping while we walk. "What?"

I shrug. "Hear me out. You could come back for Ethan's trial, but that might not take place for months. Now that we've sorted everything out between us, I want you to come back. We'll pick out a new place in Sydney, if you don't like my apartment. And we'll be together properly this time, an actual couple, not sneaking around, a boss and a temp."

Morgan stops walking, and when she looks at me, she's frowning. "Are you asking me to take a leave of absence from my new job? Or move there permanently? Either way, it's not going to happen, Luke."

Oh. "After Ethan's spectacular meltdown and then . . . ," I trail off, not wanting to specifically reference sex in the shower. But she lit up my world. *Again!*

"And then?" she presses, starting to sound annoyed, which is the opposite to what I thought would happen.

"Then the whole fantastic time in your shower. We are made for one another. I thought—"

"You thought what? Now that my crazy ex is locked up, I'll just pack up my life and follow you to the other side of the world?" Her voice rises slightly. "Or that now we've had sex again, I'll be so unable to resist you, I'll need to move wherever you want to live. You're almost as bad as he is, assuming you know what I want."

The comparison to Ethan stings. "That's not fair."

"Isn't it? You seem to have decided on how I fit into your life, without actually asking me what I want."

Jamming my hands into my jeans pockets, I start walking again. She can keep up, or catch up, because I'm not going to stand here having my words twisted. "I invited you into my life, Morgan. That's not a federal offense."

She's walking alongside me again, silent, thoughtful. "My sister is getting married in this year. I want to be a part of that, not just show up on her wedding day. My family is here. My life is here. I have the best job I could have ever hoped for."

I don't point out the obvious, that none of that means shit if you don't have someone to love. The right person. The one who loves you back and can't live without you. I guess I'm not all that for her. I think if I was, then she'd put me first in a way that Anong and Isla never did.

"God, Luke, I can't believe we're going through this again, this time on my home turf. What's the point in going over the same old problem?"

I want to argue, to tell her we could make it work, but it suddenly occurs to me that she's right. Even if I blurt out how much I love her, that won't solve the problem of distance, not even by an inch.

Instead, without exposing how my heart is breaking, I say, "You're right. I'm sorry."

She looks surprised at my quick capitulation. "Really?"

"Yes. I just . . . I want to be with you. But I shouldn't have assumed."

Morgan's expression softens. "I want to be with you too. And the pisser is I don't know how. But I'm sorry I went off on you. I guess I'm a little touchy after what happened today."

"Understandable." And it is. I shouldn't have broached the subject on the same day as that nut tried to force his way back into her life. Taking her hand, I link our fingers together again. "We'll figure it out," I say without any conviction because for the first time since I arrived in Boston, I'm not sure it's possible. "For now, let's enjoy the time we have." Even though it's only days before I have to return home.

She squeezes my hand. "Clover invited me over for dinner with the three of you tonight."

"I know. She texted me, too, demanding I bring you back to the house. But we don't have to go. Do you want to?"

Morgan hesitates. I wonder if she's thinking what I'm thinking—that I'd rather be alone, just the two of us, preferably eating pizza in bed.

"Yes, let's go. I can't keep you all to myself, when I know your family misses you as much—"

When she interrupts herself, my heart starts beating faster. "As much as you do?" There I go, assuming again. But I'm sure I'm right this time.

Nodding, she turns her face up to me. "Yes, I'm going to miss the hell out of you when you leave. I'm already feeling it. And eating with Clover and Adam like we're a committed couple won't fix anything."

"I know." And I do. We're still heading for heartbreak, and all the Henley candy in the world can't sweeten it.

Morgan

Watching Clover and Adam together during dinner makes my chest ache. They move around each other with such ease, finishing each other's sentences, sharing private smiles. This could be Luke and me, if we weren't separated by oceans.

"I want you to meet my family," I blurt out, interrupting a story about Ivy's latest adventures.

Luke's eyes light up. "Really?"

"Yes." I glance at Clover, who's beaming. "If you have time before you leave."

"I'll make time," he says, reaching for my hand under the table.

Later, when we help clean up, Clover corners me in the kitchen. "You two seem better."

"We're not," I admit. "We're just . . . pretending everything's fine."

She hands me another plate to put in the dishwasher. "You know, Adam and I put off having a real relationship for a while. I wouldn't let him into my personal life, so it was really just—"

I'm glad when she stops herself because I so don't want to hear about her sex life. Then she smirks. "Now, he says I led him on a *merry dance*. But when we were in the thick of it, he had choicer words. One time, he drove off, angrier than I'd ever seen him. But he came back."

"Our problems are different."

"Why?" she asks, her eyes so like her brother's.

"Because . . ." I struggle to find the words. "Because Henley Confectionery needs Luke in Sydney. I know he's itching to get back right now. What's more, he *wants* to be there."

Her sympathetic expression saddens me, showing me she understands the very real impasse we're facing. "I don't want to leave my family. Clover, I love your brother," I finally say the words that I've kept hidden in my heart. "But he can't be my everything, taking me a world away from where I want to be."

She hugs me. "I still think you'll work it out in the end."

I must look like a kid who has lost her puppy because she adds, "After he goes back, I'm taking you shoe shopping. There's literally nothing better to lift your spirits." Her words manage to evoke a small smile from me, even more when she adds, "We'll take your sisters, too."

Luke was quiet the rest of the evening, probably seeing no path forward and without even the promise of cute new shoes. When we pull up outside my building, neither of us moves to get out of the car.

"Come up," I say before he can ask. Just because we can see the end date on "us," that doesn't mean we should deprive ourselves of the best sex I could ever imagine.

He kills the engine. "I want to, more than I want my next breath." I guess he feels the same way—about the sex, I mean. "But I don't want you to feel used."

"Are you kidding me?" I ask. "I'm the one who should be asking you if you'll feel used."

Finally, that brings the first genuine grin to his face that I've seen all day. It makes my heart hurt, knowing I won't see it again. At least, not for a long time, although I'm starting to consider whether Sydney to Boston could be the mother-of-all long-distance relationships. The frequent flyer miles alone might be worth it.

In my apartment, we don't bother with pretense. He closes my front door with his foot since our hands are busy undoing and tugging and tearing off. Our clothes form a trail to my bedroom. Once there, we start fast with me on my back spreading for him and Luke taking no time before spearing me with his cock. I close around him like a clamshell, hands on his smooth, broad back and my legs around his hips.

We don't speak as we give and take and climb the orgasmic mountain. Surprisingly fast. Before he has time to slide his hand between our slick bodies, which are rocking in perfect synchronicity, I gasp as my climax ripples through me in long, shuddering waves.

"Morgan," he sort of grunts my name when his body tenses and he comes. I feel him spurt deep inside me, and it makes my eyes well up with tears. Not letting go, we clutch one another for a few silent minutes. And then, rather than getting up or going to sleep, we start over, slowly this time, savoring every touch, every kiss and nibble and lick and— *oh God, yes, right there!*

By the time he flips me over onto my stomach and puts the head of his cock against my swollen pussy lips, we are slick with sweat, and my muscles are trembling.

Luke slides his hard length into me and also reaches around to cup my mound, applying exquisite pressure above my pussy with the heel of his hand. *How does he know what I need?*

Then as his hips start to rock, languidly drawing out then blissfully thrusting in, his finger strokes my happy clit. I make some crazy sound that's definitely not a real word, and he speeds everything up. I'm raking the sheets with my fingers when he adds a kiss, dropped on the back of my neck, to our sexy equation.

"Luke," I say on an outward panting breath. He turns the kiss into a nip and my desire gushes between my legs.

"You feel so good," he says against my skin before nibbling on me again. I fly over the edge, hearing myself moan while he keeps rubbing my clit and surging in and out like a maniac.

"Come with," I manage, still bucking through a mind-blowing climax. And he does, pressing deep and holding still until he comes—rather fierce and hard. It makes me proud to have unraveled him like this.

Luke releases me, and I roll to my side, while he puts an arm around my waist, fitting my back to his front. I can feel his heartbeat pounding between my shoulder blades.

After a few minutes, during which my emotions flit from happy to sad and my thoughts skitter, wildly searching for a solution, I give up and recall he'll finally meet my family tomorrow.

"My parents and sisters will adore you," I say softly.

"I'm looking forward to meeting them." He sounds as though he means it.

$♥$♥$♥$

The next evening, my prediction proves true. Even though we spend the day together, mostly in the same position as we're in now, in the sheets, we arrive at my parents' house separately. Luke will be going straight to the airport from here and starting his travels around midnight.

I'm standing at the front door, with it open when he drives up. My parents welcome him like a long-lost son and are immediately charmed by his easy manner and genuine interest in our family stories. As I did at his grandparents' ranch, he scrutinizes the family photos on the walls and asks questions.

Katie keeps shooting me meaningful looks. Pru, who has promised to give us an hour and a half before she has to go back to the hospital, asks him if he knows anything about the first-ever BiVACOR artificial heart transplant in Sydney.

Looking startled, he tells her no, while we give her a hard time about her choice of small talk. Katie's fiancé, Keith, who is a genuinely sweet guy, laughs.

"You got off easy," he says to Luke. "Pru questioned me on my last proctology exam when we first met."

Everyone laughs. "Just looking out for you," Pru defends herself. "You do eat a lot of meat."

Katie and I make wide eyes at each other over our crazy sister.

"Who's hungry?" my mom asks.

"I brought wine," Luke says, indicating the brown paper bag that my mom set on the dining room table when we were giving the grand tour. "But you don't have to serve it tonight, of course."

My dad opens it and pulls out two bottles of Penfolds' Cabernet-Shiraz.

"I thought it would be Henley's Reserve," I say, having told my family how much I loved the Australian chardonnay.

"Apart from my grandfather's wine, which isn't sold outside of ten square miles from our ranch," Luke explains, "this is my favorite wine. To me, and others agree, it tastes like a slice of Black Forest cake."

Everyone gasps. My parents exchange looks, and Katie is nudging me so hard with her elbow, I nearly fall over.

"What is it?" Luke asks. "Did I say something wrong?"

"Tell him," Pru says, looking at me.

"It's nothing really." My sisters groan at my lie. "OK, well, it's actually pretty cool because my mother is kinda known for her fabulous Black Forest cake. We were just eating one the other day."

Luke grins, almost blushing. All he says is, "I'm sorry I missed that cake."

"You didn't," my mother tells him. "Of course I made one, along with an *Apfelkuchen*."

"Apple cake," I translate for him, wrinkling my nose.

"Morgan," Mom scolds. "What's that face for?"

"Because you didn't need to bake two things," I tell her. "It's overkill."

"What if Luke doesn't like chocolate?" she protests.

"Mom! He makes chocolate candies for a living," I remind her. Everyone laughs at her silly blunder as her eyes widen.

"*Entschuldigung,*" Mom says, using a classic German word meaning "my mistake."

"You can never have too many desserts," my dad chimes in.

I can see the wheels churning in my mother's head, as she thinks about another chocolatier. Suddenly, she blurts out, "The Bridegroom Oak," making me groan. Wanting to nip in the bud any romantic notions she might have, I explain to her, "I've already told the story to him and all the Sydney employees."

Luke is clearly enchanted by my family. "May I open the wine? I'd like to know if you all taste the same chocolate and cherry that I do." Dinner is a success, not only for his delicious wine—"it *does* have the flavors of Black Forest cake," Katie declares—but also his appreciation of all my mother's cooking.

Much later, when Pru and even Katie and Keith are long gone, and my parents have wished Luke safe travels and retreated upstairs, I walk him to his car. Our hands are clasped and we're sort of leaning on one another, like broken-hearted invalids who can scarcely walk.

"I see why you can't leave them," he says.

My heart squeezes painfully. "Luke . . ."

"No, I get it. Really." He turns to face me. "I love you, Morgan."

I suck in a quick breath, hardly able to believe he just said those words. Reaching up, I touch his cheek.

"I love you, too."

We smile at one another, then he sobers. "I can't ask you to choose between me and your family, any more than you can ask me to abandon my duty to mine."

My moment's happiness is instantly dashed. "So, this is it?" My voice breaks. "We simply give up?"

He pulls me close, and I breathe in his scent, trying to memorize everything about this moment. But he doesn't answer. There's really nothing left to say.

We both know the truth. *Sometimes love isn't enough.*

When he kisses me goodbye, it tastes like regret and all the possibilities that will never be realized. As I watch his taillights disappear into the night, I wonder if time will be our friend or foe. Will it help us both to heal our hearts and find love elsewhere? Or condemn us to endless longing for the one person we were supposed to be with for the rest of our lives?

For now, all we can do is let go.

25

Luke

The waterfront restaurant sparkles with city lights reflecting off Sydney Harbor, but I'm barely noticing the million-dollar view. That is, except to recall when I brought Morgan to the brew and burger joint about fifteen minutes west of here. That was the night we first had sex.

Had sex hardly covers what we do between the sheets. I guess I finally have to admit that I'm a man who *makes love* in bed with the right woman.

I don't realize I've released a long, weary sigh, until the people I'm dining with fall silent.

"Sorry," I say. "Just getting hungry." I lie. I have no appetite.

My friend Hudson shoots me yet another apologetic glance across the white tablecloth while his wife, Lily, resumes chatting with her visiting sister, Ruby. I shouldn't have let Hud talk me into this double date. I knew better. But after two months of moping around my home and office, I thought I'd try connecting with someone who isn't ten thousand miles away.

Ruby is everything I should want in a woman. She's wearing a deep-red dress, showing off curves that would make most men salivate. And her smile lights up her entire pretty face. God knows I noticed women before Morgan Anders walked into my life. Many times, I've been attracted to a beautiful face, feeling that spark of possibility.

Now, my brain keeps making unwanted comparisons—Ruby's laugh is too high-pitched, her eyes aren't that mesmerizing deep blue that I miss so much, and when she touches my arm, I feel nothing but awkward discomfort.

The only remotely interesting thing about this evening is that Ruby lives in the Barossa Valley, near where they make my favorite wine.

What a coincidence, I think, tuning back in as she describes the Penfolds vineyard, which she's been to numerous times. Even that reminds me of sharing those bottles of Cabernet-Shiraz with Morgan's family, watching her mom's eyes light up when I told her it tasted like Black Forest cake. The memory makes my chest ache.

"So, Luke, what's your take on wine and chocolate pairings?" Ruby asks, touching my arm again. "I always say they're a match made in heaven."

"Well, I tried dipping grapes in chocolate once," I say, attempting to lighten my mood. "But the vintner threatened to have me arrested for grape abuse."

She laughs, a genuine sound that should be endearing. "You're really not selling me on moving to Sydney," Ruby says. "I mean, what kind of person willfully ruins perfectly good grapes?"

I force a smile. "The kind who'd rather eat chocolate than drink wine."

"You're funny." She leans closer, giving me a view of her cleavage that would have once had me planning our next date. "I like funny."

The waiter arrives with our entrées, saving me from having to respond. Hudson ordered the lobster for everyone, and as we dig in, I try to contribute to the conversation. But my mind keeps drifting to Morgan, wondering what she's doing right now. It's early morning in Boston. Is she having coffee? Hopefully alone. Getting ready for work? Dating someone new? The last thought makes my stomach churn.

"Luke?" Ruby's voice brings me back.

"Sorry, what?"

"I asked if you've ever visited the Barossa Valley wineries?"

"Oh. Yes, several times." I suppose I should say something about going out that way again so we can meet up, but I don't. I can't because it would be a lie.

"You should come visit when I'm home," Ruby suggests. "I could show you some hidden gems most tourists never find."

Hudson clears his throat, clearly sensing my discomfort. "Ruby's quite the wine expert," he says, trying to help. "She's even thinking of opening her own wine bar."

"That's wonderful," I say politely, but my enthusiasm falls flat. Even to my own ears, I sound distant.

By dessert, Ruby has stopped trying so hard, and I feel like a complete ass for wasting everyone's evening. When we say goodbye outside the restaurant, she gives me a knowing look.

"Whoever she is," Ruby says softly, "I hope she's worth it."

I can only nod, grateful for her understanding. Is Morgan worth me spending the rest of my life alone, missing her? I can't answer that because I keep thinking we're squandering a gift by not being together. And it's not only me who's hurting. I felt her pain when we parted, and I'm just as distraught over being the one to cause it.

What a fucking mess! Back home, I pour myself some brandy and call Lark's number, not caring that it's seven in the morning her time. She answers on the second ring.

"Either you're drunk dialing me, or you just had a disaster of a date," she says by way of greeting.

"The date was fine. The woman, Ruby, was nice." I take a sip of scotch. "*I* was the disaster."

"*Ah.*" There's rustling on her end, and I picture her settling into the oversized chair she keeps by her bedroom window in the Upper East Side. I stayed with her when I was there for Mom and Dad's anniversary party. "Still thinking about Morgan?" she asks.

I almost tell Lark what a stupid question that is. Both my sisters know by now that Morgan is the one for me. But I believe I'm about to ask the biggest favor of my life, so I don't want to say anything insulting. Instead, calmly, I tell her the truth.

"She's all I think about. It physically hurts to wake up in the morning after dreaming I'm with her, only to find myself alone. For the first time in my life, Australia feels like the edge of the world, like I've been banished to some remote outpost on Mars." The admission of my private emotions and my own weakness costs me something. But Lark needs to understand why I'm about to ask her my next question, and that I'm not doing it lightly.

"Would you consider trading positions with me?"

I hear her gasp before she snaps back, "What?"

"CEO positions. You take Sydney, I'll take New York."

"Luke . . ." She pauses, and I pray she's not going to reject the idea without stopping to consider. When she does speak, her first words aren't about her life there or about me. "What about Gramps and Nan? And the ranch?"

I sink onto my couch, running a hand through my hair. "Mom and Dad are coming back here for six months anyway. I'm picking them up next week." After Gramps's stroke scare, they'd started planning an extended stay.

"Besides, Dad is more than capable, and he'd kick either one of our asses if we said otherwise. And Nan has already hired some help, just to keep Gramps from doing too much."

"True." She's quiet for a moment. "You must really love Morgan to even consider leaving Australia."

"I do." The words come easily now. "But I don't know if New York will be enough of a compromise. She might need Boston or nothing."

"Then why are you calling me instead of her?"

"Because I needed to know if this is even possible before I get her hopes up. Again." I take another sip of brandy. "Lark, would you want Sydney?"

"Honestly?" There's a long pause, which amounts to torture while I wait. "I'm getting tired of the New York social scene," she says. "All these wealthy guys wining and dining me. They seem so fake. And if I go to one more eclectic, zhuzhed-up church that has been renovated into a pseudo-ethnic restaurant, I will scream."

I can't laugh along with my sister, not while I'm still waiting for her final answer.

Then Lark says, "At least in Sydney, I'll be closer to Gramps and Nan while they need family around. And Mom and Dad will be there at the same time. Three generations on the same continent doesn't happen much in our family."

Hope blooms in my chest, and I don't point out that Clover brough the next generation to the ranch already. "So, that's a *yes*?"

"It's a strong *probably*." I can hear the smile in her voice. "I need at least two weeks to wrap things up here. And you'll have to take my apartment on the Upper East Side. I don't want to let it go."

"Done. And I've kept the apartment nice and tidy for you here in Sydney." I look around at the take-out cartons, plates and cups on every visible surface, even some stray dirty laundry that I must have thrown on the floor and forgotten. "Just the way you left it."

"You're really gone for this girl, aren't you?" Lark's voice softens. "To give up being close to the ranch."

"I can live without her," I admit. "But I can't be happy."

"That's actually pretty romantic." She chuckles. "Who knew my brother was such a softie?"

We talk logistics for another hour, discussing everything from the timing of the switch to how to handle the board of directors. By the time we hang up, I'm already planning my trip to Boston. Although Morgan and I have texted one another sporadically since I left, we haven't spoken or video-chatted. I think we both knew it would be too painful. Now, I consider calling and telling her the good news. But I hold back.

Am I afraid? Yes. What if I tell her I'm upending my entire life for her, and she says, "No, thanks." Obviously, that's not what I think will happen, not for a second. But after both of us putting family ahead of one another, I want to look in her eyes when I make my pitch. NYC is not Sydney, but it's also not Boston. I only hope it's enough.

Suddenly, I'm exhausted, and with the thought of seeing her again, I think I'll be able to sleep. Lying in bed, I don't count sheep. I think about what I'll need to do to switch places with Lark, and what I'll miss besides Gramps and Nan.

I'll definitely bring Morgan a case of the LLB she loves so much. *What the hell!* I'll bring a dozen. Plenty of room on the corporate jet.

$♥$♥$♥$

Two and a half weeks later, with my personal "stuff" going directly to NYC, I touchdown at Boston's Logan Airport, hoping Morgan is home from work. But I'm prepared to wait. I can't wipe the smile off my face, nor slow the fast pace of my heart as the driver speeds me toward her Southie apartment.

Arriving at Morgan's building, gifts in the trunk of the limo, I finally text her:

Are you home?

No reply. Of course I should have determined this fact beforehand. I wait what feels like hours but is probably ten minutes. It's 6:30 p.m. What if she's on a date? Maybe she rethought her life and got engaged to Dominic Russo. She might be slurping down his noodle this very instant.

Calm down, I order myself. Don't jump to conclusions. Besides, I went on a date with a voluptuous woman in a killer red dress. And it meant absolutely nothing. Morgan might be on a date with some chiseled stud, but why would I let that bother me? She said she loved me. I text her again:

Hey, sweetheart. Where are you?

Still no reply. My mind starts racing. Why won't she answer? Why *can't* she answer? Maybe she's in the shower. Seems an odd time to be showering. Alone! Why else would her phone be off at this time of the evening? And if her phone isn't off, why isn't she responding?

True, we've barely texted over the last eleven weeks and three days because it was too fucking painful and pointless, but still, I have to believe she would reply to any message from me.

I get out of the back seat and pace the sidewalk. The lights are off in her apartment on the second floor. Taking a deep breath, I try to relax. Obviously, she's not home. Or she's having hot monkey sex this very instant, right above me.

Dammit! Why did she ever put that ridiculous term in my head?

Her car! I jog over to the gated driveway leading to the underground parking garage, putting my hands to the vertical bars like a prisoner. I can see her car parked in her space about ten yards down on the right. That's weird.

Has a gas leak rendered her unconscious upstairs? Did Ethan escape from jail? I call her, which I should've done in the first place. It rings once and goes to voicemail. I listen simply to hear her sweet voice before hanging up. My chest tightens with this anticlimactic delay. I don't have her parents' or her sisters' cell phone numbers.

Think, I order myself. She hasn't vanished off the face of the earth.

Clover! I didn't tell her and Adam that I was coming. Mostly because I couldn't trust my sister not to spill the beans. And secondly, because I booked a room at the Ritz. I wanted privacy for our passionate reunion in the lap of utter luxury. There's a suite with my name on it, with champagne cooling and a case of Lemon, Lime, and Bitters. And roses. More than Ethan sent by about two hundred.

I was torn between the classic floral symbol of love and the Australian national flower. But a golden wattle sounds like something on a turkey's neck, so I went with roses.

"Come on, Clover. Pick up!" I yell, back to pacing the South Boston sidewalk. A glance over to the limo driver, I see he's staring at me, probably thinks I'm a madman. At least I didn't bring a billion roses in the car with me.

She answers on the second ring. "Hey, what's up?"

"Where's Morgan? Is she all right?"

After a pause that makes every pore in my body break out in a sweat, she says, "How'd you know she's not in Boston?"

"I didn't. But she's not at her apartment."

"Are you here, in the city? You little turd! Why didn't you tell me? I would've got the guest room ready and—"

"Clover, shut up! Where. Is. Morgan?" By the last word, I'm yelling again. Then I have a weird thought. Did we cross in the sky? Is she in Sydney?

"Germany," my sister says. "On business."

Something about the way she added those last two words makes my skin prickle. "Is she there alone?"

My sister does some bizarre laugh that's supposed to be light but comes off fake as shit. "Alone? I mean, there are like . . . What? . . . Eighty million people in Germany?"

"Clover!"

"She went with some hotshot she's training in cyber nerdy stuff. I don't think she had a choice. Her boss told her—"

"Hotshot," I repeat, interrupting her. "As in a really good coder and programmer or as in he's hot looking?"

"Bohhh-ttthh," my sister says, her voice rising as she draws the word out. "I met him once."

"Aaahhhhhh," I scream, head back, looking up at the nighttime sky, stars just starting to show as twilight turns darker. In Germany, it's about one in the morning. Plenty of stars. Plenty of hours to spend beneath the sheets before morning. With . . . ?

"What's the hotshot's name?"

"Why?"

"Just tell me." I hope it's Floyd or Melvin or—

"Max," she says softly. "Maxwell Alexander."

"Jesus!" Better than being named after a garden herb. I'm envious already.

"Morgan doesn't care about names," Clover reminds me. And my sister's right. I think of Morgan's body arched under mine, and the only thing that mattered was how we touched one another.

"Just text me where she is, please, and I'll be there by morning." So what if I've just been in the air for the better part of two days with a short stop in Los Angeles?

"It won't be morning. It'll be—"

"Shut up, Clover," I say and hang up.

Seven more hours of flight time before I can see Morgan's face and find out if she's willing to make a life with me, somewhere between her world and mine.

26

Morgan

Beyond my desk, the Berlin skyline stretches before me, a mix of old-world charm and gleaming modernity. I'm staring out the window, seeing nothing. The same nothing I see when I stare at my laptop screen. Although I was supposed to be conducting a final review of the cyber security system I've installed at the headquarters of a major music streaming platform, my mind refuses to cooperate.

Lately, it wanders, and at the most inopportune times, too. Always back to a certain scrumptious billionaire who has probably forgotten all about me by now. His last text was weeks ago.

Just checking in with my favorite person.

I replied to his usual text:

I'm OK. You?

Yup. Goodnight, sweetheart.

That's pretty much how most of our exchanges have gone, ever since he drove away from my parents' house. Anything more is too painful. And now that our weird relationship has fizzled out, I'm suddenly his "sweetheart." *Go figure!*

"Earth to Morgan," Max's voice breaks through my reverie. He's leaning against my temporary work station, his casual slacks and sport coat making him look like he stepped out of a magazine. Compared to most of the employees here, where they take business casual to an entirely different, more relaxed level than in the states, Max is decidedly overdressed. As am I, in a knit dress and heels.

Most of the music execs in the other rooms are wearing jeans and hoodies—visual reminders of Luke's travel outfit the first time I met him. But then, I can relate nearly everything to some experience I had with Luke. From making coffee to my morning shower, he's in my thoughts and memories until, some days, I think I might go nutso.

"The final run-through meeting is in ten minutes," Max said. "Ready to dazzle them with your expertise?"

I force a smile. "Born ready."

"That's what I like about you, Anders. All business." His green eyes twinkle with interest that I'm choosing to ignore. "Though I wouldn't mind seeing what you're like off the clock."

"Max . . . ," I start, but he holds up his hands in surrender.

"Just putting it out there. Can't blame a guy for trying."

I close my laptop, stand up, and stretch, grateful that Max takes rejection with grace. He's brilliant, attractive, and firmly planted in my world of tech and coding. But he might as well be the Hunchback of Notre Dame's less handsome brother for all I care. My heart apparently didn't get the memo about moving on from a chocolatier who can ride a horse and crush grapes, and who had no answer to my question: *Should we just give up?*

I haven't so much as smiled at a guy since Luke left. And I don't see any reason to start now. But I'm glad to have Max with me on this trip. I've been spacing out lately while training him. This morning, I trust that I didn't really need to do another review. I made sure there were no bugs yesterday, and then let Max do a final check earlier today.

"Let's go," I say, and we head into their super chic, dance-club inspired conference room. It's wild and totally inappropriate for serious work, but when in Rome!

After a successful presentation, Max and I are taken for a celebratory dinner with the company's executives to Night Kitchen, where our merry group occupies three tables on the second floor of the highly rated restaurant, serving inspired Mediterranean dishes. No bratwurst and sauerkraut here.

After eating sweet potato tabbouleh and an octopus merguez ragout, I'm disappointed but not surprised that there's no Black Forest cake on the dessert menu in the heart of such a quintessential German city. Not in this chichi place. Anyway, the brioche bread pudding soaked in crème brûlée is a pretty amazing.

I'm feeling no pain when Max and I walk back to our hotel, after I've had two BASIL-mango cordial and gin drinks. I should've stopped at one, but I just wanted to say the name to the server again. Our rooms are next door to one another, and he helps me put my card into the slot before pushing the door open for me.

"You OK, Anders?" He looks amused, also interested, as I step past him and turn to say goodnight.

But I tear up immediately, thinking of Luke and how he took care of me the last time I let cocktails go to my head. I wish I could click my heels and transport myself to Sydney.

"Hey," Max says, his tone sympathetic. "You're really not all right, are you?"

I take in a ragged breath. "I'm fine. Just missing someone."

"A guy," he guesses, leaning against the door frame. "An idiot if he let you get away."

"No, it was mutual," I say, realizing the gin has loosened my lips.

Max offers me a small but sexy grin. "Maybe I can help. I could take your mind off him. Or at least try."

I stare at him, at his handsome face and killer bod, and I feel . . . nothing. I want Luke. Only Luke. I'm in a world of trouble, possibly staying celibate the rest of my life.

"No, thanks," I say, as if he's offered me a cookie or a free movie ticket or even a different kind of ride than the one he's suggesting. "I'll have to pass. You'd be wasting your time."

With that, I push the door closed, and he has to jump back to keep from getting his fingers squished.

"Goodnight, Max," I say softly, knowing he can't hear me. I've sobered rather quickly, at least enough to drink a whole bottle of water put out by the hotel maid.

The following gray and cloudy morning, unusual for July, I'm in the lobby waiting for Max to appear so we can share a ride to the airport. Next to the concierge desk, there's a rack of guide books, which I'm idly flipping through when I gasp. The Bridegroom Oak! There it is, in full color, and the little voice inside me roars to go see it. *Three hours away!*

Shaking my head, I try to tamp down my irrational excitement. I would miss my flight. I can't do anything so impetuous.

Like flying to Australia for a three-month job.

Like giving my heart to a guy who lives on a different continent.

Go see it! It sounds ridiculous even in my head, but I can't shake the pull of visiting the tree I've heard about all my life. My Oma on my dad's side used to tell us girls all sorts of German fairy tales, but the story about the ancient tree in the Dodauer Forest was the most fascinating one of all. Because it was real.

I'm biting my lip, probably wearing a thousand-yard stare when Max is suddenly beside me.

"You daydream harder than anyone I've ever known," he quips, and I assume I'm forgiven for closing the door in his face. "You ready to go?"

"No," I say. "You go without me. There's something I want to do."

"Wait, you're staying? In Berlin?"

"No, I'm going to Eutin to see about a tree."

"Morgan," he says, looking serious. "Are you having a nervous breakdown? Is this one of those times when I should stick to you like glue or force you onto an airplane?"

I'd like to see him try, but I'm not being fair, going all space-cadet on him. "No, Max, I'm fine, really." I look him directly in the eyes, so he can see I haven't become a wild-child, about to disappear into the forest never to return. "Tell Charlie I'll be back to work in a few days. Don't worry. I'm not going to do anything stupid. Good work, by the way," I add. "But you better get going, or you'll miss the flight."

"Take care," he says and disappears out the hotel door.

Now I need a plan. Luckily, there's a helpful concierge right beside me. In a few minutes, I'm racing for the 10:07 a.m. train from Berlin Central Station, which I catch by the skin of my teeth. It's not until I'm on the train, traveling in Germany for the first time without a fluent speaker, either my parents, grandparents, or even Max who took German in college, that the magnitude of my impulsive quest hits me. I think about how my sisters, and I used to laugh at this ridiculous old tradition and the desperate romantics hanging their hopes on a freaking oak tree.

Now, I think, *I'm about to become one of those desperate romantics*.

Around noon, I check for messages besides the strange one from Luke, asking where I was. I noticed it first thing this morning when I turned on my phone, before I got dressed. Unsure how it could matter so many hours later, I'd shot back only a question mark.

There's nothing more from him now, so I text my sisters and even Clover, who has become a real friend, telling them of the silly adventure I'm on. Partly to make them smile, partly in case I do disappear into the forest, run down by a wild boar that the guide book says are a common sight.

I'm snacking on chocolate made by Milka, as well as Knoppers wafers, both of which I bought onboard the train, when I hear my phone ping.

From Katie, who's always up early because she's a teacher:

I can't believe you're going there! I'm so excited for you.

From Pru, who's always awake because she's a resident:

Ask the tree to send me a lover.

I laugh at her text. She's gorgeous and doesn't need help from a tree in that regard. She'll find a man when she stops spending seventy-five hours a week at the hospital.

From Clover, who I'm fairly certain likes to stay in bed with Adam wrapped around her, I get nothing in reply.

The train ride to Eutin takes me through pristine countryside that looks straight out of my family's photo albums. Rolling hills, neat farmhouses with red-tiled roofs, and forests that seem to hold centuries of secrets. And all of it under an unusually thick canopy of clouds.

Closing my eyes, I remember how my grandmother first described the Bridegroom Oak—"Ein magischer Ort für verlorene Herzen." *A magical place for lost hearts.* The right place for me, if ever there was one.

After four hours of travel, including a short bus ride, I drop off my suitcase at a small, two-story, pink and white "pension," a family-run hotel I booked while riding the rails. The owner has given me a cozy room on the second floor.

Intending to walk the last part of the journey, I'm glad I have plenty of hours of sunlight left. Still, I retrieve a sweater from my suitcase before I head back downstairs.

And that's when someone turns on the faucet in the sky, apparently, because the downpour is tremendous, despite the clouds being the same pale gray as the furniture in my Sydney apartment.

"Nope," I say out loud. I've waited this long. I'm not swimming to the tree, bedraggled and freezing. Besides, after all this travel and only sweet snacks, I'm famished.

After borrowing an umbrella—*ein Regenschirm*—I head out in search of a decent brauhaus pub. Not hard to find. Grabbing a table, I'll wait out the storm, eating pork sausage and roasted potatoes, or *Bratkartoffeln*, with a local Eutiner beer.

I'd forgotten how much German I've picked up from my family, but even if I didn't speak a word, everyone here speaks English, and most are friendly.

After my delicious meal, there's still no sign of the rain letting up. Despite toying with the idea of heading to the tree anyway, sort of a romantic, reckless notion, I opt to wait until morning, with the promise from my hotel host that it will dawn clear and sunny.

$♥$♥$♥$

Grateful I waited, since it turns out to be about a thirty-five-minute walk, first I stroll along a one-lane road with no painted lines and then onto a marked path taking me into the "Dodauer Forst." It's a little scary, until I pass a couple coming the other way.

"Bräutigamseiche?" I ask, referencing the Bridegroom Oak about the same time as I see a small wooden sign.

They smile, nod, and point at the sign.

"Danke schön," I say, as politely as possible.

Realizing I'm not German by my crappy accent, the woman adds, "Not too far."

After a few yards, I can see the clearing around the five-hundred-year-old oak. Its massive trunk and spreading branches are even more impressive than the pictures suggested. I can't take a photo, however, as my phone died last night, and that's when I discovered I'd left my charger in the hotel room in Berlin.

Now that the couple has left, no one else is here. There's a covered bench and a board with a forest map. Surrounding the tree is a picket fence and a path to the famous knothole that everyone uses. There's even a ladder. *Here goes nothing.*

Standing before the tree that has seen centuries pass and plenty of foolish humans, I pull from my pocket the letter I wrote on the train yesterday. When I started the trip, I swore I wouldn't do anything so idiotic as writing a letter to Luke. I simply wanted to see the Bridegroom Oak in person. I didn't even have a proper piece of paper with me, so I wrote on the back of the printed Berlin hotel invoice, with a pen I had in the bottom of my purse.

My letter is already worn from how many times I've folded and unfolded it, second-guessing every word. Taking a deep breath, I read my obsessively tidy cursive one last time:

Dear Luke,

This is probably the most ridiculous thing I've ever done. I'm standing in a forest in Germany, about to leave you a letter that you'll never read in a tree you'll never visit. But maybe that's exactly why I can finally say everything I should have said in Boston.

I've loved you for longer than you know, maybe since that first night in your office, when you flipped me over onto my back and gazed down at me with eyes that really see me. I felt like the only woman in the world that night. And I've never stopped loving you, even when I convinced myself that letting you go was the right thing to do.

You asked me to stay in Australia with you, and I didn't. I said goodbye and ran away. Then you came 10,000 miles to Boston and asked me to return to Australia with you. Again, I said no, because I was scared. Scared of leaving everything I knew, scared of becoming someone who follows a man across the world, scared of losing myself the way I almost did once before with the wrong man.

Again, I said goodbye to you, breaking my own heart.

But now, what terrifies me most is never knowing what we could have been and the life we could have together. Never waking up to your smile again or hearing you say my name.

I swear, each time you say it, you cause my heart to skip. How do you make my harsh name sound pleasant and feminine?

I know now that I'm strong enough to leave everything behind, if you still want me. Loving you has changed me in ways I never expected. You taught me that sometimes the biggest risk is not taking one at all.

I'm not sure if there's a way for us to bridge the distance between Boston and Sydney, but I'm ready to try, to do whatever it takes.

We've already endured too many goodbyes, don't you think? I keep hoping we've said our last one, and the next time we meet, it'll be forever.

If by some miracle you ever read this, know that my heart is still yours. It always will be. I'm ready to put you first and live wherever you are.

Love,

Morgan

My hands shake as I fold the letter again and slide it back into the envelope I bought in Eutin and have already addressed to Basil L. Henley, c/o Bräutigamseiche, Dodauer Forst, 23701 Eutin, Deutschland. Then I climb the wooden ladder. The knothole is less than impressive. Smaller than I imagined, the opening is about the size of my open hand, and painted with a yellow circle so it can't be missed. The space inside looks dry and clean, protected from the elements.

There's a letter inside already! Irrationally, my heart starts pounding as I reach in and retrieve it. *What if it's from Luke?*

"Morgan, you have lost your ever-loving mind," I say aloud. The envelope is written in German and is most definitely not for me. I replace it and slide mine in, too. But I don't descend the ladder immediately. I rest my forehead against the ancient bark for a moment.

"Bitte," I whisper, not sure if I'm praying to the tree, to God, or just to my own foolish heart. "Please."

"Morgan."

Sweet Mother! I have lost my mind. I can literally hear Luke's voice, despite knowing that's utterly impossible.

"Morgan," I hear him again. "Don't fall."

Clasping the ladder rails with a white-knuckle grip, I turn my head ever so slowly.

"Luke," I mouth the word, unable to find my voice. How can he be here, looking real and absolutely kissable, wearing gray jeans and a dark-blue T-shirt? It's an even bigger shock than seeing him at Clover and Adam's house.

Maybe he really is a magical Willy Wonka.

He's also grinning like a Cheshire cat. "I don't suppose there's a letter in that tree addressed to me."

27

Luke

I've never been more grateful for Clover's meddling nature than I am right now, watching Morgan perch precariously on that wooden ladder, her letter disappearing into the ancient oak's hollow. Morgan's trail had gone stone cold when I arrived in Berlin early yesterday to find out that she and this Max character had enjoyed a big festive send off the night before and then checked out of the hotel yesterday morning.

I watch her rest her forehead on the tree as though she's praying.

"Morgan," I call out after a few moments because my heart is thundering, and I can't wait to touch her a moment longer.

She doesn't move. "Morgan," I say again, this time a little worried. "Don't fall."

Slowly, she turns her head. When I see her whisper my name, I can't help smiling. I haven't felt so happy and so right where I should be in my whole life.

Yesterday, when the Berlin hotel's concierge informed me she'd checked out, along with Max, I was ready to go back to the airport. Then Clover finally got her ass out of bed midday and immediately texted me that Morgan was going to visit some ancient tree.

I don't know where she's going exactly, but there's an oak involved. Helpful?

Luckily, yes! That little clue told me exactly where my woman was going, and I rented a car and followed. Arriving late in Eutin, in a driving rainstorm, all I could do was get a room and keep trying to text Morgan, but her phone was off.

"I don't suppose there's a letter in that tree addressed to me." I'm unable to keep the smile from my face.

She grips the ladder like it's her lifeline. "How can you be here? Are you real?"

"I am," I say.

Morgan looks dazed, like the time she got drunk with my sister in Sydney, but this is from pure astonishment. I would feel the same in her shoes.

"What are you doing here?" she asks.

"Looking for you. Come down so I can kiss you properly."

She descends slowly, keeping her head turned and her eyes on me as if afraid I might disappear. When her feet touch the ground, I close the distance between us in three strides and encircle her with my arms. She's warm and curvy and . . . mine, all mine, fitting against me perfectly. My hands slide up her back, one tangling in her hair while the other spreads wide, holding her more tightly against me.

Her blue eyes are taking me in, still looking shocked, until I lean down to kiss her. Capturing her lips with mine, I pour months of longing and regret into the kiss. She melts, her muscles relaxing against mine while her fingers clutch my shoulders through my shirt.

The sweet taste of her, the soft whimper that escapes her throat, sets my blood on fire. I deepen the kiss, claiming her completely, telling her without words everything I've been desperate to say since the night I left her parents' house. When we finally break apart, both breathless, I keep her close, unwilling to let even an inch of space between us.

"I've been chasing after you since yesterday when I arrived in Berlin," I say against her hair. "When I got to your hotel, you'd already left. No one could tell me where exactly you'd gone." I brush my thumb across her cheek. "Until I talked to Clover."

Then we stay silent for a few minutes. I'm not sure how long, but we're both soaking up the miracle of being together in this ancient place when so many things could have occurred to keep us apart. When I finally lean back and look down at her, Morgan's eyes shine with tears.

She sniffs and wipes her face on my shirt. "Do you want to read my letter?"

I nearly laugh because it sounds so pedestrian, to stop and read a handwritten letter after days of flying followed by a speeding car ride. Moreover, the irony of my techno geek lady taking pen to paper isn't lost on me. In fact, I feel honored beyond anything. After stifling my laughter, I answer her question truthfully.

"I want to read it over and over every day for the rest of my life." But when she pulls away, turning toward the ladder, I stop her. "I'll read it after," I say, taking both her hands in mine. "I already know what's in my heart, Morgan, regardless of what your letter says. Unless you've written anything in it about being over me." After how she kissed me, I'm betting no, but I ask anyway, "Did you?"

"No." She gives me a quirky smile. "Just the opposite."

I drop to one knee on the wood planks leading to the ladder, ignoring the pebble digging into my kneecap. "Being apart has only confirmed what I knew in Boston—that you're the missing piece of my soul."

Pulling out the ring box I've been carrying since Sydney, I snap it open, hearing Morgan catch her breath even before I hold it up like an offering to a goddess. The morning light filtering through the leaves above us makes the blue diamond dazzle like the very center of a flame. When I first saw it, the stone reminded me of Morgan's eyes, and the opals on either side represent Australia, where I first made her mine.

"Love might be a dog's dinner, but I want to eat every messy bite with you. Morgan Anders, will you marry me?"

Her eyes are like saucers for a second, and then the most beautiful smile breaks across her face.

"Yes," she whispers, then more loudly, "Absolutely yes!"

Rising to my feet, I slide the ring onto her finger just before she throws herself into my arms, nearly knocking me backward. We're both laughing as I lift her off her feet and spin her around. Only then do I hear clapping and realize a few other people have made the pilgrimage to the tree on this Sunday morning.

"I have no idea what a dog or his dinner has to do with it, but I love you," she says.

I guess she really does because she's already wearing my ring before her busy mind starts thinking about the possible roadblocks to our happily ever after.

And here they come now. "But Sydney—"

"Is *not* where we're going to live," I interrupt. "I've arranged to switch positions with Lark. I'm taking over the New York office."

She draws back, staring at me in shock. "What? But your grandparents and the ranch!"

"Will be there for us to visit. I hope you'll go back with me to stay for a couple weeks or a month at a time, and I want to take our kids there some day. But *you* are my future, Morgan. My home is wherever you are."

$♥$♥$♥$

Morgan

My heart feels as though it might burst. This man, this incredible man, has thought of everything. Luke has put me first in a way that leaves me breathless.

"I still can't believe you're here," I say, touching his face again to make sure he's real. "That you followed me across the world."

"I'd follow you anywhere."

Now I know what it means when people say eyes can dance. Luke's golden-brown gaze is like a flickering fire. When he puts his arm around me and we start to walk away from the oak, I suddenly remember.

"My letter!" I exclaim, turning back toward the ladder. Then I recall the history of the forester's daughter and her ardent chocolatier's son. "I think it's better luck if you go get your letter out of the oak."

Looking bemused, Luke climbs the ladder and peers into the knothole, then he looks down at me and makes a face. "You had to go and tell the tree my name is Basil?" Folding the envelope in half, he tucks it into the back pocket of his jeans before descending. "I will read it and memorize it," he promises, "afterward."

"After what?" I ask innocently when he puts his arm around my shoulders again. We start walking, past another couple who offer us *"Glückwunsch,"* or congratulations, on the engagement they'd witnessed. Now, we're part of the long romantic history of the Bridegroom Oak. I'm floating with pure happiness.

"Your hotel or mine?" Luke asks, making me shiver in anticipation. I honestly don't know if the soft-spoken family who runs the small guest house would approve of my bringing this hot and handsome hunk back to bang in my cute little room.

Getting into Luke's rental car parked near the path—"No Batmobile?" I tease—we stop at the pension anyway so I can gather my things. Then we head north to his hotel. It turns out to be an historical estate from the fourteenth century, renovated into a sprawling spa on the Dieksee lake.

The original, large manor house is still standing, painted white with a glossy black roof. It's flanked by what used to be working buildings, like stables and an iron smith. Those closest to the manor are now lodging and event rooms, all their exteriors refurbished in muted-peach color siding with red tile roofs. Branching out from the main house, like arms, these smaller structures border a central oval riding ring. Currently, there are people on horseback cantering inside it.

"You're kidding me," I say when he drives up to the stately manor house at one end. "You found a place with riding?"

"Don't worry," Luke says, turning off the engine and shooting me a wicked smile. "The only thing being ridden today is you. Hard, fast, and often."

His teasing words have my pulse racing and my panties soaked. My cheeks feel hot and must be scarlet when a bellhop opens my door, while Luke gets out the other side, letting a valet take the wheel.

Horny, needy, and thoroughly aroused, we run inside.

"Hurry," I say when we cross the luxurious lobby, Luke giving a quick wave to the uniformed staff behind the reception desk. But it takes forever since, every few yards, he pauses to pull me close and kiss me, as if he can't bear not touching me. My body hums with anticipation. The kiss on the majestic staircase makes my knees buckle, but we manage to stay upright *and* fully dressed while hurrying along the wide corridor to his room.

His magnificent, old-world suite! Paneled walls, wainscoting, long-elegant drapes, and white-painted furniture. Even as I discover later, a chandelier above the bed.

Once inside, Luke's playful mood shifts to something more intense. He backs me against the door, his hands framing my face.

"I've missed you so much," he murmurs, then sears my lips with another kiss. He drops to his knees again and undoes my jeans, sliding them down. I cannot breathe when he tugs my panties to the side and kisses my pussy with equal passion.

"You are so ready for me," he murmurs, parting my nether lips and sucking my clit like it's a sweet candy drop. I sink my fingers into his hair, lean my head back and let him drive me wild. When he inserts his fingers, I feel my wetness drip between my thighs.

No lover has ever made me so out-of-my-mind turned on. I fly apart in seconds. *Seconds, not minutes!* And I can scarcely believe this man is now mine.

As I start to sag down the door, Luke stands, pausing to help me step out of my jeans, and then the race is on to the other side of the suite and the big bed. Same Scandinavian pale wood and white down comforter as in my cozy little room at the pension near the Bridegroom Oak, although on a much more luxurious scale.

As usual, we have sex twice, the first time fierce and fast, and the second time slow and sensual. Although in my mind, I'm now thinking of it as *making love.* So mushy, but true. When he finally slides his stiff cock into me during the encore, I cry out his name with exuberance, overwhelmed by the completeness I feel and the utter bliss.

When we're cocooned in the hotel's sheets and each other's arms, I say, "I'm glad you came to Germany. Any normal person would have stayed in Boston with his sister and waited until I returned."

"I'm not a normal person," he says quietly, his breath against my temple. "I'm a candy billionaire." I feel his mouth smile, and it makes me giggle.

Then he adds, "Besides, Clover told me about Maxwell Beefcake."

My giggle becomes all-out laughter at the ridiculous name. When I get it together, I look him squarely in the face and ask, "Were you really worried about Max and me together? Is that why you followed me to Berlin?"

Luke's eyes narrow slightly, then he releases a pent-up breath. "A part of me may always have a sliver of jealousy, thinking of you with another guy. I can't help it. You're gorgeous and smart and—"

"And I'm yours," I add.

"I'll have to keep reminding myself. Anyway, I like surprising you. After flying across the world and having my big Boston moment fall flat, I thought, what's a jaunt across the Atlantic to Germany?" He pauses. "Oh, shit!"

"What?" I tense. I knew there'd have to be something wrong. Everything is too perfect.

"There's a hotel room at the Boston Ritz that I never checked into."

I relax. "So?" I ask, tracing the kookaburra tattoo on his shoulder with my fingertip. I even love this bird. "Are you worried about your deposit?" I tease.

He grins, then says, "There are a lot and I mean an obscene amount of dying roses someone has to clean up."

"Oh my." But I'm beyond flattered, thinking about what he did and went through, just for me. "I wish I'd been there when you texted me outside my apartment, and I wish I could've seen all those flowers."

He strokes the flat of my stomach, each of us touching the other simply because we can. "I promise I'll reenact the whole thing. I was like Marlon Brando in 'A Streetcar Named Desire,' yelling up for my Stella."

"You didn't yell my name, did you?"

"Not really, although I did scream in frustration. I think I worried the limo driver. But I promise I'll fill your life with flowers from now on."

I wear a sappy smile at my sheer good fortune. This man loves me and is going to cherish me. Even better, he's going to let me love and cherish him right back. I want him to know the bottom line, how true I will always be to him.

"Max is a good-looking guy, and we've been in close quarters for days," I confess. Luke frowns, his jaw tightening. I add, "And a couple times, he let me know he was interested."

Luke straight up growls, and I quickly put him out of his misery. "I want you to know I had zero interest. Nothing, nada, zilch. I was too busy pining for you and much too much in love to see him as anything but a fellow cyber geek. Ditto to noticing any other guys again, ever. OK?" He nods and puts on his own sappy smile to match mine.

"So now to our new reality." I don't want to talk seriously, but we have to. "You leaving Sydney and taking over from Lark and living in New York—it's such a huge change for you, as well as for me. Are you sure about this?" I ask, still touching his skin, this time making patterns across his chest.

He catches my hand, bringing it to his lips. "The only thing I'm sure about is that I don't want to live without you anymore. Everything else we'll figure out together."

I look at my ring, sparkling in the sunlight streaming through the second-story window. "Together," I agree, and let him drag me on top of him so we can kiss again.

An hour later, he gets up to retrieve my letter. "I'm going to take good care of this," he vows and frame it for our kids. "If it's age appropriate for them to read, that is."

"I didn't write you a dirty letter," I protest, and then stay quiet while he reads it—once, twice, before putting it on the bedside table. He keeps his back to me for a few moments, and I can tell he's moved by my words. Hopefully, he's reassured that we're a forever thing, now he knows I was prepared to go to Sydney to be with him.

When he looks back, his eyes are bright, more gold than brown in the light.

"I love you, Morgan Anders."

"I love you, Ba . . . Luke Henley." No need to start off our engagement by annoying him.

"I need water," he announces. "You want some?" What with our sweaty and rambunctious reunion, we're both dehydrated. But after the water, we need more sustenance. Room service obliges, by bringing up an assortment of savory *Vorspieise*, or appetizers, and coffee.

When Luke's phone buzzes somewhere in his pants pocket on the other side of the room, I'm reminded that mine's been dead for too long.

"Can I borrow your power cord? I left mine in Berlin." Still in the thick hotel robe he wore to answer the door for our tray of snacks, he obligingly gets up to find it. "And my phone's in my purse," I add. "Can you get it for me, please?"

For my part, I'm "busy" leaning against the headboard, two down pillows nestled behind me, and drinking superb *Milchkaffee.* "I have to say, the bedding is superior in Germany. Every bed I've been in has exceeded my expectations."

"We'll get down comforters and mattresses for our home," Luke says, reaching for my purse on the tufted chair. "Down everything. Do they make down towels?"

Imagining myself covered in feathers while trying to dry off after a shower, I smile when he suddenly freezes, looking at something he's pulled out of my purse.

"What's wrong?" I ask.

"You've been cheating on me," he says quietly, causing me to sit up straight to see what he's holding. I nearly spill my coffee. He raises my crumpled Milka wrapper in the air. "This is *not* a Henley chocolate bar."

I laugh so hard, I have to set my cup down on the table beside me, holding my stomach until I fall back against the pillows. I can't remember ever laughing so hard with anyone let alone a sexy man.

Our future might not be as smooth as the center of a Henley truffle, but I know our life is going to be a fun—and passionate—adventure.

EPILOGUE

Six months later

Luke

The Manhattan skyline glitters outside my office window as I review the latest sales figures for our new Bridegroom collection. As soon as Morgan and I got settled in New York City, I got to work with my development team on six German-inspired chocolates. Hazelnuts, walnuts, coffee, apricot, apple, and even a creamy marzipan that actually tastes good are some of the ingredients.

The Henley chocolatiers and I brought them to market on a fast schedule. They've been available for just over a month in a custom candy box Clover designed for us. The cardboard looks like oak, due to a wood-grain print, and the top is a framed transparent window to see the chocolates. A gold oak leaf seal completes the package. The response has been incredible.

I pick up one of the "Morgan" truffles from the box on my desk. It's our nod to the Black Forest cake. Deep, dark kirsch-infused chocolate hides a brandied cherry nestled in the thick, white creamy center. Every time I pop one in my mouth, I'm reminded of my wife—sweet and sophisticated on the outside, with a passionate, juicy core that only I get to taste.

The thought makes me grin. I've become *that guy* who can't go more than a few minutes without thinking about his wife. The joint board, NYC and Sydney, is thrilled. Not because I finally found someone who could sweep me off my feet and settle me down, but because the new line is making Henley Confectionery a shit-ton of money.

My phone buzzes with a text from Morgan:

Leaving the conference. Meet you at home.

I reply:

On my way!!♥

I'm already reaching for my jacket and sliding my phone in my pocket. The new line of German chocolates was my tribute to finding the love of my life at that ancient oak tree, but Morgan's been busy too. She has developed her own security systems software that she started back in Sydney, when I was chasing her like a lonely horndog.

Her cyber security program is revolutionizing the industry. She didn't just *attend* a conference. She was the main speaker. My brilliant, beautiful wife is making her own fortune. Although she jokes it's small compared to mine, it's no small accomplishment at all, and I'm so fucking proud of her.

The drive home takes longer than usual thanks to midtown traffic, but thoughts of Morgan waiting for me make it bearable. The penthouse we took over from Lark overlooks Central Park, and as I ride the private elevator up, I'm already loosening my tie. The doors open directly into our foyer, where the scent of the flowers I left for Morgan to find upon her return welcome me.

"Morgan?" I call out, dropping my briefcase and shrugging off my jacket.

"In the bedroom!" she calls back.

Just where I want her. I'm already hard as I walk down the hallway. She is my everything. She is my home.

$♥$♥$♥$

Another six months later

Morgan

I stretch languidly against Luke's warm body as sunlight streams through our floor-to-ceiling windows, washing our bedroom in happy yellow tones. Saturday mornings have become sacred in our household—no alarms, no rushing, just tangled limbs and whispered conversations.

Luke has cured me of being an early riser on weekends, though I suspect his special methods of persuasion have a lot to do with my willingness to linger in bed.

"Good morning, beautiful," he murmurs, his voice deliciously rough with sleep as he trails kisses along my bare shoulder. "How about a Morgan for breakfast?"

I laugh, rolling my eyes at his favorite joke. The double-entendre about his precious Morgan chocolate truffles never gets old for him.

"Can't wait to eat my Morgan," he continues, his hand sliding down my naked hip. "Nothing better than enjoying another Morgan first thing in the morning."

"You're insatiable," I say, but I'm already melting under his touch, my body arching toward him instinctively.

"Only for you," he whispers, capturing my mouth in a kiss that quickly turns from tender to hungry. "Get naked. Now. Please."

Another of his favorite jokes. Since he said those words so much when we first moved in together, I've learned it's best to sleep nude, especially on weekends.

"I'm already naked," I point out, smiling as his hands roam appreciatively over my body, until his fingers dip low and I suck in a breath.

"So you are." His voice drops to that husky register that never fails to send shivers down my spine. "That's very convenient."

As his lips find mine again, I'm reminded of something my sister Pru said at our wedding reception, and I say it now: "When it's right, it's easy."

Not without work or compromise—we've had our fair share of both—but at its core, loving Luke is the easiest thing I've ever done.

He rolls on top of me, his weight delicious and familiar. We proceed to enjoy what some people might call "regular vanilla sex," if a star-spangled climax can ever be considered regular. It's our lazy morning sex, as opposed to our nighttime escapades, which have become more adventurous.

Sometimes warm chocolate is carefully poured on certain trembling areas, only to be licked off a moment later. And he enacts the occasional torture with a down feather, the feel of which drives me to begging.

But vanilla is perfect before breakfast coffee, and soon, I'm lying breathless, resting my head on his chest, listening to his heartbeat gradually slow to normal. When I glide my fingers across his warm skin, my diamond-and-opal engagement ring catches the morning light, sending prisms dancing across our white down comforter—a reminder of our time in Germany and the promise we made there.

"Katie called last night," I tell him, twisting my hand to play with the dancing light. "The ultrasound went well. Everyone's healthy. They're having a girl."

Luke grins, his eyes crinkling at the corners. "*Uncle Luke* has a nice ring to it, whether your family or mine."

"It does," I agree. "Although *uncle* isn't quite as good a word as *husband*. Merely thinking it—*you're my husband*—still hasn't gotten old."

He holds my hand flat against his heart. "Neither has introducing you as *Mrs. Henley*. It's pretty cool, in fact."

Life isn't just good—it's extraordinary. Occasionally, I have to pinch myself to make sure I'm not dreaming. I don't take for granted getting to live this incredible life with him.

We split our time between NYC and Boston. Having a billionaire husband means a private jet is just a phone call away, and I can go see my family on a spontaneous whim and be there in an hour. But I'm not relying on *his* fortune. I'm making my own mark in the world, too. We're partners in every sense, supporting each other's dreams.

Our families have blended so well. His parents welcomed me like a third daughter, and we've hosted a couple of massive parties with all the Henleys, the Bonviers, and the Anders. We're also determined to remain bi-continental whenever possible. When New York was gray and slushy this past winter, we spent two months at Gramps and Nan's ranch. I got to teach them both to use video chat so we could stay better connected once we came home.

Clover says Nan's face pops up on her phone at all hours, usually an up-the-nose shot—and she loves it. Fortunately for my sanity, even Jasmine had to finally face facts and move on, getting engaged to a cattle rancher. We'll never be best buds when I'm in the Hunter Valley, but the awkwardness and animosity are gone.

"I was thinking," Luke says, his fingers playing with my hair. "Maybe we should look at that brownstone on East 78th Street. The one with the garden. It might be good to have more space."

I prop myself on one elbow to look him in his fabulous topaz-colored eyes. "More space? For what exactly?"

He raises an eyebrow, his expression serious and tender. "For the future and whatever comes next for us."

My heart flutters at the implication. We've talked about children, abstractly, as something we both eventually want. But the way he's looking at me now makes me wonder if "eventually" might be shifting toward "soon."

"I'd like that," I whisper, surprising myself with how much I mean it. If *uncle* is good, imagine what a kick Luke will get out of being *daddy*.

The smile that spreads across his face is dazzling. Sometimes, everything between us is so perfect it scares me a little. But then my husband looks at me the way he's looking at me right now, like I'm everything he's ever wanted or needed, and that fear dissolves into pure, unadulterated joy.

Leaning down, ignoring the hunger pangs that are starting, I whisper, "Again, please."

And because he loves me as completely as I love him, Luke gives me exactly what I ask for. When he settles between my thighs, I wrap myself around him, still amazed at how perfectly we fit together. We may have needed a magical German oak tree to get here, but now that we've found our way, it seems all we did was follow a twisty path to its inevitable conclusion.

To compromise.

To home.

To us.

The End

ABOUT THE AUTHOR

Jane McBay is the pen name of *USA Today* bestselling author of historical romance, Sydney Jane Baily. She wanted to write about strong, sexy men who know how to treat a woman BUT aren't wearing top hats and shiny Hessian boots.

Trading carriages for limos and horses for private jets, she's dreaming up mouthwatering billionaires with big . . . hearts. They're paired with clever, passionate females who have a hard time resisting these intriguing men. *So why bother?*

Give in, have fun, fall in love.♥ They do. And you will too! *NO* cliffhangers. *NO* frustration. *ALL THE FEELS*. You're welcome!

Contact her through her website, JaneMcBay.com.